Taylor Gray grew up watching too much TV and reading far too much romance. Now she's a writer, she calls it research. She spends her days scribbling illegible notes in a notebook and wishing she could type as fast as her characters thought. She lives in a house overtaken by plants and pictures with her husband, son and cat.

- facebook.com/TaylorGrayAuthor
- instagram.com/taylorgrayauthor

Also by Taylor Gray

The Autumn Falls series
Autumn Falls
Silver Sky
Redemption River
Starlight Mountain
Midnight Promise

REDEMPTION RIVER

TAYLOR GRAY

One More Chapter
a division of HarperCollins*Publishers* Ltd
1 London Bridge Street
London SE1 9GF
www.harpercollins.co.uk
HarperCollins*Publishers*
Macken House, 39/40 Mayor Street Upper,
Dublin 1, D01 C9W8, Ireland
This paperback edition 2026

1

First published in Great Britain in ebook format
by HarperCollins*Publishers* 2026
Copyright © Taylor Gray 2026
Taylor Gray asserts the moral right to be identified
as the author of this work
A catalogue record of this book is available from the British Library
ISBN: 978-0-00-879760-7

This novel is entirely a work of fiction. The names, characters and incidents portrayed in it are the work of the author's imagination. Any resemblance to actual persons, living or dead, events or localities is entirely coincidental.

Printed and bound in the UK using 100% Renewable Electricity
by CPI Group (UK) Ltd

All rights reserved. No part of this publication may be reproduced, stored in a retrieval system, or transmitted, in any form or by any means, electronic, mechanical, photocopying, recording or otherwise, without the prior permission of the publishers.
Without limiting the exclusive rights of any author, contributor or the publisher of this publication, any unauthorised use of this publication to train generative artificial intelligence (AI) technologies is expressly prohibited. HarperCollins also exercise their rights under Article 4(3) of the Digital Single Market Directive 2019/790 and expressly reserve this publication from the text and data mining exception.

For Emily

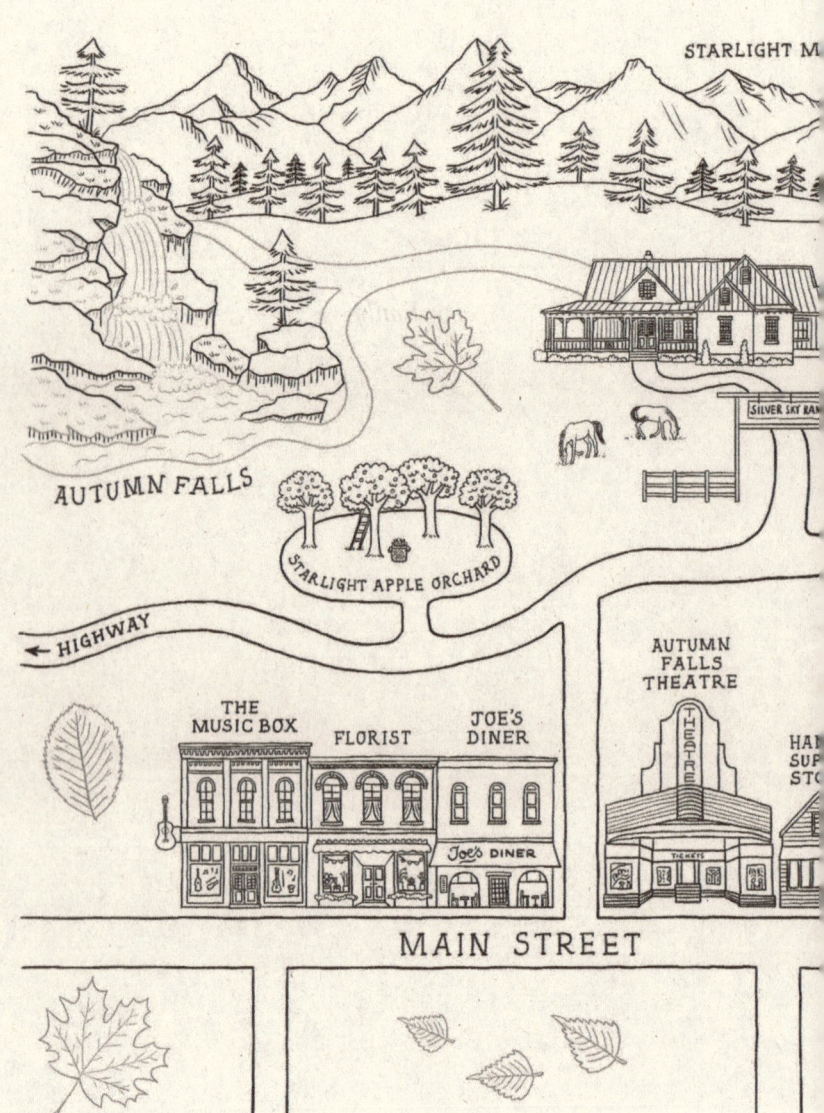

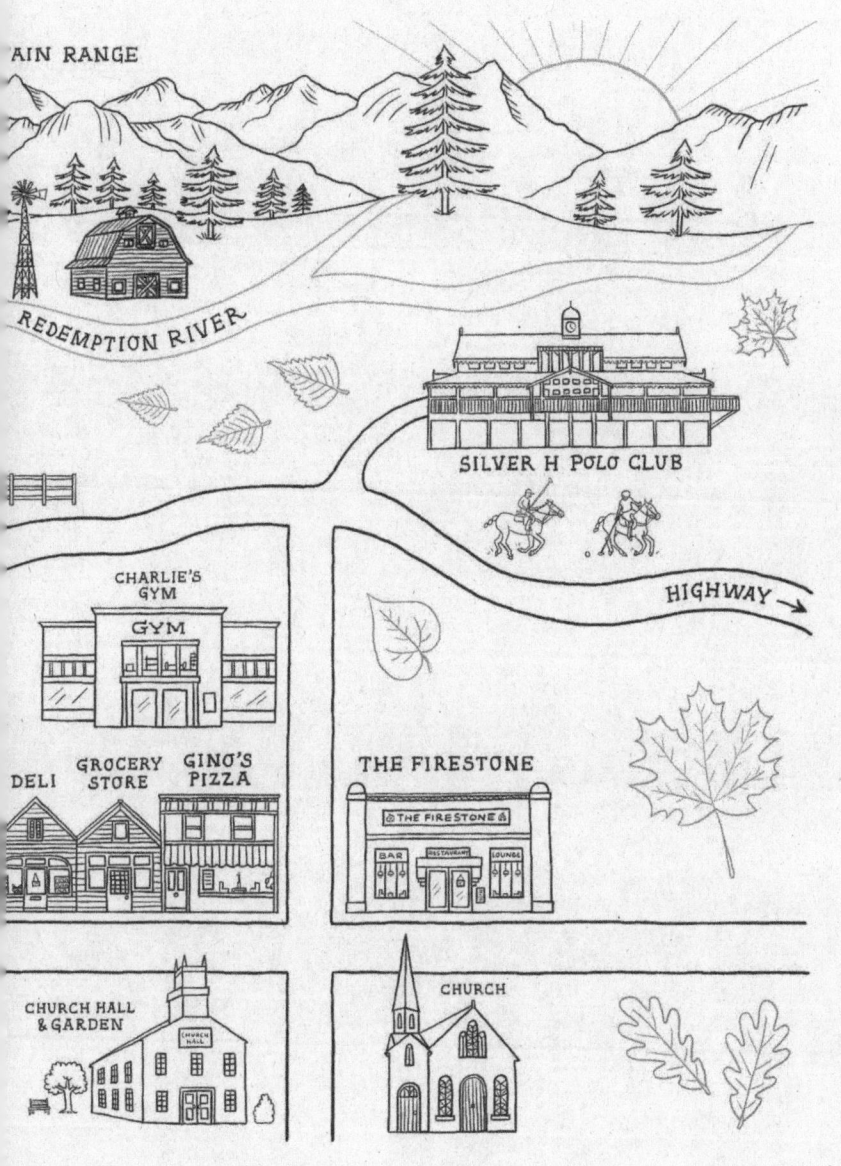

Playlist

Already Over - Sabrina Carpenter
august - Taylor Swift
Two Ghosts - Harry Styles
You're So Vain - Carly Simon
Vodka Cranberry - Conan Gray
Used To Be Young - Miley Cyrus
ceilings - Lizzy McAlpine
North - Clairo
You're On Your Own, Kid - Taylor Swift
Homesick - Noah Kahan, Sam Fender
Kooks - David Bowie
This Town - Niall Horan
the 1 - Taylor Swift
Lovefool - The Cardigans
Satellite - Harry Styles
I know it won't work - Gracie Abrams
"Slut!" - Taylor Swift
Butterflies - Kacey Musgraves
Dreams - Fleetwood Mac
Rein Me In - Sam Fender, Olivia Dean
If You Ever Want To Be In Love - James Bay
18 - One Direction
What If I Love You - Gatlin

Chapter One

Brodie Carter loved a good wedding. Reclining back in his seat, arms stretched across the empty chairs either side of him, the summer sun dipping behind the mountain and the air sweet from the scent of the orchard, he could safely say that his brother Logan's was turning out to be a great one. Not only was Brodie very fond of the bride, Bella —she was like the older sister he'd never had—but the bridesmaids were very easy on the eye, too. The orchard, belonging to Bella's parents, was strung with lights and lanterns and looked sensational, the food had been delicious, the music was exactly what he would have chosen himself, and he hadn't had to talk to his dad yet, which was another plus. All in all, a very good wedding so far.

"Brodie, why aren't you dancing?" His younger sister, Willow, flopped down next to him.

Brodie reached forward for his champagne. "I want Logan to have some of the limelight."

Willow snorted a laugh as she poured herself a glass of water. "Well, don't sit there too long, it's boring without you." She gulped down her drink, still panting from the exertion of dancing, holding her red curls in a bunch on top of her head to cool down.

Brodie was about to stand up and say, let's go back, then, when suddenly Willow jumped up and said, "Hey, look, there's Maeve!" and was gone again, over in the direction of the back door of the house, where a rather bedraggled-looking blonde was standing scanning the crowd.

If Willow hadn't brought his attention to her, Brodie wouldn't have given Maeve a second look—the hair pulled haphazardly back, the no make-up, the rumpled floral-dress-and-black-boots ensemble that was more suited to a day at the park than a wedding—except now his attention *was* on her, there was something about her face that intrigued him. He sat forward to get a better look, observed the dark, tired eyes with their slight downward slant at the corners. And the mouth, the plumpness of the top lip and the pale pink gloss. And beneath the messy hair, he made out the almost perfect heart-shape of her face. All things the untrained eye might miss, but Brodie's eye was not untrained. Years of hard work had gone into being able to spot a hidden gem in the crowd. Something about this woman—Maeve—appealed and Brodie was never one to let an opportunity pass him by.

He watched as she smiled widely at Willow approaching —nice teeth—and let herself be drawn into a hug. And then Bella was there, too, looking even more beautiful—and serene in comparison to Maeve, who was gesturing to her crumpled dress with an apologetic face and shaking her head while Bella tugged her arm forward in the direction of the bar.

Brodie lost sight of them, so with the absence of anything else to do, stood up. And, not in any hurry, strolled, hands in his pockets, in the same direction, lifting his chin just a touch to try and get a better look.

"Who are you looking at?" His twin brother, Noah, came up next to him.

Brodie frowned good-humoredly. "I'm not looking at anyone."

"Brodie, I can tell when you're checking someone out." Noah was holding a mug of coffee that Brodie presumed he'd gone into the house and made himself. Given the chance, he knew Noah would happily be back on the ranch rather than dressed up in a suit having to make small talk with townsfolk. Unable to handle any formality for long, Noah had ditched his tie, undone the top buttons of his shirt and rolled up the sleeves. His long hair flopped forward over his eyes, but he had at least made the effort to shave.

"I wouldn't say I was checking her out necessarily but, when in Rome and all that..." Brodie nodded in the direction of the blonde at the bar.

Noah looked in the direction Brodie was pointing. "Maeve?"

"Apparently so." Brodie narrowed his eyes. "Looks vaguely familiar."

"She was the year below us at school," Noah said. "Remember? Hung out with Ethan's friend Piper?"

Brodie only vaguely remembered his brother Ethan's friend Piper let alone one of her friends. He shook his head.

They both looked again to where Maeve was pouring herself a glass of water at the bar.

Noah said, "She was clever. Doctor now, I think. She'll see straight through you."

Brodie glanced witheringly at him. "Well, I like nothing more than a challenge," he said dryly and, leaving his brother smirking into his coffee, swaggered over to where the three women stood at the bar. "Hey."

Bella's face lit up when she saw him. "Hey, Brodie, are you having fun?"

He put his arm round her waist and pulling her close said, "Of course. More importantly are *you* having fun?"

"Best day of my life," Bella's smile was so wide she could barely contain it.

Just seeing her so happy made Brodie laugh. "Logan's a *very* lucky man!" Letting her go, he reached for a glass of champagne from the bar so he could clink his glass to hers.

Someone cut in to draw Willow away from the conversation and Brodie took the opportunity to turn in Maeve's direction and say, "I don't think we've been introduced."

Bella said, "Oh, sorry. Brodie, this is Maeve."

He raised his glass in her direction and said, "Nice to meet you, Maeve."

She smiled back, holding her mineral water up a

fraction. Didn't seem particularly bowled over by Brodie's presence, which always appealed to him.

He narrowed his eyes and said, "Year below at school, right?" as if he never forgot a face.

For some reason that made Maeve laugh, almost despite herself, and she said, "Yes." But rather than adding anything more, she turned her attention to Bella and said, "I really am *so* sorry I've missed your big day. Work was just crazy busy."

Brodie tipped his head, watching, intrigued at what seemed to him to be a deliberate brush-off.

"Don't be silly." Bella squeezed her arm. "I'm just happy you could pop by." Then she turned to Brodie and said, "Maeve's a doctor in the ER."

"Impressive." Brodie thought of Noah saying that she was too clever to fall for his charm, the idea of it amused him. "Save any lives today?" he quipped.

"Yeah, I did actually," she replied flatly.

Brodie's lips twitched, both from the unaccustomed sting of a snub and in self-rebuke at his flippancy. *Must do better.* Beside him, he saw Bella raise a brow, clearly tickled that Maeve wasn't the usual putty in his hands.

Before he could redeem himself, however, Logan came over to join them.

His older brother was so relaxed and happy, he looked literally ten years younger, his hands threading round Bella's waist as he stood behind her. "You made it!" he said to Maeve, who was all smiles for Logan, Brodie noticed.

There was some chat about an emergency in the ER, how Maeve couldn't get away. She asked all the right questions, listening intently to the details of the wedding, and Brodie did the same, even though he'd been there and seen it first-hand. But while they talked, he let his eyes subtly skim over her: her pale—ringless—fingers holding the glass of water, the way the buttons on her dress had been done up so quickly that she'd missed one and he could see the shaded skin of her stomach; the curl of her hair that settled enticingly just below her collarbone. Yes, he was very intrigued, even more so because she seemed completely disinterested in him.

Over on the dance floor the song changed and Willow whooped because it was one of her favorites, and turning back to their group said, "Come on, let's dance!" Reaching over, she yanked Brodie by the sleeve of his jacket.

He laughed. "All right, I'm coming," he said, then he turned to Maeve, his arm outstretched in invitation. "You dance?" he asked.

"No," she replied, deep, brown eyes steadfast.

Chapter Two

Maeve slipped away from Bella and Logan's wedding as soon as politely possible and walked fast down the sidewalk, berating herself for even going. In retrospect, it had been a dreadful idea. She'd had the perfect excuse not to go and yet she had *wanted* to be there, to congratulate her friend, Bella, see her in her beautiful dress looking happy and content and living the dream she deserved. So she had risked the possibility of bumping into Brodie Carter, but from what she knew of Brodie, she'd presumed he'd be far too distracted with the other more glamorous guests to take any notice of her.

But then he'd sidled over, looking all effortlessly gorgeous and Hollywood-esque in his pale blue suit with his artfully mussed hair.

She shook her head up at the cloudless sky at her own stupidity. *What* was she thinking? She could only blame tiredness from her twenty-four-hour shift for clouding her judgment. But of all the people there, why had Brodie had to come over to the bar the ten minutes that she was there? *"Why?"* she said out loud.

She dropped her head, looked down at her boots pounding the sidewalk. Perhaps he'd already worked his way round the available females in the crowd before she arrived, and the sight of fresh pickings was what drew his attention.

Her house was a block from the orchard. She could see the rusted wire fence that marked her little garden in contrast to the white picket fences of her neighbors. She really should get it replaced. If only she had time. All she wanted right now was sleep. Since leaving the hospital she had fantasized about her soft white sheets and the precious calm of her bedroom.

She reached her front gate and was just going to unlatch it when she heard the sound of running footsteps on the sidewalk behind her.

She glanced and what she saw made her stomach tighten.

Brodie was coming toward her, at not quite a jog, more of a languid lope, his suit jacket undone, his expression knowing, which only made the panic rise to Maeve's throat.

He came to a stop in front of her, unruffled by the exertion, running a hand through his still perfect hair, and said, "Stanford Stadium. I was doing a solo concert. You were there with Ethan's friend Piper Adams. Ethan got you backstage passes. You were wearing a little pink skirt and silver boots. Yeah?"

Everyone in Autumn Falls knew the story of the Carter brothers forming a band and auditioning for a TV talent show to cheer their mom up when she was undergoing chemotherapy. No one had ever expected them to win, let alone go on to become the world famous, multi-platinum boy band, Silver Sky. Nor that Brodie Carter, when the band split, would go on to have a chart-topping solo career. But looking at him now, with his glinting eyes and razor-sharp cheekbones, radiating an effortless confidence, it was obvious that he was destined for stardom.

Maeve found herself struggling with how to reply, and in her panic went with the knee-jerk reaction of denial. "I don't know what you're talking about."

Brodie's mouth stretched into a crooked, cocksure grin. "Sure you do. I remember that skirt."

She shook her head. "I really, honestly don't know what you're talking about."

He laughed, dimples in both cheeks, eyes creasing slightly at the sides. She thought of all the women who went weak at the knees at that laugh, at that laser-like attention. She had of course fallen for it herself, dressed in the pink leather skirt and the silver cowboy boots she'd borrowed off Piper after much cajoling. "That really doesn't sound like something I'd wear."

But she had worn it. And dressed in something completely different to her normal style, her make-up done by Piper who was amazing at that kind of thing, and just totally relieved to have a break from her grueling college workload, she had felt like a different person. A person who had the confidence to respond when she saw Brodie's eyes light up at the sight of her—everyone at school had loved Brodie and he'd never even cast a glance her way. So to see that smile focused on her alone, when only half an hour before she'd heard his name chanted by a stadium full of fans, girls next to her crying when he sang the first note while his face was beamed around the stadium on giant screens, it had been intoxicating.

While all the brothers had their fanbase, as the lead singer, Brodie's star had always shone that little bit brighter, with that magical tone to his voice, even more so when he was up there on his own.

It made Maeve flirt back a little when he flirted. To allow herself a little fun having been cooped up with her books since her second year at Stanford began. It was beguiling to be caught in the glow of someone as famous and beautiful and charming as Brodie Carter was then—that's what she told herself when she tried to rationalize it later.

Now here Brodie was, leaning up against her neighbor's fence post, arms crossed, his knowing—almost mocking—smile still in place. "You can deny it all you like, I know it was you. I'm terrible with names but I'm good with faces." He paused, his mouth tipped up. "And skirts. And silver boots."

Maeve was about to shake her head dismissively, considered perhaps even just walking away up the garden path and leaving him standing there, when to her absolute horror, from behind her, a little voice said, "Hi, Mom. I saw you through the curtain, Carole said it was okay for me to come out."

Maeve's body froze rigid, the blood pounding in her head as she took in the scene in snapshots, every word like an echo, images suspended in time. The music from the wedding in the distance. The rattle of the metal fence as her daughter, Zoey, swung from it, her untied shoelace. The navy Jackson General Hospital fundraiser sweater she had on that Maeve wore to do the gardening and Zoey had taken a shine to—even though it came down almost to her knees when she wore it. Her fluorescent-yellow leggings, her favorite red polka-dot bobble hat, and the wisps of hair that had come loose from her braid.

Then her precious little arm as she stretched it out toward Brodie, the cuff rolled over like a sausage, and said, "I'm Zoey. Nice suit."

Watching Zoey's fingers, pale and tiny when clasped by Brodie's big, tanned hand, Maeve could barely allow herself to look at his face as he said, "Pleasure to meet you. I'm Brodie. Not a bad outfit yourself."

Zoey looked down at herself as if to check what she had on and said, "Thanks." Then she turned back to Maeve. "What were you talking about?"

Maeve said, "Nothing," her voice strained and thin.

Zoey frowned. "Why have you got your stressed face on?"

Maeve tried to ignore her. "Go inside, I'll be there in a minute."

Zoey didn't move. Instead, she looked to Brodie, giving him a proper once up-and-down as if he might provide some answers.

Clearly more than happy to oblige, Brodie said, "I was just reminding your mom about a time we met a while ago." He paused to think back.

Maeve watched him mentally calculating, her heart thumping like a drum.

"It must have been one of the first concerts I did without the band," he said. "So, when was that, about eight years ago?"

Zoey said, "I'm eight." Grinning with pride at the fact. Dimples in both cheeks.

Maeve found herself struggling to breathe.

Chapter Three

B rodie felt the moment that the words registered in his brain. He went from thinking, *cute kid*, to just wallcoming-down blankness. Maeve was staring at him, pale face suddenly flushed red at the cheeks, eyes momentarily pulsing with panic before she blinked and looked away.

All the while, the back of Brodie's mind was whizzing like a rollercoaster but he wasn't listening. As if his body sensed danger, he felt an instinctive urge to back away, to ignore. "Okay," he said, one foot stepping back. "Well, that was all I wanted to say."

The kid was still swinging on the gate, the squeaking noise piercing the air as she watched him with eyes as big and round as one of Noah's cows.

He thumbed behind him. "I should get back to the wedding."

"Yep," Maeve replied, now cool and calm, like she'd drawn on her unflappable, doctor persona in the brief moment it had taken Brodie to get his words out.

"Okay," he said again, unable to pull out one of his usual charmingly witty one-liners. Like his head had nothing in it. Taking another backward step, he stumbled on a piece of loose paving, then laughed and said, "Need to get that fixed." All the while he felt the scrutiny of the kid's wide eyes.

He raised a hand to wave before turning on his heel and striding away in the direction of the wedding music, chin raised a touch, trying not to think of those huge bovine eyes following him.

When he was almost back at the orchard he reached up and loosened his tie, undoing the top button on his shirt, then he shrugged off his jacket. Everything suddenly felt too constricting. His skin hot, like he had the flu.

Around the side of the main orchard house, he could see the lights of the dance floor, the air strobing with color, the leaves of the apple trees illuminated, he could hear laughter and the buzzing hum of chatter. The clink of glasses. He walked up the front drive, lit with tealights and strung with white wedding bunting, remembering how smug he'd felt when his recollection of Maeve that night at the concert had flashed into his mind, he'd laughed as his champagne glass touched his lips. He'd found himself driven by a conceited desire to tell her what he had decided she already knew and had been haughtily pretending she didn't. He'd arrogantly assumed that people didn't forget a night with a celebrity.

He strolled back into the wedding reception, trying his best to appear blasé, and hooked a glass of champagne from the bar. But his hand was shaking so he put it back down on a table. Then he stood with his hands in his pockets, not totally sure what to do with himself.

Noah sidled up. "So, how'd it go with Maeve?"

"Maeve?" Brodie frowned, feigned nonchalance. "What about her?"

Noah laughed, deep and satisfied. "She blow you out?"

Brodie could feel sweat trickle down his back.

I'm eight.

"No," he scoffed, like the idea was absurd. His mouth was dry, he needed a drink but knew Noah would clock his trembling fingers.

"What are you talking about?" It was Ren, Noah's girlfriend. One of Brodie's new favorite people, he admired anyone who could keep his monosyllabic brother on his toes. She looked adorable in cream hotpants and a lacy vest.

"Maeve," Noah said.

"Maeve and Zoey, Maeve?" Ren clarified.

"Know any others?" Noah replied dryly.

Ren whacked him affectionately on the stomach. "I was just checking!"

Willow appeared from the dance floor, guzzling down a glass of water. "I'm boiling!"

So was Brodie.

"Why were you talking about Maeve?" Ren asked.

"Brodie likes her," Noah replied as if it were fact, grabbing an OJ from a passing waiter and thanking him.

Willow took a glass of champagne. "You know she's got a kid?"

"I don't need to know!" Brodie said, exasperated. "I don't even know why we're talking about Maeve!"

"Ooh, defensive." Willow sniggered.

Noah raised a brow, clearly enjoying himself. "You *did* get the brush-off."

Bella came over to join them. Draping her arm round Brodie's shoulder, she said, "Who? Maeve?"

Brodie tipped his head back. "I hate you all!"

Noah laughed out loud.

Ren crossed her arms and, looking thoughtful, said, "Who's Zoey's dad?"

Bella shook her head. "Don't know."

"No one talks about it," Willow added, sipping her champagne.

I'm eight.

"I never knew you lot were such gossips!" It was probably the first time in his life Brodie had ever taken the moral high ground. Noah spluttered into his drink in surprise, but Brodie didn't care, he needed to shut this down or his heart was going to fail. "You should be ashamed of yourselves."

Chapter Four

When Brodie rang on the bell of the small cream wooden house with the green awning and gable and the squeaky metal front gate, he heard the kid shout, "I'll get it!"

He had to hold onto one of the struts of the porch to stop himself turning away as she appeared behind the glass and grinned when she saw him. "It's the blue suit guy!" she yelled behind her.

There was a clatter from the kitchen as Zoey opened the door, her hat discarded now, her long fringe half over her eyes. "You're back."

"I am," he said, wondering if his heart had ever beaten so fast. He felt like he'd made a mistake.

"You forget something?"

He shook his head.

Maeve appeared at the end of the hall. She looked at him like perhaps she'd known he would come. Her face, however, didn't give anything away.

They stood for a second in silence before Maeve said, "You'd better come in."

Brodie went into the house. Zoey watched his every step.

Maeve waved a hand at the clutter in the corridor and said, "Excuse the mess, I haven't been home—" Brodie noticed that her cheeks were flushed again, realized she wasn't immune to the tension pulsing in the air.

He shook his head to say the mess didn't matter and glanced around, but barely took it in other than some mismatched furnishings and piles of washing on the stairs. When they got into the kitchen, the table was covered in tiny colored beads.

Zoey sat down, one leg crossed underneath her and said, "We're making bracelets."

"Nice," Brodie replied, dazed by all the glittery paraphernalia; the thread, the beads, the charms—all scattered over the red-checked tablecloth. He thought of the clean lines of his Malibu beach house, the white sofas and the minimalist surfaces.

He glanced up at Maeve and caught her watching him. Her beautiful heart-shaped face and deep brown eyes were now like a painting—distant from him, untouchable.

"Take a seat," she said, moving some medical textbooks from a spare chair round the table. "Can I get you a drink? Coffee? Glass of wine?"

It was painfully polite.

Brodie sat in the rickety wooden chair and said, "Just a glass of water, please." His mouth was very dry.

In the homespun kitchen, surrounded by kid stuff,

colorful plastic beakers on the drainboard and unopened mail piled up on the countertop, he had the thought that he had stepped unwittingly onto the wrong stage, that he would be ushered away any minute, directed to where he really belonged.

Maeve went to pour him a glass of water and when she placed it on the table in front of him and sat down opposite said, "Zoey, honey, why don't you go and watch TV?"

"No, you said we could make bracelets." Zoey frowned. "I've been waiting all day."

Brodie watched Maeve rub her forehead. She looked more tired than before, dark circles under her eyes. But he couldn't feel sorry for her. Right then, he wasn't sure he could decipher a single coherent feeling from the tangle in his head.

Zoey tucked her hair behind her ears, and looking at Brodie said, "Do you want to make a bracelet?"

"Sure," he replied.

She handed him the thread.

Sitting at the table, it felt like there was an abyss of sharks and creatures of the deep beneath him, but Zoey's presence meant he was balancing precariously on the surface, pretending not to look down.

"You make a knot at the end then you just start threading, like this," Zoey held up one that she'd made earlier. All purple and pink with a tiny silver starfish charm.

"I like that," Brodie said admiringly while his stomach clenched and he wondered if he might be sick. He went to pick up a bead and tried to concentrate on threading it on the string. He remembered doing the same with his sister as kids.

Opposite him, Maeve picked up a bracelet that she'd obviously been making before he got there and appeared to be focused on threading white beads. She wouldn't look at him. Zoey was concentrating intently on hers, too, tongue between her teeth as she worked.

Brodie kicked Maeve under the table to get her attention.

Her head shot up.

He raised his eyebrows.

She raised hers back as if to say, *what?*

He did a sharp nod in the direction of the kid then pointed to himself.

He watched Maeve roll her lips together as she contemplated. Then after what looked like a steadying breath, she gave a tiny nod.

The world paused.

Brodie lost time. Who knew if he was breathing. He almost laughed thinking, *lucky there's a doctor in the house*.

His head tightened. His face got hot. He wondered if he might pass out. He felt an overwhelming urge to correct her, to look around and see if all his brothers were about to pop out and laugh at the joke, to wind back time and make Maeve do something other than nod.

He was sweating in his pale blue shirt. His mouth was dry again, he couldn't swallow. Blood whooshed in his ears. He focused on Zoey's pink fingernails as she clutched the thread. For some reason he thought of the white sofas of his

Malibu house again, all pristine, with the view out to the ocean.

"You're meant to be threading beads!" Zoey's voice sounded so loud he startled in shock and immediately picked up a yellow bead shaped like a heart, but when he looked down he realized his hands were too shaky to get the bead on the thread. He fumbled it and dropped it, then bent down to try and find it on the floor. Under the table, he saw only a dry breakfast Cheerio, then spotted the yellow heart over by Zoey's feet. Small bare feet with tiny little toes.

He thought he might be sick. He jerked up and bashed the back of his head on the table.

"You okay?" Maeve asked, jumping up from her seat.

Brodie stood up too quickly, rubbing the back of his head. "Yes, fine. Sorry."

Maeve was standing, mouth closed, eyes blinking unreadably—could be relief or could be fear, she was still wearing her slightly crumpled floral dress that a mere hour ago he had found so intriguing. Just like that, Maeve was now a forever presence in his life. No longer just a pretty heart-shaped face. She was the mother of his child.

His child.

Brodie's vision blurred.

Zoey was leaning down to pick beads up off the floor that had fallen when Brodie bashed the table. "They're everywhere!" she exclaimed. Then, "Oh, there's a Cheerio!"

Maeve said, "Don't eat it!"

Zoey came up with a grin on her face, like she had definitely just eaten the Cheerio. All Brodie could see was her cheeky, dimpled smile and self-assured eyes. All of a sudden, a smaller, female version of him staring back.

"You know, I should get going," he said.

Maeve nodded. "Okay."

He had no gauge of her emotions; he was thinking only of how quickly he could get to that front door.

"But you've only just started." Zoey held up his bracelet with one bead on it.

"Another time, I promise," he said, heading out the room. And he was gone before there were any goodbyes.

Heart pounding, he almost ran back to the orchard where the wedding party was in full swing for the evening. He stood on the threshold surveying the scene as he caught his breath. The Autumn Falls band had taken over from the DJ; his mom on guitar, Hank Murphy on keyboard, Bella's friend Claudette on the mic. He saw Logan and Bella, noses touching as Logan whispered something to make her laugh; he saw his sister dancing with Ren, and the other ravishing bridesmaids now with their hair down and their shoes kicked off as they danced. Brodie grabbed a drink off a passing waiter, downed it in two gulps. Then running his hand through his hair he blew out a breath, pushed the last half-hour out of his head, and jogged down to the dance floor, plastering a wide smile on his face.

Chapter Five

Maeve had told him.

Her eight-year secret was out, just like that.

She had gone from bone-shatteringly tired to wide awake in an instant.

Zoey was in bed and Maeve was sitting alone in the living room, perched on the edge of the couch, hands clasped in front of her. How would Brodie react? Would he take Zoey away? Argue in court that she'd hidden the truth from him? Fight for sole custody?

No. She had to stay calm. She'd known that one day this would happen.

She flopped back against the cushions. Closing her eyes, she saw that night at the concert. Saw her and Brodie chatting, saw him laugh at something she'd said. She remembered the welcome surprise in his eyes at the laughter and the warm feeling of success in hers. As the evening had worn on, the sense of Brodie's famousness had lessened. She watched it fade before her eyes as he wound down. With his brother around, he became almost bashful, laughed more easily as he relaxed, then suddenly, he was Brodie from school again. The boy she'd been in the school play with but had only managed to pluck up the courage to speak to once.

That night, though, he was super attentive, interested in everything she had to say. She remembered Piper nudging her. Brodie taking her hand to pull her down the stairs to some underground dive bar that Ethan had chosen. Dark and sweaty.

All her life, it was, *work hard, Maeve, don't get distracted.* So of course, she said she had to go home, she had piles of work to do the next day. Brodie had frowned. "Why would you go?! It's only just beginning," he said, and he'd slung his arm around her shoulder and pulled her close. "You can't leave!" He grinned then, leaned down and whispered, "You're the only reason I'm here."

Now in the dusky living room, Maeve's eyes flew open. This was not the time to be thinking about *that* night.

She'd had boyfriends before and after Brodie. Never anything serious—she was always too busy—but occasional dates with guys at medical school, or doctors at the hospital. But whoever it was, no one—and she was loathe to admit it—had ever come close to matching that one night with Brodie. A night that for him was one of too many to count, but for her was…

Don't think about it, Maeve.

It wasn't just the first kiss, that moment he put his hand on her cheek and dipped his head with a knowing smile on his face, eyes sparkling like she was the only person in the world, or the touch of his hand, cool on her back, and the tickling trace of his fingertips up her bare leg, that she remembered so exquisitely. It was the other moments, too, like when they sat up talking, the skyline lit up out the window of his hotel room, wearing his T-shirt as they laughed about things she couldn't remember now but that were so funny she was almost crying. Or when he made her a cup of hot chocolate because he said hotel hot chocolate at midnight was one of his favorite things, and she didn't believe him so he made it for her and they sat up drinking it in bed like an old married couple. Or when he challenged her to a game of *Super Mario* and she surprised him by knowing where the secret rooms were that he didn't.

It hadn't been just a mistaken night. It had been, if she allowed herself to admit it—which she rarely ever did because the consequences had rewritten it—one of the best nights of her life.

Chapter Six

The wedding celebrations went on into the early hours. There was an after-party at Logan's polo club, the Silver H, for anyone who wanted to carry on. And Brodie chose very much to carry on. He needed as much distraction as he could get. When the Silver H closed, he ended up taking a cab with his sister and a bunch of other guests into Jackson. The following day there was a brunch at the ranch, hosted by his parents. Brodie rocked up in his pale blue suit and his sunglasses and picked up where he'd left off. If there was a still a crowd, still a party, still a distraction, Brodie was there. He didn't want to go back to his condo. He didn't want silence. He didn't want to have to think. But even he struggled to keep going for thirty-six hours, before the sun set on the Sunday evening celebrations and Logan swept Bella off to the airport for a honeymoon. It was coming up to polo season, so they weren't going away long as Logan had to be at the club, so Brodie had offered them the penthouse suite in the mock

Tuscan castle at his vineyard in Napa. Handing Logan the keys, Brodie finally had to admit defeat and go home.

Brodie's condo building was nearby the Silver H polo club. It was new and fully serviced and felt very similar to living in a hotel, which he usually found strangely comforting. But tonight, as he lay on his bed, dressed in a T-shirt and Calvins, hands clasped behind his head, staring up at the ceiling, it felt coldly impersonal and, if he was honest, a little bit terrifying.

Now he was alone, he kept seeing Zoey's cheeky grin after she'd eaten that Cheerio. He wanted to close his eyes and go to sleep, same as he'd wanted to just dance at the wedding and chat amiably at the brunch, and forget about it, but it was like he had a new shadow, hovering there in the background of everything he did: dancing with his sister. *You have a kid*. Laughing at Bella's speech at the brunch. *You have a kid*. When he was with people, Brodie could distract himself, get up and go and talk to someone else, have another cup of coffee, eat another smoked-salmon bagel. But at home on his own, the shadow engulfed him. Walking in the door. *You have a kid*. Taking a shower. *You have a kid*. Trying to go to sleep. *Kid, kid, kid*.

Brodie got up and looked out the window. He could see the polo field in the shadowy moonlight. Thought about the horses all soundly asleep for the night. He wanted to be soundly asleep. He wasn't a stranger to staying up all night, but it was always by choice. When he chose to sleep, Brodie slept like a log. As soon as his head hit the pillow he was out.

But tonight. The shadow wasn't letting him sleep.

How could she not have told him?

A child. That was a massive responsibility. Life-changing. He thought of his mom saying, *You have to be selfless to be a parent.*

Brodie exhaled. *Selfless.* Not a word in his vocabulary.

Maybe the kid wasn't his?

The answer to that question came with those big wide eyes and the dimples. The kid was definitely his; she was beautiful, charming. And she looked like him.

Brodie stared at the clock, it was 4 a.m. On the ranch, Noah and his dad would be getting up soon. He remembered those dark, cold mornings of his youth, the tired silence as they ate their oatmeal, the list of jobs to be fought over. The backbreaking work. Brodie had hated it. Didn't just hate it, he detested it. On the ranch, he was like the kid not picked for the football team, the hindrance.

You have a kid.

He shivered.

He squeezed his eyes shut. He put the pillow over his head. He didn't want this. He didn't ask for this.

Maeve clearly didn't want him to be a part of this.

He'd leave tomorrow.

He moved the pillow from his head and put it behind his head again at the idea. He'd get a couple of hours sleep now, then get up, pack his bag, and go to the airport. He was meant to be meeting friends in San Diego in a few days, he'd just arrive early.

Brodie rolled his shoulders, he felt better. He plumped the pillow and turned onto his side, pulled the cover up over him, knew now that he'd be able to sleep. He loved the airport. Loved the freedom of it. The world his oyster.

He woke up five hours later, the sun streaming in through the window, the familiar sounds of the polo club filtering into the room, the shouts and the crack of the mallet, the smell of freshly cut grass.

He rubbed his eyes, reached for the glass of water by his bed, saw his blue suit on the chair.

You have a kid.

He stopped still. He could hear his heart.

There was her face. Small, perfect, the exact combination of him and her mother.

He suddenly imagined the look on his own father's face were he ever to discover that Brodie had fled from this revelation. There would be no shouting, no scoff of disgust or reprimand, there would simply be a slight pursing of the lips; perhaps his dad would slip his hands into his pockets, with a look in his eye that said Brodie had done exactly as he would expect.

He stood up and looked out the window, at the sun glinting on the lush grass of the polo field.

You have a kid.

He knew in that instant there was no escape. If he got on a plane the shadow would follow him, but worse, so would that imagined I-thought-as-much look in his father's eye.

Brodie rang the buzzer again. When no one answered he looked in through the window, cupping his hands to try and see better. The piles of washing were still on the stairs. He went back down the porch steps and turned to look up at the upstairs windows.

"They're not in," came a voice from the neighboring garden.

Brodie turned to look at who was speaking and saw a gray-haired woman eyeing him with suspicion. Presumably Carole, the babysitter, whose house Zoey had appeared from the day before. "Do you know where they are?" he asked, flashing her his best smile.

She folded her arms across her ample chest and didn't smile back. "I imagine they're at school and work."

Brodie often forgot about normal life. Jobs, school, commitments.

The neighbor watched till he was off the property and back in his Aston Martin. For some reason, the sports car felt childishly showy under her gaze, so he slipped on his sunglasses and pulled away without looking back. Headed straight in the direction of Jackson General Hospital.

Chapter Seven

"Brodie, I'm at work, you can't just turn up here." Maeve stood with her arms crossed in front of the double plastic doors of the ER. She was exhausted. She had barely slept since she last saw him, terrified of this very moment.

"Why didn't you tell me?" Brodie didn't seem to care where he was. He had that air about him that he breezed into places and got what he wanted without even trying.

Maeve glanced round the room, every eye in the place was on Brodie. The people waiting to be seen, the nurses at the desk, the janitor, even a patient on an IV drip waiting to be wheeled to the elevator. He mesmerized people. She closed her eyes for a second, then, with a resigned sigh, ushered him to follow her into one of the side rooms. Shutting the door she glanced at her watch and said, "I don't have much time."

He nodded. Then repeated his question. "Why didn't you tell me about her?"

Maeve swallowed. "I tried."

Brodie seemed surprised by that, as if he'd already played out how the conversation would go. "When?"

"When I found out. I asked Piper to get your number from Ethan. I rang you, I left you a message to tell you to call me, that it was important. You never called back."

Brodie laughed, incredulous. "Do you know how many women leave me messages telling me it's important and to call back?"

Maeve looked up, met his eyes.

The words hung in the air between them. As if Brodie properly heard what he'd just said, he ran a hand through his hair.

"I left loads of messages," she said.

Brodie paced the exam room, which was set up with a couple of chairs, a bed and a desk. He stopped by one of the chairs, rested both hands on the back and said, "You could have told my mom, she would have got hold of me."

"Why should I?" Maeve bashed the desk without thinking. "I wanted to tell you!"

Brodie turned away and looked down, tight-jawed, at the bland hospital floor. "If I'd known why, I would have called back."

"And then what? Your PA would have rung me and sorted out logistics? Brodie, my life literally imploded when I found out I was pregnant with Zoey. You weren't my top priority. I tried. I tried to reach out to you and you didn't get back to me." She could feel her heart thumping. That wasn't what she'd meant to say. She'd rehearsed this, she'd feared it. She thought she'd come to terms with it, she'd waited for the moment, knowing it would happen one day, but now it was just a muddle of words. How could any of it convey what the last eight years had been like for her. "So, to be honest, Brodie—" she shook her head "—I wasn't really thinking about you at the time. And then—" she crossed her arms "—well, I guess I watched you get more famous, and then you got married and you lived in that big house and had everything anyone could want."

She remembered his wedding announcement. Him and a fellow pop star. Everyone said it wouldn't last, some claimed it was a publicity stunt, but for Maeve it was another reason to keep away from him. He was rich, married, and lived in a mansion. In contrast, she had very little to offer.

She glanced out the window at the trees and the blue sky. It was hard admitting her own fears and mistakes but she had promised herself that if he ever asked she'd be frank. "I didn't want you to swoop in and take Zoey away." She looked over and met his gaze. Eyes that she'd seen on posters and on the TV, eyes of a celebrity that she could convince herself, *had* convinced herself, weren't really real. "I had nothing, you had everything. I was young and I was afraid."

He stared at her for a moment, frowning. He was so good-looking that when he frowned it was hard to believe he was actually annoyed, more that he was acting the part of annoyed.

It was hard to believe that he was the father of her child. If there wasn't such a serious issue between them, she would find herself tongue-tied in his presence. Yet the existence of Zoey was like a shield against his stardom.

She looked at her watch again. "I have to go." She started walking to the door, then paused and turned back. "Listen, if you want, you can come for dinner tonight. But I don't want you to fly into Zoey's life, go, 'Wa-hey I'm your dad,' bamboozle her and fly out again. I won't let that happen, Brodie."

"That wasn't what I was going to do," he replied but from his telltale swallow before he answered, she knew it was exactly what he would do and that he knew it, too.

"If you want to get to know her, that's fine," she continued, forcing herself to be matter-of-fact when really she wanted to run home, wrap Zoey in her arms and lock all the doors. "But you're not telling her who you are yet. You decide first what you're going to do. This is not one of your conquests, Brodie. This is a little girl who has no idea you're her dad."

Brodie nodded to show that he'd heard but then instead of answering, he looked away. He squeezed his temples with his fingers. "This is all too fast for me," he said, eyebrows drawn together, almost pleading. She noticed the honeycomb tan, the expensive sneakers, the fun red sunglasses looped at his collar. "I can't think straight."

She put her hand on the door handle. "That's the thing with children, Brodie. There's no time to think straight. This is it, you're either in or you're not."

Chapter Eight

Brodie swung by the Silver Sky Ranch on the way back from the hospital, shaken, a bit lost, and in need of a distraction.

Pulling up in the driveway, he took a moment to look at the big family house with the trailing rose round the door bursting with pink flowers, the sweeping landscape behind with the pines pointing up to Starlight Mountain, the dewy green of the pasture and the almost beacon-red of the barn roofs in the sun. Everything felt like he was seeing it for the first time, in some new light, like there was now a before and after version of Brodie Carter.

Shuddering at the idea, he got out the car and ambled over to the horse barn to see if anyone was about.

He just had to take it a day at a time, not stress. That was his mantra in life. See where the day took him.

You have a kid.

His legs wobbled and he almost stumbled, it was a

feeling akin to his yacht yawing at ninety degrees in the Atlantic waves.

There were a couple of horses in the paddock, the only one he knew the name of was Blue—Noah's horse—because he was strictly forbidden to ride her. Noah was very protective of his horses.

Brodie went up to the fence and whistled and a striking palomino came straight over. "Hello, girl," he said, rubbing her nose and letting her snuffle his hair. "I don't have anything for you, sorry." He breathed in the warm scent of her, felt the softness of her muzzle. "Aren't you lovely?" He wondered if Zoey could ride a horse. He frowned at the thought, didn't know where it had come from. Didn't want similar intruding on his every day.

"Well, isn't this a sight for sore eyes." Noah was leaning in the open doorway of the barn watching, arms crossed, smirking as Brodie got all schmaltzy talking to the horse. "Don't usually see you venturing this far from the house."

"Ha-ha." Brodie stepped away from the affectionate mare and threw his brother a withering look.

Noah strolled over, remnants of the smirk still on his face. In his plaid shirt, scruffy T-shirt, mud-splattered jeans and boots, this was the version of his twin that Brodie knew best. "What are you up to?"

"Not a lot." Brodie tried to imagine the look on Noah's face if he told him about Maeve. Knowing Noah he'd probably just nod, let the information sink in. Brodie's stomach felt coiled like a spring.

"You okay?" Noah asked.

They didn't share a twin's sixth sense but they could read each other pretty well.

"Fine," Brodie replied stiffly. He was so wound up, anyone could probably have sensed it. Noah would never push it, though, never asked too many questions. "You?"

Noah glanced out to the far pastures. "Gotta go round up some cattle. You want to help?" he offered, although they both knew the answer.

Brodie wondered if being out in the saddle might actually help relax him, but his agreement would raise too many eyebrows, incite too many questions. "You know me, terrible with a lasso."

"Bit of practice usually helps," said a voice behind him.

Brodie rolled his eyes before turning round. There was Emmett Carter, saddle over his shoulder, hat half hiding his face, beard more white now than it was black. "Hi, Dad."

"You here to help?"

Brodie swallowed, no one made him as nervous as his father. Except now, perhaps Maeve. "I was just stopping by."

"It would be a darn sight more useful if you were here to help."

Silence.

While Brodie searched in his head for an answer, Noah looked at him supportively. Emmett waited for a beat, letting the message sink in, then said, "You staying long? Nice if you told your mom what you were doing."

Responsibility, obligations. Would Brodie have to say this kind of stuff to Zoey?

Behind them, the screen door to the ranch house banged

and his mom, Martha Carter, appeared. "Brodie! Oh, I'm so glad you're still here. I thought maybe you'd already left!" she called over as Emmett carried on in the direction of the barn. "You want to stay for dinner?"

Brodie glanced at his father's broad back and couldn't imagine anything worse than sitting opposite him for a whole meal. Whether he'd made up his mind or not about accepting Maeve's invitation, he said, "I can't, Mom, sorry, I got plans."

As Martha made her way over, Noah raised a brow and said quietly, "You get lucky at the wedding?"

Brodie had a moment's confusion at the question, as if his days of "getting lucky" were already a whole other lifetime. "Not in the way you'd think."

Noah laughed. "What does that mean?"

But Brodie found he couldn't tell him. Couldn't or didn't want to. "Nothing," he said with an easy laugh. To voice it made it real. At the moment, Maeve and Zoey were like his childhood Star Wars figures; all set up in his bedroom but only existing if he decided to pick them up and play. Tell his family the truth about Zoey, and he could only imagine the snowball effect. They would be drawn in and consumed by the Carters. He would lose any agency as they became part of their combined lives. He would be tied to the ranch and Autumn Falls, whether he liked it or not. No escape. He would regress, back to being the boy his father saw him as; the useless one with nothing to offer except a better than average singing voice. The thought made a shiver of what could only be fear run through him. "Right, I'd better go."

Martha said, "So soon? I wanted to show you how the

shop's getting along." Her latest venture was The Silver Pantry, an old barn she was converting into an organic produce and lifestyle store.

But Brodie was already on his way, his T-shirt feeling suddenly tight, his skin on fire again, his legs taking him away as fast as politely possible. "Yeah, I really want to see that! I'll come by tomorrow." He smiled wide to counterbalance his mom's face of disappointment. But the easy grin faded the moment his back was turned.

Chapter Nine

The door flew open. "Brodie!" Zoey had obviously been waiting there for him to arrive.

Brodie had been sitting in his car for the last ten minutes debating whether or not to drive away. "Zoey, isn't it? Right?" He pointed at her, looking mock-confused.

She giggled. She looked super cute in a Taylor Swift T-shirt and tie-dye shorts.

He grinned. Then handed her a massive box of beads and charms that he'd bought from the toyshop in town on the way over.

He'd walked into the shop like he was trespassing, eyes suddenly awash with stuffed animals and Lego sets and, quite frankly, things he'd never thought he'd need to see again in his life. The girl behind the counter had chosen the bead box for him.

Zoey gasped in delight. "Wow!" Then almost immediately, "Mom is going to go nuts."

"Why?" Brodie couldn't understand how he'd managed

to do something wrong without even setting foot in the house.

"Because this is, like, a Christmas present." Zoey marveled over the fancy box.

Brodie chilled out. He owed the kid eight Christmas presents—one for each year Maeve had denied him. He readied himself with that comeback as Zoey raced ahead toward the kitchen and he strode down the hall, defensively righteous, behind her.

But then in the kitchen he saw Maeve listening, rapt, as Zoey showed her the box and together they forensically examined each little compartment, pointing out the tiny pliers and beads stamped with the letters of the alphabet. When Maeve looked up, there was no annoyance on her face, she just bashed Zoey on the shoulder and said, "Have you said thank you?"

"Yes," Zoey replied immediately without taking her eyes off the beads. Then she paused and said, "No." She looked up at Brodie and said, "Thanks, Brodie."

He nodded. "You're welcome." He wanted to say, *I'm your dad*. Instead, he looked at Maeve. "These are for you," he said, handing her a bunch of flowers, equally over the top. Where the bead box seemed fun in its lavishness, the bouquet seemed immediately too expensive, gaudy even, among the everyday-ness of their home.

During his very short-lived marriage, they'd paid a guy to refresh the flowers in their house what seemed like every day.

Brodie did his best not to think of those days. He was at the height of his solo fame but lonelier than he'd ever been.

Celeste M. was similar levels of famous as him and model-beautiful. They looked good in photos together, everyone said they were the perfect couple. His management team were delirious at the idea of marriage. In retrospect they were playing at being grown-ups, with their huge house and their little dogs.

Aside from growing up at the ranch, his marriage was the only other touchstone he had for family life. Five minutes in Maeve and Zoey's house was enough to tell him that his attempt had been as bad as the *National Enquirer* suggested it was.

As Maeve thanked him for the flowers, he took an instinctive step away, hands in his pockets, on the pretense of taking a look around. He didn't want to tell Zoey he was her dad. That would be a very bad idea. He peered into the living room, at the wooden floors and the shagpile rug, the coffee table covered in papers and felt-tip pens, the iPad propped up, a book open on the well-worn couch.

Behind him, Maeve said, "This was my grandmother's house. I haven't had time to do much to it so don't judge me on the furnishings." She said it kind of jokey, but he wondered if the whole time she was thinking, *he's going to annihilate me in court*.

"It's really nice," he said, turning round, hands still in his pockets. On the wall behind him was a pair of moose antlers and a watercolor of Starlight Mountain at sunset. "Homely."

She made a face. "That's a polite way of putting it."

He laughed, couldn't help himself.

She smiled, then tucked her long hair almost self-consciously behind her ears.

It was strange interacting with her. On the one hand, there was obviously some attraction because they'd slept together—although she was completely the opposite of his type. On the other hand, she was a total stranger and effectively the enemy—she'd kept knowledge of his daughter from him for eight years. But *enemy* didn't feel like the right word. Because as he turned at the sound of a million tiny beads hitting the floor to see Zoey looking up guiltily holding the overzealously ripped packet in her hands, he was secretly—shamefully—quite relieved that Maeve had never told him.

She went to get the dustpan and brush and Brodie pulled up a chair next to Zoey. "So, what are we making?"

"Name bracelets," she said, "like Taylor Swift." She pointed to her T-shirt emblazoned with Taylor's face.

Brodie tipped his head in acknowledgment. "Gotta love Taylor." Then he got his phone out his pocket and said, "I went to one of her concerts a while ago, I've got a video—"

Zoey gasped. "You went? Really?"

"Yeah," Brodie laughed, swiping through his phone photos to find it. "Next time she's touring, I'll take you—if you want?"

Zoey looked like her world had paused. "Mom, did you hear that?" She looked down at her mom's head as Maeve swept up beads.

"That would be incredible, honey, wouldn't it?" Maeve's head came up and she smiled at her daughter, sharing her enthusiasm.

Brodie couldn't help but feel a little smug at Zoey's reaction and thought now might be the time to really blow her mind by telling her that when he was in Silver Sky, he, too, used to fill out stadiums with girls wearing T-shirts with his face on them. He reclined in his chair and said, "Yeah, you know, Zoey, I used to be in—"

"The year above me at school," Maeve cut in before he could finish. She stood up with the dustpan and brush. "Brodie was in the year above me at school," she said again, more definitively, her eyes locked on his in warning.

Brodie frowned.

Zoey said, "Yeah, I know, you told me that already," and gave her mom a look like she was losing it.

Maeve put the dustpan full of beads on the floor by the back door to deal with later and said, "Did I? Silly me." Then she mouthed something at Brodie that seemed like gibberish at first, until she did jazz hands and sternly shook her head and he realized it was actually "*No bamboozling*."

Annoyed that he wasn't able to wow Zoey with his past, Brodie briefly wondered what else he had to offer, then turned back to the task in front of him and said, "So, what name are you doing?" He nodded toward Zoey's bracelet.

Zoey made an exasperated face. "Zoey!" she said, as if he and her mom were equally perplexing.

They had pizza and salad for dinner. Water in glasses with tiny clouds printed on them.

For some stupid reason, when Maeve had said come for dinner, Brodie had imagined some three-course thing, where they might start with a glass of crisp white wine and end by breaking out the good bourbon to discuss logistics.

His phone pinged as he was reaching for an extra slice of the pepperoni and he paused, got it out his pocket and read the message. It was his friends in San Diego checking what time he was arriving.

"Mom says no phones at the table," Zoey admonished.

Brodie glanced up from the screen, saw Maeve looking anywhere but him. "Sorry," he said. "I didn't think. Yes, that's very rude."

Zoey nodded in agreement.

For a moment, Brodie thought longingly of San Diego. Imagined lying on the deck of the yacht, cracking open a beer and casting his fishing line while being able to scroll on his phone to his heart's content.

Later, as they were having scoops of vanilla ice cream and sprinkles, and had talked all about Zoey's day at school and she'd recited the lyrics to a number of Taylor Swift songs, Brodie said, "So, what do you want to be when you grow up?"

"A vet, a YouTuber, an actress," she replied without pause, lifting up her hand to count them off. "And I'd also like to run an animal sanctuary."

Brodie's mouth turned down, impressed. "Well, they are very complementary professions."

Over the other side of the table, he heard Maeve either scoff or laugh as she scooped up her ice cream. He surprised himself by hoping it was a laugh. He'd noticed that every time he and Zoey spoke, Maeve reached for her water or patted her lips with her napkin to hide her face as if having to take a moment to calm herself down.

Zoey looked confused. "You think?"

"Why not?" he said, turning to look directly at her. "You train as a vet, you set up a little sanctuary in the back yard, you film yourself saving some cute little hamster with a broken leg, post it on YouTube, follow up with videos of it limping around on its little crutches." He did an impression. Zoey snorted when she laughed, which made her laugh some more. That made Brodie laugh, too. "You'll have like ten million followers in no time," he said, still smiling.

Zoey turned to Maeve, "See, Mom, I *can* be a YouTuber when I'm older."

Maeve nodded, her smile less overt than Zoey's. "Looks like it, doesn't it?"

Brodie realized that this choice of profession must be an ongoing argument, and he felt momentarily like he'd messed up. But then, how was he to know?

Zoey sat back all smug and said, "Can Brodie come for dinner every day?"

Brodie swallowed. This was fun and everything, but the idea of sitting around the table every evening eating pizza and ice cream and talking Taylor Swift made his palms start to sweat.

Luckily, before she could answer, Maeve's pager went off. Brodie was about to quip, *No phones at the table*, when she picked it up and said, "Oh, no!"

"That means Mom's gotta work," Zoey said matter-of-factly.

Chapter Ten

Maeve had never been more relieved to be called in for an emergency. She stood up from the table. "Sorry, Brodie, I'm afraid we'll have to do this again another time. Zoey, I'll call Carole, okay?"

"Oh, I hate Carole," Zoey moaned.

"You do *not* hate Carole."

"She makes me wash my face with a flannel."

Brodie sniggered.

Maeve threw him a glare. It was bad enough him dazzling Zoey with his Taylor Swift tickets—she couldn't imagine the reaction when her daughter found out about Silver Sky—but there he was, all crease-eyed and chilled sharing a joke with Zoey, arm looped casually over the back of his chair. She had tried to convince herself that she could handle this, that she could be mature enough to let him into their lives, but she wanted him gone. Out the house. Out of her space. He was too handsome, too funny, too laid-back. He was on a different stratum of society to her, one with money and power and chiseled good looks. What did he want? What was he planning to do? She wanted him to disappear back to his waterfront Malibu mansion that she'd seen pictures of in *Architectural Digest* and that had original Keith Haring prints on the walls and a snazzy, temperature-controlled wine room.

"I can babysit," he said, eyes smiling as if nothing could be easier or more obvious.

"No." She replied too quickly.

"Yes!" said Zoey at the same time. Then scrunched up her nose at her mom and said, "Why not?" She turned to Brodie. "We could watch Harry Potter."

"Only if it's one of the first four," he said without missing a beat. "I haven't finished reading book five yet."

Zoey giggled.

Maeve realized she was doomed.

Her daughter scrabbled off her chair to go and set up the TV. On her way she stopped and said, "He can do it—babysit—can't he, Mom? Please." She held her hands together pleadingly.

Brodie watched, smiling dazzlingly from his chair. Innocently casual, the ball now in Maeve's court.

She wanted to say no again. Every fiber of her being screamed no. But she had to be rational. He was a Carter. They were good people. He was Zoey's father—whether she liked it or not. He was, underneath it all—maybe—the same guy from school who everyone loved, who charmed the teachers and the lunch ladies and was the star quarterback but also the lead in the school play, and who sang for the old people at the charity Thanksgiving meal. He was Brodie Carter, not the Big Bad Wolf.

But still. She wanted him to go.

She thought of all the times she had imagined something like this happening and how in every scenario she'd pictured herself cool as a cucumber, confident in her own role as Zoey's mother and humbly open to this man coming into her child's life. What she hadn't counted on, however, were her own involuntary emotions. The insecurity when he came armed with extravagant perfectly-pitched gifts, the terror when she realized how much money—and therefore power—he had at his fingertips. But most of all, the envy, the bone-deep jealousy inside her when he made Zoey laugh so effortlessly. She could look into the future and see the relationship that they'd build, shooting off to Taylor Swift concerts in his open-top car while posting it all on YouTube. He was Fun Dad.

She didn't want to be jealous.

She needed some space to think. The world she had so tightly controlled was unraveling before her eyes. "Let me go and get changed and think about it."

Once in her bedroom, she called Bella. "Would you trust Brodie Carter to babysit your kid?"

"Yes, of course," Bella replied, no hesitation. Then she paused. "Why? Is Brodie looking after Zoey?"

"Kind of," Maeve replied, screwing up her face, not ready for questions. "Can you not mention this conversation to Logan, please?"

"Okay—are you all right, Maeve?"

"Fine," she sighed. "I'm fine. Gotta go."

Maeve went back downstairs, changed and ready for work. "Okay, you can babysit."

Zoey whooped.

"But there are conditions."

Brodie's lips twitched. "Absolutely," he said, as if he wouldn't expect anything less, though she wondered if anyone had said no to him in his life.

Behind her, she caught Zoey doing a little victory dance and shooed her away into the living room before going over to pull out the chair opposite Brodie.

"You don't leave the house," she said. "Neither of you, either separately or together."

Brodie shook his head. "No, ma'am."

She cocked her head. "Don't do that."

"What?"

Maeve didn't reply because she knew that he knew *what*, judging by the smirk on his face.

"Sorry," he said, holding up his hands. "I'm not very good at being told off. Ask my brothers."

"I'm not telling you off, Brodie. I'm not your teacher." She tipped her head back.

"No, of course not." He smirked again, seemingly unable to help himself.

She pushed her chair back. "I'm going to call Carole."

"No," he held his hands up again. "Please don't. Sorry." He schooled his features. "I'll be serious." He shook his head like he was trying to rid himself of his childishness. "Okay," he said, gravely. "I'm ready." He rolled his shoulders back. "Can I take her to the movies?"

"Brodie, I just said, don't leave the house."

"Did you?"

She put her head in her hands. Her phone bleeped and her pager went off again. "I really have to go. Please, Brodie, don't go anywhere, don't anything. Just—" She sighed. "It's a school night. Zoey has to be in bed at eight. By your standards, it's boring. You watch TV, she goes to bed, you sit here on the couch for the rest of the evening. You go up if she gets scared. It's not glamorous or exciting —it's just—" she felt weirdly guilty saying the word "—parenting."

His mouth opened slightly as if he was going to protest but then he seemed to reconsider and gave a small lift of his chin to show he'd understood. "I hear you," he said.

She narrowed her eyes, trying to look behind the charm and the beauty and the little turn up of his mouth that clearly got him everything he ever wanted. "Do you?"

He nodded. "Yes, ma'am."

She sighed.

He bit down on a grin. "Sorry."

Maeve ignored him. She had no choice but to trust him. He was the dad. And as much as she wanted it to be, this wasn't only *her* chessboard now. "Just look after her."

Before he could reply, Zoey appeared in the doorway. "Are we going to the movies?" she asked with an excited grin in Brodie's direction, like she'd listened in on some of what had been said but had felt too guilty to eavesdrop on all of it.

Brodie shook his head. "Nah, sorry, kid, we have to stay in."

"Why?" Zoey whined. "Just 'cause Mom says…" Her

eyes immediately zeroed in on Maeve like she was the worst person in the world.

Maeve flinched.

But then Brodie said, "No, that's not it. It's school tomorrow. No one goes out on a school night. Not even me." He made a face like the idea was pure madness. "On a school night," he said, strolling in the direction of the living room, "you want to get cozy and sit on the couch and watch Harry Potter—but actually not the third movie, either, because that is *terrifying*."

Zoey followed him, Maeve could sense her daughter's wariness, like she knew she was being played, but as long as Brodie was involved, she would play along herself. "Can we have popcorn?"

Brodie glanced back at Maeve who would normally say no because they'd already had ice cream but didn't want to give any more fodder to being Mean Mom, so she said, "Yes, it's in the cupboard above the toaster."

Brodie tipped his head. "Harry Potter and popcorn. That's like my *perfect* evening."

There was Zoey's sweet tinkling little giggle.

"Okay, I have to go," Maeve said, kissing Zoey and throwing Brodie another warning glare. "Have fun." Then she left before she could change her mind. But once outside, she glanced back at the cozy, low-lit living room, the film paused and ready on the TV, and knew this was the start. Good or bad.

She looked up at the sky, offering a silent plea: *please don't let him break her heart*.

Then she caught sight of Brodie, watching her watching

them, his eyes creasing, and a grin spreading wide when she noticed. He raised a hand in a casual wave. Maeve's stomach tightened at the ease of it all for him, all chocolate-box handsome, sprawled on the couch, prodding Zoey in the ribs to wave, too. Brodie Carter was in her living room. She waved back, then turned quickly away, refusing to even contemplate what his presence might do to her own heart.

Chapter Eleven

The birds were singing when Maeve came home. Finches and sparrows clung to the feeder that her grandma had hung in the aspen tree. She had sat with Zoey as a toddler pointing out all the tiny birds that relied on it. Maeve kept it topped up in her grandma's memory and Zoey could name every bird species that fed from it. Now, however, the birds just served as a reminder that it was morning already and she hadn't had any sleep.

The house was silent when she walked in. She'd let Brodie know as soon as she found out herself that she wasn't going to make it back till morning and given him Carole's number but he'd texted back a thumbs-up emoji and said all was good, he could stay.

Maeve felt weird about the idea of him being in her house. His zippy little car parked outside. His shoes in the corridor.

She peered into the living room to see Zoey asleep on one couch under her comforter and Brodie asleep on the other, tucked up under her grandma's quilt that usually lived on the back of the couch. She paused in the doorway watching them sleep. Brodie on his back, legs too long for the space so his feet poked out the end. Zoey curled up like a mouse, all her stuffed animals positioned around her. Maeve imagined the scene, the total lack of bargaining that would be needed for Brodie to allow her to decamp downstairs. Zoey would have loved it.

Brodie opened one eye as if he could sense Maeve in the room. Then both eyes. Then he stretched and said, "What time is it?"

"Seven," Maeve replied, feeling a strange intimacy at the fact he was waking up, stretching in front of her, his hair unkempt. He sat up and rubbed his face.

The night they had spent together eight years ago, he'd been up and dressed when she'd woken up. All traces of the Autumn Falls boy were gone and the famous person back in place. "Gotta go to work," he'd said, like he was off to the office. With a quick peck on the forehead, he'd left, saying, "Enjoy the room service." She'd gathered up her belongings and fled, couldn't imagine anything more humiliating than sitting around eating eggs Benedict as a consolation prize.

She said, "Sorry it took so long."

He shook his head. "Not a problem." He yawned again. "I slept pretty well, actually."

Maeve never slept well at other people's houses. Brodie was obviously one of those people who could sleep anywhere, or, she thought wryly, had a lot of practice.

"Mom!" Zoey woke up. "Brodie let me sleep on the couch!" Her tone was gleeful.

"So I see." Maeve raised a brow in mock-admonishment at her daughter, as they both knew it wasn't really allowed.

Brodie frowned. "You said you always do it!"

Zoey bit down on a guilty grin.

Maeve said, "You were very lucky." Then, "Now go and get ready for school and I'll make you breakfast."

After much cajoling, Zoey gathered up all her plushies and went upstairs to change.

Brodie followed Maeve into the kitchen. He'd slept in his jeans and a T-shirt. He watched her putting toast in the toaster and said, "Have you slept at all?"

She scooped coffee into the machine. "No."

He pulled out a chair. "Aren't you exhausted?"

"Yes." She turned round to face him. "Toast or cereal?"

He shook his head. "I don't really eat breakfast. Just a coffee. Do you want me to do it?"

She didn't even pause, so unused to having another adult in the house to help. "No, it's fine, thanks."

Brodie sat down at the table. "Is this what it's always like?"

She didn't know how to answer. Couldn't work out if it was a judgment. Didn't want him to think that she couldn't cope. "Not always. It's fine," she said, flicking on the coffee machine. "I'm used to it." But it came out more defensively than she'd intended.

She felt his eyes on her back as she got the peanut butter from the cupboard and spread it on the toast.

"I want to tell her."

Maeve paused her spreading. She turned to face him, the

knife still in her hand. "I want you to wait. Let her get to know you."

He drummed his fingers on the table. Again, she wondered how often he heard the word no. "Why?"

"Brodie, you're new in her life It's too much to come in and tell her you're her dad. Last night you were about to tell her you were once as famous as Taylor Swift—"

He looked mildly affronted by the word *once*.

"I mean, I'm sure you're still as famous—"

"No, of course not." He glossed over her clumsy attempt to make it better.

It hadn't occurred to her before that he might still crave that level of fame. Sometimes, late at night, she'd go on his Instagram, see him standing with a scantily clad model on some Malibu beach with his surfboard under his arm or taking a selfie on the world's best golf course, and presumed he relished retirement.

"Anyway," she said, going back to the toast. "It's too much. She's only little. We have to take our time."

Brodie gave it two seconds' thought before seemingly accepting the rationale and said, "Maybe I could pick her up from school?" He stood up to pour the coffee when the machine was done. "Take her for a smoothie at the diner or something? You take milk?"

Maeve looked at the cups he'd chosen. They weren't her normal coffee cups. On instinct, she was about to say something about how she liked the striped ones for morning coffee but stopped herself in time. How used to living on her own she had become. "No milk, thanks."

Brodie turned so that he was leaning against the

countertop, one hand wrapped round his coffee mug. For some reason, it seemed obvious that he wasn't someone who'd use the handle.

Maeve took a deep breath and said, "If you take her out, someone will photograph the two of you together and then I—we—lose control of the narrative." She saw Brodie about to protest that she was being overly cautious, but she carried on before he could. "Why else would you be photographed with an eight-year-old?"

He shrugged. "She could be my niece?"

"But she's not," Maeve shot back.

Brodie sighed, clearly annoyed. He looked away out the window, squinting in the shaft of sunlight. Hair sticking up, faint stubble on his face. His attractiveness was a dominating presence to have in the room, took some of the air away, made it difficult to breathe. Made her want to just say, fine have what you want.

Then she looked past his profile at where he was looking and saw a sparrow on the birdfeeder and a goldfinch taking a bath in the water bowl. She thought how much she had gone through to get to this point and rolled her shoulders back, resolute.

"So how do I—we—do this?" he asked, turning back after the pause had hung for long enough without him getting his way.

"I don't know," she replied, willing the floor to open up and for him to disappear. "We make a plan." She moved to the hallway to shout, "Zoey, your breakfast is ready."

When she came back Brodie had moved so he was standing in the kitchen doorway and they almost collided.

He seemed completely normal again, any hint of annoyance gone, as if he couldn't be derailed by anything for long. "Are you working this weekend?"

"Why?" she squeezed past him suspiciously. How could someone smell so good after a night on the couch?

He followed her back into the room where she busied herself putting the toast on the table and pouring Zoey's juice. "We could go to the cabin," he said, eyes now alight as if there had never been an idea better. "It's my uncle's. It's in the middle of nowhere. No one around for miles. We used to go there to write songs. I'll call and check it's empty, but he's rarely there. Yeah?" He already had his phone out his pocket.

Maeve buttered herself some toast, she was starving—she'd barely eaten since their pizza the night before. "Brodie, I'm not staying in a cabin with you in the middle of nowhere."

That made him pause, look up from his phone and grin. "Why not?"

She tipped her head exasperated. "I don't know you."

"Oh, come on," he huffed like that was the stupidest reason he'd ever heard. "We grew up together."

"You'd barely spoken to me before—" She paused, then a little too formally said, "Before that night."

Brodie raised a brow, grinned knowingly. "We have a child together, Maeve, I think we know each other well enough."

Maeve was about to both protest and shush him, but the subject closed at the sound of Zoey thundering down the stairs and swinging round the banister to hurl herself into the kitchen. "Don't you think my school uniform's gross?" she said to Brodie, pulling at the collar of her maroon polo.

"Awful," he agreed. "But we all had to wear it."

"You wore this?" She looked down at the shirt with its Autumn Falls Elementary School logo.

He nodded. "Oh, yeah."

Zoey sat down in her chair and picked up her toast, seeming to suddenly wear the uniform with a little more pride. "Brodie loves Harry Potter, Mom. He's a Gryffindor, like me."

Maeve had taken a seat and was spreading jam on her second slice of toast. She looked up at Brodie and said disbelievingly, "You're not a Gryffindor."

Brodie's mouth opened in shock. "I am!" he said, defensively, pulling out the chair closest to him. "What are you?"

"Mom's a Ravenclaw," Zoey said, as she was chewing. "She took it twice and still got Ravenclaw."

Brodie sniggered. "Who wants to be Ravenclaw?" he said conspiratorially.

Zoey giggled back.

Maeve put her toast down. "For someone who's only halfway through book five, I don't think you're in a position to mock me."

Brodie frowned, feigning offense. "Are you making fun of me for being a slow reader?"

Zoey raised her brows. "Mom?"

Maeve sighed. "No. Yes. I suppose so."

Brodie shook his head. "That's harsh."

"Yeah, Mom." Zoey folded her arms over her chest.

Brodie leaned over to Zoey and, without taking his eyes off Maeve, whispered, "Typical Ravenclaw behavior."

Zoey nodded, wide-eyed with knowing.

Maeve shook her head, refusing to succumb to the smile tugging at her lips or the feeling of how like a family this felt. "I apologize."

"I should hope so," Brodie said allowing his own smile to spread across his face. She remembered then how the full power of his attention blinded like the sun.

She had to look away, downing the rest of her coffee and standing up, she said, "Zoey, we need to go."

Zoey nodded, holding her piece of toast between her teeth as she yanked on her school bag, then taking the toast out again, she asked, "Are you coming over tonight as well, Brodie?"

Maeve had told her they were old friends catching up, that he hadn't been in town for years, which Zoey seemed to think meant he'd be there every second of the day.

Brodie pushed in his chair and went over to the dishwasher to put his cup in. "Not tonight, unfortunately," he said, following them out into the hallway, "but maybe at the weekend." He looked pointedly at Maeve over Zoey's head as she put her school shoes on.

"Why, what's happening at the weekend?" came Zoey's muffled voice.

Maeve couldn't believe he'd mentioned it in front of Zoey and, glaring at him dumbfounded, shrugged as if she had no choice now.

Brodie chose to completely ignore the undertone and

grinned at her over Zoey's head. "Excellent," he said. "So, I'll send you directions to the cabin."

"Cabin!" Zoey gasped.

When Maeve's mouth pursed, he winked, as if a flash of his boyish charm would make up for getting his own way.

She shook her head to let him know it hadn't worked, while at the same time trying to ignore the little burst of stars exploding in her stomach.

Chapter Twelve

The cabin sat on the edge of the Redemption River, deep in the foothills of Starlight Mountain. A small wooden structure, it was built by Brodie's Uncle Joel, his mom's sister's husband. It was his fishing retreat. When Brodie rang to ask if he could use it that weekend, Uncle Joel couldn't have been happier for someone to go check on the place. Since his hip operation, he hadn't made a trip there all year. "It'll be you and a fair number of critters, I think."

Brodie hated spiders. "No problem. Thanks, Uncle Joel."

"Anytime, Brodie, you know that."

There had been many times when Brodie wished Uncle Joel had been his dad. Uncle Joel would do things like get his guitar out at a family gathering and, with no apology in the face of Emmett's derision, agree with Brodie's mom that it would be a good time for a song. Brodie would watch him and Aunt Eleanor singing so unselfconsciously together and marvel, almost wistfully, at the idea of two people aligning in such a way, while his dad rolled his eyes and sloped off outside. Just the idea of simple merriment was so alien to Emmett. The idea that his dad might laugh. Uncle Joel laughed all the time. He tapped his foot as he strummed his guitar and he closed his eyes when he felt the rhythm of the music. Brodie remembered the time when he was about thirteen and his mom said, "Brodie, sing Uncle Joel that song you wrote last week." His dad had been in the room, too. Brodie had winced, felt the embarrassed shame of preferring to sit in his bedroom writing songs to riding out on the land. And yet also a shame deeper, that his mom would never say, "Brodie sing it to your dad." But he sang Uncle Joel the song he wrote anyway, and even though his dad didn't look up from his catalogue, afterwards Uncle Joel blew out a breath and said, "You've got some voice, kid. I can feel all the hairs on the back of my neck standing up on end." Then he'd laughed, as if he couldn't quite believe it. "Some voice."

Brodie sometimes wondered if his whole life's ambition centered on those words—someone finally finding value in something he did.

Brodie's Aston Martin wasn't built for the dirt track that led to the cabin. It bumped along on the ruts in the earth and he heard the scrape of metal, but the view when he pulled up was worth it. The morning sun glinting on the glassy water, the reflections of the pines so clear, so perfect that it was hard to tell real from imaginary. Above him, the sky was the cobalt-blue of a child's painting.

Twice he had picked up the phone to call and cancel the weekend, and twice he'd told himself not to. There was still time to leave and pretend he'd never known about Zoey, just live his life as normal. It was how he had dealt with most other things up to now. But then he would remember her smile when she ate the Cheerio off the floor, or when she appeared in the doorway in her pajamas with all her stuffed animals when he was babysitting and said with big hopeful eyes, "It's more fun down here." When he looked at her, he saw himself. That was hard to walk away from.

Brodie got out the car, took off his sunglasses, and stood for a moment just taking it in. The warm, reddish wood of the cabin, the old Adirondack chairs on the veranda, the curls of old leaves, the creak of the boards as he took the steps up to the front door. He put his hands in his back pockets and looked out over the river, remembered driving here with his younger brother Ethan every time they wanted to get away, write the songs for the new album. He could hear the echo of the easy laughter, the conversations that didn't halt to take in the view, the idle pushing open of the door and dumping their bags, grabbing a cold beer, chucking themselves down on the Adirondacks, still without thought, without notice, maybe even yanking off their T-shirts and jeans and diving into the cool, clear water. They had taken it for granted, that time, that enjoyment, that purpose. And yet, what was happiness if not the times you were fully in the moment, taking life for granted?

"Brodie!" The sound of Zoey's voice made him turn and smile as she careened down the path. "This is amazing! Can we swim in the river? Hey, look there's a swing! Do you think it's haunted? Wow, a canoe!"

Brodie blew out a breath, senses overwhelmed by her enthusiasm. "Slow down, kid. Where's your mom?"

"Over there." She waved absently behind her like her mom and the journey were already forgotten, pulling her Crocs off and dipping her toes in the cool water.

Brodie jumped down off the veranda and walked round the side of the cabin where he saw Maeve locking the car, which she'd parked further up the track to avoid the potholes, something he probably should have done. She hadn't seen him, and he watched her unnoticed as she stopped, closed her eyes for a moment and took a breath in. Most people would be enjoying the fresh country air, but it looked more like she was steeling herself for what was to come. Eyes closed, she looked softer than he'd seen her before, her blonde hair in a braid over her shoulder, bangs swept either side of her face. Her skin was still pale, the circles under her eyes darker than they should be, and he wondered how many more emergencies she'd covered that week. She wore baggy brown cords cinched with a battered leather belt and a thin yellow T-shirt. He wouldn't pick it for someone as an outfit, but it suited her. In her hand was a straw sunhat which she pulled on when she opened her eyes and started making her way down the slight slope. It was then that she saw him. He waved guiltily at having been caught watching her. "Hi."

She raised a hand. "Hi."

"You find the place okay?"

"Fine."

"Well, welcome." He gestured to the cabin and the chocolate-box scenery and smiled; the sun broke through the pine trees dusting everything in glitter. He leaned against the cabin wall, folded his arms across his chest, felt a little flutter of pride at being able to bring her to a place of such beauty, maybe even wow her a little. He'd actually never brought a woman here and wondered suddenly why not. It was perfect.

But Maeve seemed unfazed by the majesty of the place. As she came and stood next to him, her attention was focused first and foremost on where Zoey was. Once she'd seen her paddling in the shallows, she turned his way, locked him with her serious gaze and said, "You can put that smile away, Brodie. I'm here for Zoey, that's all."

He was caught momentarily off-guard by the statement. Was he really that obvious? But then, as she raised a brow to make it clear that she could see straight through him, he felt the guilty-as-charged grin start to spread over his face and did his best to hold it in check. He tipped his head. "Understood."

Part of him wondered if it was easier to flirt with her than remind himself that she hadn't told him about his daughter. That every time he saw her something in his brain always knocked in warning to say, *this isn't your friend*. But he hated having that kind of pressure in his life. And he hated having to feel that way about anyone, especially a woman, especially one as pretty and, despite the outfit, downright appealing as Maeve.

She leaned round him to look at the little wooden cabin. "This is very nice," she said, as if now that was cleared up, she could acquiesce to the charm of the place.

"No one's been here for a while so there might be lots of spiders inside." He shuddered at the idea.

It was Maeve's lips that twitched this time, her eyes lighting up in a way he'd never seen before. "You afraid of spiders, Brodie?"

He paused, sensed her goading and said, "Not in the slightest, I just thought you might want to know."

She slipped her hands into the pockets of her pants. "I'm fine with spiders."

"Good," he said. "Me, too."

Maeve kicked the dry leaves on the ground with a smile on her face. Brodie found himself grinning, too. Standing side by side, not looking at each other.

Chapter Thirteen

"Brodie!" Zoey shouted, from the shoreline. "Come and see the fish!"

Brodie immediately loped away in the direction of the shoreline where Zoey waited expectantly.

Maeve watched him go and, kicking off his flip-flops, stand ankle-deep next to her daughter and look where she was pointing. He was wearing khaki shorts and a gray marl sweatshirt with the sleeves pushed up, and beside Zoey in her cut-offs and red-and-white striped T-shirt they looked like something out of a fashion shoot, the epic scenery stretching out ahead of them. It was a good reminder after that unexpected weird almost-flirtation that had taken place, that things with Brodie were always too perfect. At school he'd had his pick of the best-looking girls. He was on all the first sports teams—she'd watched him sometimes in the Friday Night Lights polo games with Jack and Logan, whizzing up the pitch, loving it, grinning delightedly at the competition of it all. His words, his mannerisms, his clothes, it was all super slick and faultless but, as she'd discovered, he didn't hang around when you woke up in the morning. He had the big lavish wedding but then the catastrophic divorce, he had the number-one solo career but then canned the third album and got sued by his record label; his mom was forever sighing about how he flitted into the ranch laden with gifts but was gone before anyone could have a conversation with him; his sister complained about how he'd seduce her friends and then leave her to pick up the pieces. He was like a magpie. He picked up anything shiny then dropped it when he got bored.

She watched her daughter lie down next to him on the end of the jetty, their noses almost touching the water so they could spot the giant fish, and felt a lump of concern in her throat. Zoey was ever-so-shiny.

Maeve put her hands on her hips and watched Brodie flick water in her face pretending to be a fish and Zoey screeching then laughing and giving him a shove.

She was ever-so-shiny and ever-so-vulnerable.

And even though Maeve knew all those stories about Brodie, he was like an illusionist, he could make you unbelieve everything you knew just with that dimpled grin.

She sat down on the edge of the veranda and kept her eyes fixed on her daughter. *Please don't break her heart*, she mouthed silently as Brodie whipped off his sweater, chucked his phone on the jetty and dived into the water, beckoning Zoey to do the same. Her daughter glanced back at her to check it was okay to jump in fully clothed and Maeve smiled and nodded, who was she to stop them?

She had to keep her distance from Brodie's golden

charm, if only because it would be her job to pick up the pieces of Zoey's heart if it all went wrong.

But, she told herself, for now they were there and it was for Zoey. And Zoey—currently screeching at the coldness of the water and splashing Brodie—was having the time of her life.

Maeve went to open the door to the cabin but it was locked. She thought about calling to Brodie to ask where the key was but that would interrupt them and pause the fun. She needed to put the milk she'd brought in the fridge, make up the bed in case they did decide to stay—which she still hadn't made up her mind about—but she couldn't do any of that.

Brodie hauled himself out of the water and beckoned Zoey to do the same, then he pushed her in and she cackled with glee. He did it every time she got out.

When Maeve swam with Zoey it was to teach her to swim.

No, she had to tamp down the envy. She wouldn't allow it.

With nothing to do, and reluctant to let her daughter out of her sight for too long, Maeve sat on one of the Adirondacks and watched them. The weather-beaten wood was smooth, almost soft, as she laid her hands on the rests. She kicked off her shoes and stretched her legs out in front of her. She didn't close her eyes, she would never close her eyes while Zoey was in the water, but she allowed herself to sink down into the chair because there was simply nothing else for her to do. Her body resisted at first, alert, as if the chance to relax was a trick, but after a while she felt her shoulders begin to drop. She stayed sitting and watching until she heard Zoey say, "I'm hungry," and Brodie say, "I'm Brodie." Then, "You have to hunt what you want to eat." Zoey gasped. And Brodie nodded, as if he'd never said anything more serious. Then Zoey's bottom lip trembled in a way so familiar to Maeve that she was already out of her chair and walking toward her when Zoey burst into tears.

Brodie's eyes widened, perplexed, as he dried his torso with his T-shirt. "I'm just kidding! Seriously! I've got a bunch of stuff to eat—chips, Pop-Tarts, popcorn—there might even be an apple if you really search for it."

Maeve stroked Zoey's wet hair, making sure not to look at Brodie half-naked. "D'you hear that? Pop-Tarts."

Zoey turned to look warily at Brodie. "Are they chocolate?"

He made a face as he yanked on his T-shirt. "What other flavor is there?"

Maeve rummaged in their bag and pulled out a towel, which Zoey wrapped around her sodden clothes while Brodie unlocked the cabin and pushed open the door. "Ladies first."

Maeve eyed him suspiciously. "Are you basically sending me in to find the spiders?"

Brodie scoffed. "Certainly not." Then to Zoey he said, "That would be very un-Gryffindor behavior."

Maeve picked up her bag, and sweeping past him muttered, "Seeing as you definitely cheated on that test, I wouldn't be surpris—" But she never finished the accusation because she was immediately distracted by the interior of the cabin. She walked in a few paces then turned in a circle to try and take it all in. The main room was small with timber-clad walls and thick ceiling beams. Huge windows at either end made the best of the views. Two huge couches dominated the main living space, covered with big cushions and plaid blankets. On the wooden floor were dark, patterned rugs, worn threadbare where they'd been walked on over the years. The furniture—the tables and sideboards—looked handmade, as if when his uncle realized he needed something, he went outside and knocked it up from wood he found in the forest. The rough walls were hung with tapestries and big paintings and photographs that fitted the landscape. Maeve had never been anywhere more perfect.

"It's good, huh?" Brodie said, pride in his voice.

She walked further into the room, ran her hand along one of the soft blankets on the back of the couch. "It's amazing."

Zoey had run off already and shouted, "This is my room."

"Zoey, we're not definitely staying," Maeve called back.

Brodie frowned. "I thought you were."

"I thought we could just play it by ear." Maeve turned and leaned against the arm of the couch. "I don't want it all to be too overwhelming."

Brodie waved her concern away as unwarranted. "Zoey's having a great time."

"We've been here half an hour."

"There's no point putting an end on it before its begun, that's asking for trouble." As he spoke, he went back out onto the veranda to pick up a massive grocery store bag and hauled it into the kitchen.

Maeve followed, picking up her own smaller bag of supplies.

"You gotta loosen up," he said, unpacking champagne and the cereal with marshmallows in it, his tone half-joking, as if he knew it was an annoying thing to say. "Go with the flow."

She narrowed her eyes. "Don't."

He paused, lips twitching. "Sorry."

"Brodie," she said, unpacking her own groceries. She noticed that she had bought the sensible things like milk and bread. "The only way I've got through the last eight years is by planning and organizing, by not *loosening up*."

She regretted saying it immediately. The atmosphere of the room shifted and his movements lost their underlying joviality.

As he took the milk from her to put in the fridge, she waited for the comeback, the cool reply about how if she'd told him about Zoey, then he could have helped with that burden. She knew he was more than justified in saying whatever he wanted in that regard, and she braced herself.

But it never came. Instead, his features softened into that infamous grin, and he shrugged and said, "It's never too late to learn."

Chapter Fourteen

Brodie had pictured Maeve hiding away in the cabin while he and Zoey hung out, but after the moment in the kitchen, she seemed more amenable to his suggestions. Maybe she felt she owed it to him.

When Brodie suggested they all take the canoes out, Maeve's reluctance was only visible in her slight hesitation before she said, "That sounds fun!"

He wasn't certain if he'd said it to punish her or to push her out of her comfort zone. His feelings around her were still hazy, tangled with confusion.

And it was fun. Brodie went with Zoey in the two-man, and Maeve went on her own in the single. She was wearing a perfunctory Speedo but he couldn't resist the odd glance in between bouts of Zoey telling him that he wasn't trying hard enough with the paddling. He took them to all his favorite spots along the river, coves that hadn't changed since he'd last been there, fishing spots where he and Ethan would go if they needed a meditative moment to get the creative juices flowing, a dip in the rocks that created a shallow pool, which in the summer sun heated up like a hot tub. Zoey loved it, lying flat like a starfish. Maeve, he couldn't read. Her guards were so high it was lucky he could see her eyes.

On the way back, the current in the center of the river did most of the work for them and he couldn't help watching Maeve as she took the opportunity to look around at the scenery. Caught unawares, all her emotions played out on her face. The awe of the giant pines towering above them. The beauty of the sunlight reflected on the water.

"Look, there's an eagle!" He pointed. They gasped in wonder, and he felt a swell of pleasure at their response.

Then he felt stupid at his own thoughts of heroism. He heard his brothers' voices in his head. "That's not an eagle, Brodie!" Laughing. Faster than him in the canoe. Everything a race to win. He always felt it in Autumn Falls; the fear perhaps that he'd never be able to grow up.

Zoey turned around and said, "Do you think it could eat us?" snapping him out of that thought.

"If it was really hungry, maybe," he replied dryly.

She narrowed her eyes to see if he was joking and, clearly deciding that he was, said, "You're bigger, they'd eat you first."

He laughed, taken by surprise at the comeback. She turned away smugly. He stared at the back of her head, her damp brown hair in a scruffy ponytail, tendrils stuck to her slender neck. That was what it was like for your kid to make you laugh.

Your kid.

He wondered suddenly if he might hyperventilate.

Breathe, Brodie. Breathe.

He focused on a spot on the canoe, thought about calm things, like skiing down snowy white mountains, ordering an espresso after a meal, watching the NBA game in bed while the Malibu waves crashed outside his window.

His life really wasn't designed for having a child.

"Sorry, what was that?" He realized Zoey had been talking to him.

"I said, do you have a girlfriend?" she repeated, exasperated that he hadn't hung off her every word.

"No." He shook his head. "Do you have a boyfriend?"

She made a face like the idea was disgusting. "No!" Then going back to her original train of thought, she asked, "Do you want my mom to be your girlfriend?"

Brodie laughed. Momentarily, he thought about his last girlfriend, Angelina, a supermodel from Milan. They had been together for six months, seen each other approximately once a fortnight and both dated other people throughout. He was not in the market for relationships with small-town doctors who would definitely require more commitment than that.

"Zoey!" Maeve cut in admonishingly from the canoe next to them.

"What?" Zoey asked, acting all innocent. "I was only asking. You told me I should always ask if I had a question."

"Sorry, Brodie," Maeve said, ignoring her daughter, her cheeks bright pink with embarrassment.

Brodie shook his head like it was of no consequence, but

he found Maeve's blush surprisingly endearing. Turning back to Zoey, he said, "I think your mom would make a wonderful girlfriend, but right now we're all pretty happy as we are."

Zoey started paddling again, mollified. Brodie glanced at Maeve who gave him a small smile of thanks. For the tiniest moment he imagined what it would be like for her to be his girlfriend. Warmth sprang to mind. The colors of fall.

But at the same time a claustrophobic pressure on his chest that made him fear for hyperventilation again.

He started paddling with more effort, wanting to get back to the cabin and away from the questions.

But the questions didn't stop. His daughter, it turned out, was a one-girl question machine. She fired them out like bullets.

His daughter. It shocked him to say it in his head. He went back to calling her Zoey.

"Do you like ducks? I think they might be my favorite bird. What's your favorite bird?"

"A flamingo. How could you not choose a bird that stands on one leg?"

"Do you think fish can see what we see?"

"Yes."

"If you had to be a tree, which one would you be?"

"That one."

"Why do you look at your phone so much?"

"It's an addiction that I will try and break now that you've pointed it out."

Along with the questions came the activities. Brodie's body ached. They'd canoed, they'd rock-climbed, they'd walked, they'd made small houses out of branches and leaves, they'd had a diving competition, swimming races.

The pinnacle came when Zoey opened a trunk in one of the bedrooms and found all of Aunt Eleanor's pageant clothes. "Oh, my goodness!" Her eyes lit up. "This is awesome!"

Later, Zoey stood admiring herself in the mirror wearing a dress that was so big it pooled around her ankles with giant puffed sleeves and so much diamanté it glittered like aluminum foil.

Brodie caught a glimpse of himself in the mirror behind her, slumped in a chair wearing a tiara and a sash, his arms forced into a too-tight spangly jacket, his eyes drooping with tiredness.

Maeve came into the room and let out a snort of surprise when she saw him. "Oh, dear," she said, in a sympathetic doctor voice.

Zoey spun round, panic in her big brown eyes. "We're not leaving, are we?"

Having previously been aghast at the idea of cutting the weekend short, Brodie found himself longing for home, to pour a gin and tonic and have a lie down. He was exhausted, mentally, physically.

Maeve, clearly sensing his fatigue, said, "We should head home, Zo, it's been a long day. Everyone's very tired."

Brodie felt a flicker of relief at the idea.

"No!" Zoey looked like she was going to cry, all the tiny diamantés shimmered as she moved. "Please?" She turned from her mom to Brodie. "Please make her let us stay, please!"

Brodie could barely haul himself up from the chair. "You're welcome to stay," he said, and even to his ears his voice lacked conviction.

Maeve raised a brow, the corner of her mouth turning up like she could see through the lie. "I think we should probably leave you to it, Brodie, it's a lot for one day."

He rolled his shoulders as best he could in the satin jacket, willing his energy back. He thought of life in the band, the grueling tours, the jam-packed schedules with one day off a year, the promos, the interviews, the rehearsing. What had happened to him over the years? His dad would say he'd gone soft. He thought wistfully of the time spent lying on the deck of his yacht, arms behind his head, soaking up the sun.

"No." Zoey started to cry silently, her shoulders curled forward so the puffy sleeves of the gown flopped forlornly like an under-stuffed toy.

A voice inside Brodie said that he didn't need this. He'd done enough to impress the kid. They could pack up, he could jump in the car and get the heck out of there.

It was on the tip of his tongue to say, *Your mom's right*, but something stopped him. It wasn't the tremble of Zoey's bottom lip—which, while heartbreaking, was something his well-hardened heart could deal with—instead, it was the stoicism of Maeve's body language. She, too, had rock-climbed, she'd come on the walk with them, she'd been cajoled into the diving and swimming races, she'd faced a similar barrage of questions, she'd helped Zoey when her house of leaves and sticks kept falling down. The only thing she hadn't done was dress up in gaudy pageant attire, but that was only because she had volunteered to clear up after their picnic dinner. And yet she would bundle the upset child into the car and drive her back and put her to bed and wake up in the morning and do it all again.

It made Brodie feel weak. And he hated feeling weak. It reminded him of life under his dad's roof. The feeling that he wasn't good enough, couldn't cut it, didn't have the backbone to do an honest day's work. He imagined Emmett walking in now, saying, "Someone hands you even an ounce of responsibility and you crumble. Typical." His reflection in the pageant dress-up only seemed to make him more the fool.

So, he found himself saying, "Stay," louder this time, with more conviction.

Maeve tipped her head uncertainly, brows raised. "Are you sure, Brodie?"

Zoey dared to wipe her eyes and smile hopefully.

"Of course," he replied. "It's not every day Aunt Eleanor's Miss America outfits see the light of day. Here—" He took his tiara off and chucked it across the room to Maeve. "You're woefully underdressed."

Chapter Fifteen

Zoey was tucked up in clean cream sheets, under plaid blankets. "I've had the best day," she said.

Brodie was walking past the doorway and paused when he heard her say it. Now that she was going to bed—and he wasn't having to perform, could sit down and finally have a drink—he saw it all as much sweeter.

He listened as Maeve said, "Good, I'm glad. Now go to sleep because you're really tired."

He peered in without them seeing and saw Maeve kiss her on the forehead and, stroking her hair back, say, "Call me if you need anything." Then she turned the sidelight off and started toward the door.

Brodie backed away so she wouldn't catch him listening.

Zoey said, "Mom?"

"Yeah."

"He could be your boyfriend."

Brodie bit down on a smile. It was cute. The kid was persistent.

He heard Maeve laugh. "No, Zo, he couldn't."

Brodie cocked his head and frowned at how easily she dismissed the idea. He caught his reflection in an old gilt mirror on the wall. Why not? What was wrong with him? He knew he was a better-than-average-looking guy, women flocked to him.

Zoey voiced his question for him. "Why not?"

Maeve paused.

He thought suddenly that she was going to tell her that he was her dad and he felt his heart almost stop, terror chase up his spine. How flippant he'd been when he'd told Maeve to tell her. Now he realized he was in no way ready for that revelation. Maeve of course didn't say anything other than, "Because he's just a friend."

And Brodie felt his heart start up again.

He went and sat outside on the Adirondack chair, ankle crossed over his knee, looking out at the last embers of the sun rippling over the water. Thought of Maeve referring to him as a friend. It made him chuckle that she'd been forced to say it because he knew he was someone who wouldn't normally register on her friendship radar. He imagined her friends sat around discussing literature and analyzing complex medical dilemmas. He knew she thought he was flighty. But she wasn't someone he would usually align himself with. His bunch of friends were carefree and fun-loving, ring one of them up and suggest an impromptu trip to the Alps or Long Island and they were there. When any of them peeled off into the married-with-kids bracket he tended to wave them off with a wry look of pity.

He imagined them watching, dumbfounded, as he played happy families at the cabin.

Maeve came out onto the deck, her hair tied haphazardly on top of her head, wearing gray tracksuit bottoms and the yellow T-shirt. "That's a crazy view," she said.

He noticed she made no effort to dress up. Not that he would have expected her to, it just wasn't what he was used to. Usually, there would be skin-tight leggings or a flash of bare midriff. But it wasn't just that she didn't dress to impress, it was that she wore things he had an active dislike for, like Birkenstocks—with their round toes like ugly mushrooms—worn with white sports socks. She didn't seem to care what he thought of how she looked, which, he had to admit, was an anomaly in the women he met. Part of him wondered if she was doing it deliberately to put him off, but that felt too contrived for someone like Maeve. There was a possibility she *actually* didn't care what he thought.

He gestured for her to sit in the other Adirondack. "Do you want a drink?" He'd brought out the champagne and a couple of glasses. She laughed when she saw them, and he knew she was mocking his choice of beverage. Most women Brodie knew loved a glass of champagne in a mountain cabin.

"That would be lovely, thank you." She sat down in the seat next to him, sitting back but definitely not relaxed.

The bubbles fizzed over the edge of the glass and ran down the side over his hand. He shook the liquid off as he handed her the glass. "Sorry, I can usually pour better than that."

"It's fine. I don't usually drink champagne and watch the sunset."

He wondered then if she hadn't been mocking him, rather had been momentarily taken aback by the decadence.

She sipped her drink. Brodie sipped his. "You like it?" he asked, knowing that it was a loaded question.

Maeve shrugged. "Yeah, it's really nice."

Brodie said, "It's from my vineyard in Napa. It's not actually champagne—we're not allowed to call it that because it's not from Champagne—but it's up there with the best." He was showing off, he couldn't help it, he did it on autopilot around women.

Maeve smiled politely, didn't seem massively impressed with the quality of his sparkling vintage. Instead, she said, "I didn't know you had a vineyard. That must be a lot of work."

"For the people who run it, yeah!" Brodie joked.

"You're not involved?" She seemed surprised.

Brodie shrugged. "I'm not really there enough. When I am, it's great. But it's more of an investment."

Her silent nod propelled him to say more, not liking the impression she was forming of him swaggering into his vineyard a couple of times a year to taste the Pinot Noir. "I actually have learned quite a lot," he admitted because her values seemed to be different to those of the people he hung around with—who were more concerned with when the next bottle would be opened. "I didn't think I'd be that interested in vines but—" He glanced to see if she was listening. "Well, they're complicated little fellas."

"Yeah," she agreed. "John-Luke has some at the orchard. I watch him out there talking to them."

"I'll admit I've never said a word to my vines," he replied, and she laughed, mouth closed, eyes creasing as she looked down at the glass in her lap. It felt as if some of the awkwardness between them was lessening.

But then they lapsed into silence again.

Brodie hated any kind of social discomfort or unease. He knew it probably had something to do with his dad—the protracted silences that came with Emmett's stern disapproval of the boys when they'd done something wrong, silences that Brodie itched to fill, to crack a joke, to make it good again and eventually run as far away as he could.

But it was Maeve who said, "How did you find today?" and he imagined her using the same tone as she stood at the side of a patient's bed, calmly assessing.

"Good," he said. Then, "Exhausting!" Maybe to try and make her laugh and it worked. She laughed out loud, seemingly surprising herself.

"I take it that's what most days are like?" He gestured back to where Zoey was asleep, thinking he could happily shut his eyes and take a little nap.

"Yes," Maeve replied, still with the hint of a smile. "It's hardcore."

"You're telling me." He blew out a breath. The most brutal bits had been when he was just having a sit down and Zoey ran over, grabbed his hand and dragged him to look at some poor frog quivering under a rock or beg him to climb the pine tree to get a fir cone.

"It's better now she's older."

Brodie felt his eyes widen. *"Better?"*

He watched her brows draw together as she looked at him like he was joking. "Yeah, *way* better."

He shook his head. He couldn't have spent eight years doing that. He'd be a wreck. Again, the image of himself prostrate on his yacht flashed into his head. "Wow." He wondered if he was missing a trick somewhere. "And you're a doctor, too." He was genuinely perplexed.

She laughed and he thought he saw her relax a little. She leaned back in her chair and, rolling her head his way, said, "I guess—" She paused, rolled her lips together as she thought about what to say. "It's hard but you just get on with it." She sipped her drink, the condensation fogging the glass. "I got through it, that's the best I did."

"Please!" From what Brodie had seen of her so far, he imagined she'd aced it. "I'm picturing you sitting in classes with a baby strapped to your front, blazing a trail with all those crusty Stanford professors."

He couldn't even imagine getting into somewhere like Stanford, let alone with the goal of medical school. Brodie had dropped out of school at fifteen when they'd signed with the record label. They'd had tutors, but he didn't pay a huge amount of attention. Who wanted to do lessons when there were mobs of screaming girls outside and interviewers begging for an audience, and cities to explore after dark? He was living his best life, and algebra didn't register highly on that agenda.

Maeve put her wine glass down on the deck and, taking a deep breath as if bracing for something, said, "I wasn't at Stanford, Brodie."

He was intuitive enough to know that the statement meant something. He found himself wanting to rewind five minutes and go back to talking about the vineyard. He said, "My mistake, sorry, I thought you were."

She considered for a moment, then said, "I mean, I *was* at Stanford," she corrected herself. "But not when I had Zoey."

Brodie shifted a fraction in his seat. He thought about saying that his vineyard had a fourteenth-century, Tuscan-inspired castle on the grounds. Instead, he said what he was meant to say, which was, "What happened?"

She bit her bottom lip for a second, then she tucked her leg underneath her and turned his way, as if she knew she had to go through this at some point. "My parents—Let's just say they weren't too happy about the fact I was pregnant. Or, you know—" she swallowed awkwardly "—the circumstances around it."

The more time Brodie spent with Maeve, the more he could recall glimpses of the night they spent together. His main memory had been of a very pretty girl with a really sexy pair of silver boots. But he was starting to recall other stuff, too. Like a lot of laughing. And ripping open a packet of hotel hot chocolate when normally he'd ordered up expensive room service. He had an inkling they'd played *Super Mario*, which didn't usually happen on his nights with women. Either way, in his view of it there were no life-changing ramifications. No sad eyes or heads bowed in shame.

"My parents were paying for Stanford, and, well, when they knew there was going to be a baby, they decided that it was no longer the best use of their money." She glanced up, eyes narrowing in humorless amusement, like that was the polite way of saying what her parents had said. "They felt that I had not made the *best use of my potential*." She smiled wryly as she said it like she'd lived with those words, that disappointment, for a long time.

Her parents obviously had the same playbook as his dad.

"So, where did you study then?" he asked, reluctant to let go of the halcyon picture he'd painted of Maeve with a baby sling and a Stanford sweater frolicking around campus with her cooing college friends.

"Jackson University."

That made Brodie pause. "I didn't even know Jackson had a university."

She laughed and said diplomatically, "It's very small, but it's okay."

"It's not Stanford, though."

"No—" she shook her head "—it's not Stanford. But it worked. My grandma, she lived in the house in Autumn Falls, she let me come live with her. She went against my parents, which I know was really tough for her." Maeve stopped talking and reached down for the champagne glass that she'd put on the deck.

In that pause, Brodie tried to think what he'd been doing

at that time. A world tour. Having, he hated to admit it, an absolutely fantastic time.

Maeve clearly needed a subject change and, looking out toward the lake as she took a sip of the sparkling wine, said, "I've never seen the river this still, it's perfect."

The sun had disappeared behind the pines, the last shafts of light dancing between the branches and glinting off the river like silver fish.

Brodie said, "Go for a swim." He felt weirdly guilty thinking about how he'd been jetting across the globe, soaring over the crowds at various international stadiums on high wires while Maeve was living with a screaming baby—his screaming baby—a grandma, and at the same time commuting to nowheresville, Jackson to study for a medical degree.

"No way!" She looked at him like he was crazy for suggesting a swim. "I couldn't."

"Why not?"

"Because."

"That's not a proper answer." Then gesturing toward the view, he said, "Go, honestly, you won't regret it. I've got it covered here."

He had an ulterior motive for suggesting it, he craved a bit of time to sit back and relax, to think of nothing. He tried his hardest in life to avoid any kind of heavy conversation, it was a good tactic until it thwacked into him like a freight train. It seemed to be happening more and more recently. First when his older brother Jack died a few years back, and now this news about Zoey.

He tried not to think too much about things he didn't

want to, but these big moments would sideswipe him when he least expected it.

It still shocked him about Jack. He had seen him so rarely in the years leading up to his death that it was easy to imagine him still alive, living in LA, shooting his new movie. Jack and Brodie hadn't been the closest as adults, but as kids, Brodie had spent a lot of time hiding out with Jack avoiding ranch work. Jack knew all the best places to lie low. They'd spent many hours together sniggering in the gap between the wall and the chicken coop as one of his brothers called their names, trying to find them to help. They'd eat cookies snuck out from the house and talk trash. It was only when his dad's booming voice would cut across the yard with the threat of some hideous punishment that Jack would push Brodie out and make him take the first round of the verbal lashing. Jack would saunter over later when the worst of Emmett's annoyance was over. It happened time and again, Brodie never learned. When Jack died, it was like all those memories of their childhood antics flared back to life, popping up when he'd least expect it, filling him with equal amounts of disdain and nostalgia for life in Autumn Falls, a place he had previously thought very little about. Those memories had kept burning bright ever since, however much he tried to tamp them down again.

Chapter Sixteen

The last eight years were kind of a blur for Maeve. It was like looking back on running a marathon, she knew it had been hard, but the only evidence were the aches in her body and the tiredness that went deep to the core of her being. Never in all that time did she think she would be swimming in the Redemption River at twilight while Brodie Carter kept an eye on Zoey.

The water was luxuriously cool, rippling over her skin with every stroke she took. When she turned and dipped her head back, a delightful chill crept over her scalp and then as she lay fully submerged she could hear nothing but a low hum of the water. She floated like Zoey would, arms outstretched. Above her, the faint outline of the moon as the sky darkened. She felt cocooned away from the world, levitating above real life.

Then she heard Zoey calling and immediately pulled herself upright in the water and scanned the view of the cabin to see what was wrong. But all she saw was Brodie piling up logs to make a fire just in front of the veranda. She called over to ask if it had been Zoey and he shook his head. Then he smiled. That infamous crooked grin that had sold a million albums and graced posters on bedroom walls.

Maeve's insides fluttered, her breath caught. Berating herself, she started to swim toward the shore.

It was dangerous to relax too much. There were too many shadows—too much coming that she needed her strength for, her armor. She must never again allow herself to be distracted by—succumb to—that grin.

"Good swim?" Brodie asked, ambling casually to the shoreline to hand her one of the navy bath towels.

The brief interaction felt strangely intimate, like they were a couple. Their hands brushed as she took it and she was suddenly hyperaware of wearing only her bathing suit. It made her take a few steps away as she wrapped herself in the towel. "Thanks, yes, it was lovely."

Brodie held her gaze for a second longer than normal. She wondered if he, too, had felt the jolt as their hands touched. But then he just nodded and went back to the fire.

Small flames licked at the base of the pile of logs. It surprised her that he knew how to build a fire, which was stupid because he'd grown up on the ranch, but he was so golden nowadays it was hard to imagine him getting his hands dirty.

He had brought the chairs down from the veranda and placed them either side of the fire.

Part of her wanted to call it a night and the excuse of getting changed was the perfect opportunity to do so, but she also knew that there wouldn't be many opportunities where they would be alone. Especially in a setting so remote from real life. And there were things she needed to say to him still.

She rewrapped the towel around her waist and pulled her Jackson hospital sweater on over her damp bathing suit then sat down next to the fire.

Brodie perched on the edge of his chair, stoking the flames with a stick. He looked boyish in the firelight, flopping haired and twinkly eyed, like he used to at school. It made her say, "You said you used to come here with Ethan?"

Ethan was Brodie's younger brother, same year at school as Maeve. Cut class all the time. Way too cool to be friends with Maeve, but she knew him through her friend Piper, the one who'd persuaded her to go to Brodie's concert.

Brodie looked up, there was something about his eyes that made him look like he was permanently amused by a joke, the uptilt at the corners and the fan of coal-black lashes.

Don't look, Maeve. She lowered her gaze.

"Yeah, this is where we wrote a lot of Silver Sky songs. Just the two of us. They were good times."

"You miss him?" she asked. No one had seen Ethan for years. But a while back, Maeve had bumped into Piper at the grocery store and her friend had told her that she thought she'd seen the elusive Carter brother on her street. "It was weirdest thing, I looked out my window and I swear I saw Ethan standing under the streetlamp."

Maeve had said that she didn't think he'd stand under a streetlamp if he didn't want anyone to know he was there, which seemed to be the case as no one had heard from him, but Piper was having none of it. "It was him, Maeve, I know it was," she'd said.

"Yeah, I miss him," Brodie nodded without question. "He was like…" He paused trying to think of an analogy. "I don't know, I can't explain it. I can write a good song on my own, but with Ethan, it becomes something else. He can see a lyric or a melody and know *exactly* what to change to take it to another level, give a song some gravitas." Then he laughed. "I didn't even know I knew that word."

Maeve laughed despite herself.

The smile in Brodie's eyes only intensified having made her laugh.

The air seemed to still, pause on the moment.

She felt her face get warm and pulled her damp hair up from her neck. *Don't look at him, Maeve.*

They sat in silence but it wasn't the same silence as before. There was suddenly an awareness to it rather than an awkwardness. She could hear her breathing, watched the movement of his throat as he swallowed. She should have gone to bed. She tried to stay focused, willed herself not to look at him, but she couldn't help it, her gaze drawn to his side of the fire, the hypnotic blue of his eyes. *It's not real, Maeve*, she warned herself. *It's all just a trick of the light.*

"Brodie, I've been meaning to tell you…" she began cautiously.

His brows drew together. "Is this to do with Ethan?"

There was a hopefulness to the question that made her feel for him as she shook her head. "No, it's to do with your mom."

"*My* mom?" He pointed to his chest as if to confirm.

The tension dropped like a stone, gone in an instant at the mention of his mother.

"Yeah." She nodded, leaning down to pick up a twig from the ground and chucking it on the fire. "She's helped me quite a lot with Zoey."

Brodie cocked his head. "Does she know?"

Maeve winced. "No. And I feel awful about it." She bit down on her nail, a terrible habit that she'd got into at medical school, so she tucked her hands into the cuffs of her sweater. "My grandma died when Zoey was three years old. It was really sudden." Maeve remembered coming home and finding her grandma apparently asleep in her chair one afternoon. There was a bag of apples on the floor next to her that she'd obviously been given by John-Luke at the orchard as she'd walked past. She still had her coat on. Maeve had known as she stood in the doorway, she'd seen enough death at work to know that her lovely grandma was gone. She'd walked over and pressed her cheek to hers, her eyes welling with tears, and said, "Thank you for everything." Clutched her grandma's clasped hands in hers and said a prayer for her to sleep peacefully. When Maeve had stood, it felt like the world had given way underneath her.

"I was a bit of a mess afterwards for a while," she said to Brodie, who was studying her too intently for her liking, like he could see through to everything she was thinking. "My grandma had always looked after Zoey, so without her I was pretty overwhelmed by everything. One day in the grocery store, Zoey was having a meltdown and I just kind of broke down—it was a bad day," she added jokily to try and lighten what she was saying.

Brodie smiled softly.

Don't look at me like that.

Maeve tried her very best not to be distracted by the creasing of his eyes at the corners.

"Anyway," she said, forcing her gaze back to look at the fire, "your mom was there, and she tried to help me but I was *so* terrified of her getting involved that I just ran away from her. Literally, picked up Zoey and fled. She must have thought I was crazy. After that, any time I saw her, I'd completely avoid her, even though she was just trying to help. She'd come round and ring on the bell and I'd pretend not to be at home."

Brodie gave a wry smile. "She's a very persistent woman!"

"Tell me about it!"

He chuckled and it seemed to bring them suddenly closer, joined, almost like family, by such intimate knowledge of a parent's behavior.

Maeve hurried on, "I had found this babysitter who would take care of Zoey in the afternoons. She seemed great, Zoey loved her, but then things started going wrong in her life and I didn't realize quick enough. Your mom came round one day and found her passed out drunk in the hallway." Maeve shuddered at the memory of it. "It was really bad. I shouldn't have let it happen. Martha rang me at college, all calm while I was panicking, and made me tell her where the spare key was and that she would take Zoey home and not to worry." Maeve sighed as she looked up at

Brodie. "Of course, I left straight away to come and get her and there she was, fast asleep in a little crib—that was probably your crib once!—at Silver Sky. I could hardly breathe. Zoey was your mom's granddaughter and she had no idea. It was awful." She covered her cheeks with her hands. "I couldn't say anything."

Brodie sat forward, brow furrowed, hands clasped in front of him. "Didn't you think that we could have helped? Given you money? Made life easier?"

"Of course I did." She looked across at him over the fire, his wide, clear eyes reminding her so much of Zoey's. She stared, almost beseeching, as she said, "Think back, you were so famous, Brodie, you could have anything you wanted. And I'd already kept the truth from you. I didn't know how you'd react." It was a risk, her honesty, laying out her vulnerability for him, but it felt like the only way. "You were a gazillionaire and I'm in my grandma's house with a drunk babysitter barely able to scrape together the money to eat and work and put gas in the car while studying full-time. I was not in a secure place. And maybe you wouldn't have tried to take Zoey away—" the fear of him swooping in and gathering Zoey up had forever kept Maeve awake at night "—but I couldn't take that risk. I was scared, I was young, I had no one." Stupidly, she felt her eyes well up, and she was not a crier! "I know it sounds like an excuse, Brodie, but I just didn't want to lose my daughter."

Chapter Seventeen

Brodie wanted to stop her, to tell her that she didn't need to say all these things. Even though he wanted to hear them. He felt like a fraud expecting this justification because he knew, with certainty, that if she had told him at the time, bar throwing obscene amounts of money at the problem, the situation would likely have been the same—his mom would have stepped in to help.

He sat back in his chair and sighed as he looked across at Maeve, sitting with her damp hair in tendrils in her baggy sweater and towel, a haunted look of fear on her pale face, eyes glittering maybe with hidden tears, and said, "I'd like to think that I wouldn't have tried to take her away."

While he wanted to stick with that train of thought—felt a moral right to make Maeve regret her past choices—as he said it, he had a flash memory of his and his ex-wife, Celeste's demand for unicorns at their wedding. It pained him to think too much about his own ego. The addictive amusement of demanding the impossible when money was no object. The certainty that life revolved without doubt around him. He could imagine being on tour saying, "I want to see my daughter now." He thought of Celeste, cuddling her little dogs, saying, "Brodie let's have a baby. The dogs would *love* it!" And him balking. He could have shipped in Zoey for them to play with. He cringed at what he knew of his past self. It was all about the fun. Everything in his life at that time had been done for him. Even when he and Celeste realized they couldn't stand each other, they'd simply handed the reins over to lawyers to deal with it. He couldn't have looked after a child. He didn't even know how to pay his own bills when his music career ended.

"All I wanted," Maeve said, "was security—safety—and I could do that, just about, alone. I couldn't trust what might happen if I told you. I didn't know you."

Brodie looked down at his hands for a moment, then he looked up, met her gaze and nodded slowly. He watched her shoulders drop a fraction. "But like you said before, you still don't know me."

"No—" her eyes were more steely now "—but I know myself better. What I'm capable of."

Brodie thought about that for a moment. The only sound was the river rippling over the rocks. The last of the blood-red sunset giving the air an ethereal glow. He wondered if he could say the same about himself. Recalling that time of his life with Celeste was enough to make him curl in on himself, like he'd taken a hit on the football field.

Did he know himself? What he was capable of? He thought of his dad: *One day, Brodie, you'll grow up and see that life's not just fun and games.*

Maeve sat back in her chair, pulled her knees up, her bare feet flat on the edge of the seat. "I'm not looking forward to Martha's reaction when she finds out. She's been so good to me and I've, well, you know…"

Brodie ran his hand through his hair, wondering what his mom would say. He tried to imagine her getting annoyed, but all he could see was her face softening at the idea that she had a bona fide grandchild, and that it was Brodie of all people who had made it happen. "I think she'll be pretty thrilled when she finds out."

"I think she might be mad."

He shook his head. "No, she's not like that." He thought of the times his mom would come and sit on his bed and say things like, "I know it's tough, Brodie, but just because you don't see eye to eye, it doesn't mean you're not special to your dad." Brodie would know it was a lie but it made him feel better all the same. "And you're more special than anything to me, all of you are."

When his mom had gotten sick and they'd auditioned for the band, he wrote songs like there was no tomorrow. His pen couldn't move quick enough on the paper. They poured out of him like therapy. Every fear and blank, cold terror for the future came out in those lyrics. Some people said it was the songs that won them the audition. They'd certainly made Brodie and Ethan millions. They were the soundtrack still to people's weddings and funerals. An alchemy that he'd all but forgotten about.

"I *am* sorry, Brodie, that I didn't tell you," Maeve said.

Brodie could barely meet the earnestness in her eyes. Her story was like listening to something very far away, a turning off the path of his life that, even if there had been a signpost, he would have shot past at full speed. He hated to admit it, but the more he thought about it, the more he was glad, in fact, that there was no signpost. But he couldn't bring himself to say that out loud. Such a confession would undercut everything she had been through, all her fear and anxiety. And yet he felt like a fraud nodding in acceptance at what had seemed like a justification, and now her apology.

Really, all he could think was, given who he was eight years ago—he still cringed at his wedding pictures in *People* magazine with the carpet of scattered rose petals and the golden horse/unicorn-drawn carriage—he could not be certain that his daughter would be the inquisitive, strong, vivacious kid he had spent the day with.

His daughter.

He reached for a gulp of champagne. Then dangling the flute between his fingers, he said, "I'm sorry I didn't return your calls."

Maeve blinked as if taken by surprise then laughed. "I did get sent a copy of the album and a signed photo."

He winced at the idea of it, pressing his thumb and forefinger to his forehead thinking of how often he'd just turned any and all admin over to his management. "I hope you ripped it up."

"I saved it for Zoey."

He nodded, embarrassed, pleased, confused. Then he sat forward in his chair and after a moment's silence said, "You've done a really good job with her, much better than I could ever have done."

And again, clearly caught by surprise, she said, "Thanks, Brodie. I really appreciate that."

Their eyes met for a moment, hers holding a grateful smile, soft with unchecked vulnerability.

Brodie had enough experience to know he wasn't imagining the tiny crackle that sparked between them like an ember falling from the fire, a sizzling awareness that shivered through him, but the moment he felt it, the moment he saw her feel it, Maeve turned sharply away, like she'd promised herself never to go there.

Chapter Eighteen

Maeve slept better than she had in years, curled up on a twin bed next to Zoey. It had taken her a while to fall asleep, reliving the conversation with Brodie, replaying again and again the tiny nod he'd given her in understanding of her past decisions. She would never be able to put into words how important that nod had been to her, how it relaxed every muscle in her body just a tiny bit, tension she hadn't known she'd carried with her every day for the last eight years.

She told herself that was all she cared about—if her thoughts strayed to the looks over the fire that made her heart thrum, trapped and frantic, she convinced herself it meant nothing. Brodie was nothing if not a master of the lingering look.

Thick blankets hung as curtains over the windows and the sun streamed in through the cracks giving the room a pale glow and the comforting scent of warm wool. Zoey snored softly in the adjacent bed. Maeve was torn between snuggling down and sleeping longer or getting up and making the most of a few precious hours alone before anyone else woke up.

She chose the latter, and pulling on her tracksuit bottoms and an orange sweater with a hood she could bury herself cozily inside, she went to make herself coffee.

In the kitchen, she was surprised to see the coffee machine on and half full, a note on the counter read, *help yourself!* in the kind of confident slanting cursive that she imagined someone like Brodie would have.

Maeve poured herself a cup and looked around but there was no sign of him in the cabin.

Hands wrapped round the thick pottery mug, she walked outside. There were no curtains to block the sunshine now and it bathed the veranda like a coat of yellow paint, filtering through the pines and the aspens, coloring the leaves the mock gold of fall.

She took a seat on the veranda steps to gaze out at the river, warm mist hovering like clouds over the water, and sighed at the calm beauty of it all.

It was then she saw Brodie carving lengths through the water, fluid and agile, water glistening off his bronzed skin with each stroke, sun catching on the droplets as they fell from his fingertips, his hair slicked back dark. She stared with her cup to her lips. When she realized she was staring, she gave herself a shake, drank a slug of too-hot coffee and burned her mouth. And rather than think about his tanned, muscular arms, she thought how surprising it was to see him so athletically active. It put her floating-on-her-back to shame last night.

As he swam through the mist, there was a serenity to the scene that made her feel like she was intruding. He always seemed to be on show and yet this was just him swimming alone in the river of his childhood.

She was staring, again. She shut her mouth, swallowed, felt the invasion of her gaze but couldn't look away.

Before she could think about standing up and going back inside, however, he stopped swimming and, looking toward the cabin, waved when he saw her.

Maeve forced a smile and waved back. She tried to play it cool but it seemed obvious that she'd been watching him. How did raising her hand to wave back somehow feel trite and rehearsed, like she was some starstruck fan?

Brodie swam toward the shore and when he got to the shallows, strode out of the water. She tried not to stare at him, the sun glinting off his torso. "Morning!" he grinned.

"Hi." She saw his towel draped over the balustrade and when he got close enough, she pulled it down and chucked it to him, hoping he might cover himself up.

Instead, he just roughly dried himself then wrapped the towel around his waist so his chest was still on display, the honeycomb muscles and shoulders wide enough to shadow the sun as he stood in front of her. "It's perfect out there," he said, slicking back his hair with both hands.

She imagined him on a photoshoot and willed the previous version of him back, the one who hadn't known he was being watched. When she looked up, all she could see was *him*, her vision engulfed by all his glowing skin and bench-pressed abs.

"Do you think you could just—" She raised a hand and waved it in the vague region of his chest.

"What?" Brodie looked confused.

Maeve scrunched up her nose, embarrassed that she'd even said anything. "You know, dial it back a bit."

"What do you mean?" Brodie looked down at himself.

"This." She motioned up and down with her hand. "The whole photoshoot vibe."

Brodie barked a laugh in understanding. "Sorry," he said. "Is the sight of my bare chest too much for you?"

"Quite frankly, yes." All hopes of playing it cool were now out the window. "Especially at seven in the morning."

Brodie laughed as he grabbed his T-shirt from the railing and yanked it on. Then he flopped down in the chair across from where she was sitting on the steps. His hands hanging relaxedly off the armrests of the Adirondack, his head tipped slightly back, he said, "So you find me distracting?"

Maeve closed her eyes for a second, she could feel her cheeks flaming, embarrassed that she'd ever said anything. It made her defensive. "I don't find you distracting. I find you too much of a—"

"What?"

"Too much of a show, I guess."

He raised a brow, feigning offense.

She shrugged, like she was only being honest but knew she was just trying to dampen his ego to level the playing field. "Sometimes it's hard to tell with you, Brodie, what's real and what's not."

But rather than deterring him, a slow, crooked grin spread across his face as he drawled, "It's all real, baby."

Maeve shook her head in despair. She had to laugh. Across from her Brodie was grinning, all dimples and wolfish eyes, clearly very much enjoying himself.

Picking up her coffee cup, Maeve stood and said, exasperated, "Get me back to normality!"

His laugh followed her back to the cabin.

Chapter Nineteen

Brodie was still reclining in the Adirondack, half snoozing, half remembering, with renewed amusement, Maeve tucked into a terrible orange hoodie waving her hand up and down his body asking him to dial it back. He'd been very taken with her pink cheeks and attempts to justify her request.

The mist had lifted from the river. A cormorant was drying its wings on a fallen branch. The sun was getting warmer as the morning ticked on.

He yawned and stretched his arms above his head. When he let them flop down either side of him he almost jumped out of his skin to see Zoey standing on the veranda steps eating a bowl of the cereal with marshmallows he'd brought.

"We're not allowed this at home," she said, heaping great spoonfuls into her mouth.

"No, neither were we, growing up."

Zoey frowned. "So why'd you buy it?"

Already with the questions.

He thought for a second then said, "So that you'd think I was a fun, cool guy."

Her mouth was full of cereal and she tried not to laugh.

He stifled his own smile. "Can you get me a bowl?"

"Sure."

She put hers down on the veranda table and went back inside. A minute or two later, she came back with a bowl filled to the brim with cereal and milk, carrying it steadily like a tightrope walker over to where Brodie sat.

"This is great, thanks," he said, taking the overfull bowl from her, trying not to spill any on himself. "You're like a miniature servant."

She giggled again and, going to get her own bowl, sat down on the opposite Adirondack, wiggling herself back as she held the bowl steady with both hands. Her legs stuck out horizontally on the chair. For some reason, it was the most heartbreaking thing he'd seen all weekend.

He ate a mouthful of cereal, trying not to think too much about the unexpected burst of emotion at the simple sight of her sitting in a chair. As he chewed, sweet sugariness exploded in his mouth. "Wow," he said. "That is everything cereal isn't meant to be."

"It's good, huh?" Zoey agreed, mouth full, trying not to dribble milk down her chin.

Brodie laughed. "Yeah, it's awesome."

He pointed out the cormorant. Zoey asked how he knew its name. He said he figured his dad must have told him.

Then Zoey said, "I don't have a dad."

Brodie froze. He felt his heart skip a beat in a confusing

mix of both longing and utter terror. He didn't know how to reply. What should he say? There was no way he could tell her the truth on his own without Maeve there. His palms started to sweat. He wasn't even sure if he was ready to tell her. So, after slightly too long a pause, he said, "You can have mine if you want."

She rolled her eyes like he was really silly and then gasped when a fish jumped in the river. Brodie was more than relieved by the distraction. "Do you want to go fishing?"

"Do the fish die?"

"Generally, yes."

Zoey put her spoon down in the bowl and thought for a moment. "Will we eat them?"

"Yes."

"Okay."

"Good. Let me go and get changed and then we can take the boat out." He almost jumped up from his chair, he was so desperate for a breather, his heart still booming from the dad comment. As he took the veranda steps, he realized he should probably check with Maeve if it was okay to take Zoey fishing and said, "Where's your mom?"

"Doing yoga," Zoey replied, her sticking-out feet tapping to some beat in her head as she finished her cereal.

Brodie had to stop himself visibly recoiling. Yoga was another thing on his pet-hate list. Women were always doing it on the yacht in their swimwear, mainly—Brodie concluded—so that the men onboard could ogle their pert bottoms at breakfast. Cynical, he knew, but it was only because he did the same—rolled down his wetsuit before swaggering out of the surf with his board under his arm; snowboarding in just a long-sleeve white thermal and snow pants, hair mussed. He knew his best angles.

Zoey came inside with him and propped up her iPad to watch TV in the living room. Brodie went upstairs on the pretense of getting changed, but really because he was intrigued by the image of Maeve doing yoga.

On the landing, he slowed as he came to her bedroom door that was partially ajar. He could just see through the crack to where she was standing on one leg, arms above her head, eyes closed, wearing black leggings and a gray vest. Perfunctory and plain. Not a flashy athleisure print nor miniscule bikini in sight. She was *actually* doing yoga. As he watched, he found himself distracted by the glisten of sweat on her skin, her face relaxed and serene, her hair knotted high on her head, tendrils escaping round her neck. The calm simplicity of it made him catch his breath. He stepped away feeling suddenly like he was intruding, even a bit ashamed of his world view, and went to shower and get dressed.

Brodie waited downstairs, watching YouTube with Zoey, until Maeve came down to join them, pausing at the bottom of the staircase.

She was wearing knee-length shorts and a baggy white T-shirt, the ugly mushroom shoes on her feet and her hair still pulled on top of her head from the yoga, as if she was deliberately trying to repel him, and yet it was somehow having completely the opposite effect.

"Mom, Brodie's taking me fishing," Zoey said excitedly, half an eye still on the iPad screen.

Maeve nodded. "You know the fish die, Zo?"

"Yes," she replied matter-of-factly.

Not wanting to sound like the useless, unthinking parent, Brodie said, "I did tell her. She's fully prepared for the consequences."

Maeve seemed to mull it over for a moment then said, "Okay. Well, good luck."

Zoey jumped up and went to put on her Crocs. Brodie walked out with Maeve and said, "Do you want to come, too?"

She shook her head. "No. I think it's good for you two to spend some time together."

Brodie felt a twinge of unexpected disappointment that she wasn't clamoring to spend time with him. "Sure?"

She half laughed. "An hour here on my own reading my book in complete silence? I'm sure."

He found himself laughing back because, after just one exhausting day, he was in on the parenting joke. For a split-second he felt the physically impossible; both unfathomably, joyously light and yet the weight of the entire world pressing down on him all at once.

He loped over to the boat, trying his hardest to feel nothing at all.

It was a small wooden rowboat. The same one he and Ethan used to take out. Ethan loved rowing and, more often than not, that meant Brodie could just stretch out at the bow of the boat and take in the scenery or catch up on some sleep.

Today, however, he was manning the oars, Zoey saying things like, "Do the fish die right away?" and, looking at the hook on the line and the box of dried mealworms he'd found in the fishing cupboard, "Do you think it hurts them?"

By the time they got halfway to the best fishing spot on the river, Brodie—torn because he loved nothing more than to do a little fishing—said, "Zoey, would you prefer it if we just looked at the fish rather than actually did any fishing?"

Her huge brown eyes raised to his and after a little pause, she nodded.

"Okay," he said, smiling inside to himself. Then as she settled back, visibly relieved that no fish would be harmed on the trip, he handed the oars over to her and said, "Your turn."

"Ha-ha," she replied, sardonically, and looked for a second like his twin brother, Noah. It gave Brodie a bolt of shock. It was the first time he'd really properly seen the Carter family resemblance—and of course it would be when Zoey was looking at him derisively. Again, the feeling was half pride, half gut-punching horror.

"No seriously," he said, "I'm tired. Get rowing."

"I'm eight," she replied with confusion. "I'm not rowing."

Brodie pulled the oars in, put his hands behind his head and lay back. "Guess we'll just have to stay here, then."

Zoey assessed him, head tilted, beady eyes trying to see if he was serious or not. Now she looked like Maeve. He watched her covertly through half-closed lids. When he showed no signs of movement, she harrumphed and, reaching forward, took hold of the oars, heaving them practically over her head with each stroke.

Brodie opened an eye and watched. The sight made him smile. If she wasn't going to learn to fish, she could learn to row. At the thought, he felt suddenly like his dad when Emmett made Brodie do something he was clearly too young for or just reluctant to try. He realized there was a certain pride in making your kid do something they didn't think they were capable of.

He shifted uncomfortably as he lay back in the boat. It was an odd feeling, empathizing with his dad. He wasn't sure if it was good or bad.

Chapter Twenty

Maeve looked up from her book to see Zoey rowing them back to shore. The oars kept popping out of the water midway through a stroke, or sometimes missing the water completely, but she was clearly working her hardest and making steady, if slow, progress.

Brodie was leaning back, propped up on his elbows.

When they got closer, he took over the rowing to navigate the landing, and Zoey jumped out while they were still in shallow water, splashing her shorts she was in such a hurry to tell Maeve all about it.

"It's okay, we didn't kill any fish, but Brodie made me row, which was totally unfair but I didn't mind it in the end—and look, I've got a blister on my hand." She held up the soft skin of her palm for Maeve to inspect.

"That looked like really hard work," Maeve said. "Well done."

Brodie came loping over having hauled the boat onto dry land. "She was really good," he said. "A natural."

Maeve felt that tiny prickle of jealousy that Brodie could seemingly persuade Zoey into anything. She couldn't imagine her daughter ever agreeing to row if she'd asked her.

But then as Zoey proceeded to recount every second of the trip with exuberant excitement—especially the bit when Brodie had said they didn't have to do any actual fishing—as well as the faint envy, Maeve felt something else that she couldn't quite get her head round.

Brodie came and stood next to Zoey, swiping a bug or something off the shoulder of her T-shirt as he said, "You were awesome. Much better than I was at your age. This girl's got some muscles." He gave Zoey's bicep a squeeze and she flexed it proudly. "Check those out!" he added with mock amazement.

Maeve watched the interaction, the care that Brodie took around Zoey, the obvious fun they had together and realized that the feeling bubbling inside her was hope.

Maybe this could work. She didn't want to give it too much room, but just a little gap in the guards she had up around them that might allow Brodie to squeeze through—if he really tried!

They spent the rest of the day hanging out. Zoey drew pictures and pressed flowers with Maeve. Brodie taught her to skim stones and then she made him do somersaults and handstands in the water. Sometimes he'd flop down on a chair but then Zoey would yank him up again for a diving competition or similar.

When Zoey got really tired, they went inside and she watched TV. Brodie and Maeve sat on the deck again.

"What would you normally be doing right now?" Maeve asked him.

Brodie thought for a second, looked at his watch and said, "Not sure, having a long lunch somewhere. Or surfing, if I was at home."

"Home?" she asked. "Where would you say that is?"

"Malibu at the moment," he replied, "but I'm not sure if it's *home* home."

She took a sip of the water she'd brought out with her. On the grass, birds pecked at the fallen breadcrumbs from their lunch. "Where's *home* home?"

Brodie thought. "Nowhere." He grinned. "Everywhere."

She looked heavenward, his lifestyle was incorrigible. "So ... what would be your plan—with Zoey—if—When you tell her who you are?"

He shrugged, all casual. "I'll be here."

"All the time?" she asked, brow furrowed uncertainly.

"Not *all the time*," he replied, like that was crazy. "But when she wants to see me."

Maeve stood up, she found the conversation made her skin feel too tight. "What if she wants to see you *all the time*?" she asked, leaning against the balcony.

He paused, had no immediate answer. Then he grinned and said, "Some of the time she wants to see me."

Maeve frowned.

Brodie stood up, too, came to stand next to her. "I'm kidding. I'll be here. We'll work something out. Times I have to be here, times I don't."

Maeve nodded, he was too close and she couldn't concentrate. She turned and started walking toward the water. What he'd said was fair enough. But it made her heart dip a little: *times I* have *to be here*.

She would never have expected anything more than part-time with Brodie, but there was always that smidge of hope.

Hope. She kicked a stone. It felt like life with Brodie might involve a lot of it. Swept along by that persuasive smile, hoping he didn't let you down.

"Maeve," he said, standing next to her on the shoreline, "You don't have to look so worried."

She glanced at him, was it that obvious?

There was that smile. She shouldn't have looked.

But she was looking. The forest around them fell suddenly silent. She was seeing the way the corner of his mouth curved, the slow blink of his dark feathery lashes, the hypnotic lure of his sky-blue gaze. She remembered. The way his arm reached like it was right now, so close, the way she leaned slightly toward him, pulled by an invisible thread of simple want, desire to let his palm touch her cheek, to kiss and be kissed like that one fateful night, to relive a moment carved so memorably in her mind it sent a shudder down her spine.

Then she saw the long black thin legs on his shoulder. "Brodie, there's a spider on your shoulder. Oh, my goodness!" She gasped.

Brodie froze, then, glancing to his right to see the massive black spider edging its way to his neck, he went literally bananas, swiping at his T-shirt, dancing about in horror. Yanking his T-shirt off over his head and hurling it to the floor he then turned and raced into the water, diving in and fully submerging himself.

Maeve could only watch his reaction in shocked amusement.

He surfaced, said, "Do you think it's gone?"

Maeve, still stunned at the reaction, said with a laugh in her voice, "I would imagine so."

Brodie exhaled, pushed his hair out his face, said, "That was close." He shuddered. Then started out the water.

"You really don't like spiders, huh?"

"Hate them." He shuddered again. Tanned torso glistening with water, endearing vulnerability on his face as he shook out his T-shirt. No pretense at machismo, no front. As he was about to put his T-shirt back on, he paused and said, "I might get a different one."

"Brodie," Maeve said, "I think the poor thing is long gone."

"I'm not taking any chances." He chucked her the T-shirt, unable to cope with even holding it.

She walked back to the cabin, slightly behind him, carrying the shirt still warm from his skin, thinking what a lucky escape they'd all just had.

Chapter Twenty-One

Brodie got in his car with a smile on his face. In his rearview mirror, he watched Maeve's silver Volvo reversing up the craggy slope to the main dirt track, Zoey strapped in the back, her window open and her hand waving. The top was down on his Aston Martin and he sat looking sideways, waving back at intervals and occasionally pulling a silly face. It reminded him of getting into a car on tour, girls screaming and waving. He'd do something stupid like a cheesy double thumbs-up and stick his tongue out and they'd go even wilder. He'd loved the adoration at the time, he was a teenage boy, who wouldn't? But it wasn't something he craved any longer, it was a relief not to have to scour the bushes for paparazzi or hide behind a baseball cap every time he ventured downtown.

But with Zoey, the adoration was almost addictive. The hero-worship. It made his chest puff and his ego inflate from the feeling that he'd got the whole parenting thing nailed. He couldn't see Maeve because of the sun reflecting on the windscreen, but he imagined her eyeroll if she could see inside his head to his thoughts.

Maeve. He recalled the moment by the river. He'd like to kill that darn spider. Although, he probably should be thanking it. Not a good idea to get mixed up in anything with the mother of his child. That would make things far too complicated for Brodie's liking.

When the Volvo got to the main track, Zoey shouted, "See you later, alligator!"

Brodie cupped his hands and called, "See you on the moon, you big baboon!"

Zoey left cracking up and he was certain he saw a hint of a smile on Maeve's face as they drove away, something that left him feeling more smug than it should.

He turned and looked back at the wooden cabin, the reflections of the pines on the river, the rolling clouds over the mountain, and felt a warmth suffuse his body that he wasn't used to feeling.

It brought back more memories of being a kid, of coming here and messing about with his brothers—but also memories of being at home, of his mom making pancakes in school holidays. Being on the couch in PJs when it was snowing outside. Basketball in the sunshine. Days when he was too young to be any use on the ranch except for feeding the chickens.

It made Brodie pause, wrist resting on the steering wheel as he thought about the bits he had enjoyed as a kid. He'd endured the bulk of the farm work, but there were bits he'd liked: the horses, playing polo with Logan—and he'd liked riding the quad bikes with Jack and the camaraderie of big events like branding or round-ups. It was the bits between the work itself that he liked. Lying down on the grass in the scorching heat when exhaustion set in and getting one of his brothers to chuck a bucket of water over him, talking about girls they fancied at school when riding back from some mundane task or another, cracking open an ice-cold Coke after cleaning out the stables. All the bits once the job was done. Or maybe all the bits when his dad wasn't there.

With a sigh, Brodie started the engine and drove away, cautious over the rocky ground with his car, but strangely less precious about it, as if the space in his head for worrying about such fripperies was getting smaller now that it was half consumed by the idea of a child's life.

The thought made him shudder, fish around inside himself for the person who cared about the damage a rock might do to the chassis.

Then he hit the open road and it started to rain and he was distracted by trying to get the roof to close. It was a good segue. Him now tucked up in the dark enclosure of his car, music blaring over the noise of the wipers, the sun making a rainbow in the rearview mirror, which, if he still wrote songs, might be something he'd add in as symbolic of something he couldn't quite name. And something that, if Ethan were around, he'd cut out as trite cliché. The thought made Brodie smile sadly to himself. Then he stopped and phoned his brother Noah to see if he wanted to go to the Firestone for a drink.

Noah convinced Brodie that he needed to put more time in at the ranch. That their mom was really keen to show him her new Silver Pantry project. Brodie had a cynical suspicion that this sudden new shop venture was actually Martha's way of luring her children back to the ranch, give them something of hers to come and see that wasn't so tied in to their father and the ranch. Or perhaps that was unfair, and she did actually just want something that was hers. He was on the fence.

Either way, the following day, he went to visit. It was still raining on and off. Heavier through the night but summer drizzle in the day. He waited for it to stop, for the sun to burst out from behind the clouds before heading over.

The roads of Autumn Falls were still eyes-closed familiar to him, even after all those years away. When he reached the turning for the Silver Sky Ranch, he slowed, looking down toward the big gates at the end of the track, trying to imagine the life behind them. Visualizing himself coming down for breakfast as a kid, pouring out too much cereal as he was distracted chatting with his brothers, laughing, spilling the milk. Getting a massive sigh from his dad. Maybe that was why he'd brought Zoey the marshmallow cereal and been more than happy for her to fill the bowl to the brim. That sigh of Emmett's still echoed in his mind. He felt like he heard it every time he stumbled out of a club after a great night out, and so deliberately went for one more; when he pointed his skies over an off-piste sheer drop; when he flew to Hawaii because the waves were record-breaking, or held a party at his Malibu home for absolutely no reason other than that he could. Everything felt like it had been a fight against that sigh.

Brodie parked at the far end of the drive closest to The Silver Pantry building, away from the view of the main ranch. He didn't want to admit that this was to avoid his dad but that was most likely the truth.

The pantry was housed in what was once an old barn, but you wouldn't know it to look at it now. It had been pretty much rebuilt, with a porch over the large front door, galvanized buckets bursting with flowers outside, and huge picture windows. The clapboard was painted a tasteful pale gray with The Silver Pantry scrolled straight on the wood in a darker tone above the door.

The moment his mom glimpsed him through the window, she pulled open the heavy door. "Brodie! Hi, honey." She wrapped her arms round his neck, smelt as she always did, of perfume and Mom. Then she stood back and, looking down at her apron stained with summer fruits, said, "Sorry, I'm a mess, I'm making jam."

"You don't look a mess," he said, shaking his head at the very idea. "You look beautiful."

She waved the compliment away in pretense at being embarrassed but he saw her smile at him endearingly.

"So, what do you think?" she asked, gesturing to the façade.

He took a step back, glanced up and said, "It looks incredible." Then he frowned when he looked further up and saw his dad appear on the roof.

Martha saw Emmett at the same time and said, "There's a leak that we didn't discover till the rain came last night. Your dad's fixing it. I've told him to call a roofer but he insists on doing it himself. He's doing far too much at the moment."

"Why is that?" Brodie stepped further back to get a better look at his dad scowling at the leaking roof.

His mom shrugged. "Doesn't want to admit that he's getting old?"

Brodie huffed. In his mind, his dad had always been old. Old and grumpy.

"I think maybe it's because there's been so much change," Martha went on. "Logan moving back, Noah more settled." She looked pointedly at Brodie but didn't elaborate—he knew his mom disapproved of his lifestyle. "I guess it makes him think of what's been lost." She paused. "Of Jack." Her mouth tightened at the memory. "Ethan being who-knows-where. He worries."

Brodie looked up again at the profile of his father on the roof and wasn't convinced by his mom's argument. But, whether from a feeling that perhaps things were intrinsically different now that he was a father himself, or just feeling a pang of unaccustomed sympathy if what she said was true, he shouted, "Need a hand?"

"Who's offering?" His dad called back.

"Me."

There was a pause. "No, I'm okay."

Brodie frowned. Usually he'd just laugh and walk away, but today it felt different. He felt like *he* was someone different. He'd just navigated a weekend with his own kid. "I can help if you want help."

His dad laughed to himself. "I'm fine as I am, thanks. Quicker on my own."

Brodie stood with his hands in his pockets feeling stupidly ashamed at his dad's dismissal, especially with his mom watching. Not because of her judgment, but because—yes, there it was flitting across her face—of her pity. He knew if he were anyone else—Noah, Logan, even Ethan probably—his dad would have said yes. And usually he wouldn't care. But today it seemed to accentuate feelings about himself that he didn't want to acknowledge. Enhanced the image of him being the kind of person someone wouldn't want to be part of their child's life.

He felt a hollowness in his belly. So high in Zoey's eyes to so low in his father's. How pathetic it seemed to be idolized by an eight-year-old. And for what? Buying unhealthy breakfast cereal and enjoying YouTube. He looked up at his dad and wondered at the look he'd give him if he'd seen Brodie making Taylor Swift bracelets or dressing up with Zoey in Aunt Eleanor's pageant clothes.

It would be the same look as when Brodie wrote a new song as a kid—it wasn't disregard, it was blankness. Like if it wasn't cattle or fishing or similar, it didn't rank on his dad's radar and it meant nothing.

What his dad would think about Brodie having fathered a child and not knowing about it, didn't bear thinking about.

Luckily, Brodie's phone rang just at that moment cutting the tension. It was his friend Caleb ringing about their sailing trip.

Brodie looked down at the gravel path as Caleb launched into a story about all the stresses and calamities of getting the boat into harbor, scuffing the stones as he listened, laughing.

His mom stood for a while, but Brodie gestured that he'd be five minutes, so she went back inside to carry on with her jam.

On the phone, Caleb said, "So what time are you arriving?"

Brodie walked away round to the side of the barn. "Not sure I'm going to make it, actually," he said with a regretful wince.

"What?! We can't go without Brodie!"

Brodie grinned, thought wistfully of crashing through the waves, spray on his face. "I've got some stuff to deal with here."

"What the heck do you have to deal with that's more important than San Diego?"

Brodie looked in the window of the pantry at his mom ladling glossy crimson jam into rows of glass jars. "Just life stuff," he said, knowing it sounded cagey.

"Sounds to me like you've got a better offer, Brodie. Do I know her?"

"No it's..." He didn't want to explain, didn't want to have the outside world intrude, so he said, "No you don't know her."

He glanced up and saw his dad turn away like he'd been listening. Brodie sighed, of course his dad would overhear that bit.

After some more attempts at persuasion Caleb rang off.

Brodie slipped his phone in his pocket.

Above him, he heard a noise and saw a roof tile slide

down from where his dad was trying to fix the leak and had obviously fumbled it in his hands. It caught momentarily on the gutter and his dad shouted, "Watch out!" Then it fell and cracked when it hit the ground.

"Darn it." From where he was sitting astride the roof, his dad started to move himself along back toward the ladder. Fumbling roof tiles was not Emmett's style. He didn't make mistakes and wouldn't be happy about it.

"Do you want another one?" There was a pile of fresh tiles by the side door.

Emmett paused.

"Stay there, I'll bring one up," Brodie said, determined suddenly to be seen as of use, maybe just to be seen.

Emmett didn't reply but didn't move any further to the ladder. Brodie took that as a yes.

He picked up a new tile and started climbing up. He stopped at the top and stretched over to hand it to his dad.

"Thanks."

Brodie nodded.

He was about to go back down but his attention was caught by the view. He could see the whole ranch from up there. The red-rooved barns, the paddock, the pastures, right up to the mountains.

His dad said, "Something wrong?"

Brodie frowned at his tone, like he wanted him gone. "No, was just checking out the view."

Emmett gave it a cursory glance then went back to his tiling. He'd clearly seen it a hundred times before.

Brodie got the impression that he was being dismissed. He imagined if he was Noah, his dad would probably ask his advice. Noah would climb agilely over and they'd fix the roof together. Heck, they probably rebuilt the barn together in the first place.

He wasn't jealous. He didn't want that. He had a great life doing things he enjoyed. Again, he thought longingly of the sailing trip and kicked himself for turning it down.

"Are you going to stand there all day?"

Brodie stared incredulously at his dad, at his whitening beard, the battered hat forever on his head, the plaid shirt, darned and patched so much it probably didn't have any of the original material left, his face set in such familiar stern lines. But then, before his eyes, his father suddenly seemed older—maybe frailer—than he normally did. Or perhaps that was the reality, whereas all Brodie ever saw was the fearsome memory.

He had grown up terrified of this man. Always on guard around him for the constant reprimands, the dressing-downs, the sighs of discontentment, the looks. But what he struggled most with was that feeling of being disliked but endured. The impenetrable disappointment, like his dad put up with him because he had to. There was no love, no respect. If he had to give one of his children away, Brodie knew he would pick him. Even Jack, while he and Emmett fought, had been a good ranch hand when forced, and a ruthless competitor. Brodie just never came up to par. He liked fun and jokes, meeting new people and having a good time—everything his dad despised.

Looking at him now, head bent over his work, he thought that as a father, Brodie would never want to be like him.

And yet, he found himself wanting to tell him about making Zoey row and how she'd enjoyed it in the end. What did he want from Emmett? Pride?

Being his son held him in eternal thrall to this man. And yet his father seemed to have no idea how monumental his role was in Brodie's life.

"Have you ever liked me?" He didn't mean to say it out loud. Or maybe he did. Maybe it was time.

"'Scuse me?"

"You heard."

Emmett put his tools down and sat for a moment contemplating the question, head bent, eyes obscured by his hat.

Brodie couldn't hear anything but the thumping of his heart. He felt like a child. Like Zoey. He imagined them in a similar situation—her huge brown eyes staring plaintively back at him desperate for something he had no idea if he could give.

His dad looked up, eyes narrowed so thin, so disdainful, that Brodie could barely see them. "My job as a parent wasn't to be your friend, Brodie, it was to make you a man."

Brodie felt his taut muscles quiver in shame at the coolness of his dad's words.

"To teach you the value of hard work, responsibility and respect. So you could go out in the world and make good decisions. Find purpose. Marry well. Start a family of your own." He seemed to leave a deliberate pause so they could both recall Brodie's disastrous marriage to Celeste. He saw his parents, having only met the bride once, at the lavish wedding, sitting among crowds of celebrities, out of place and uncomfortable. Then their faces when he welcomed them into the sprawling mansion he'd bought, complete with a Japanese water garden filled with koi carp and a butterfly house.

His dad's ensuing silence suggested that he had failed on all accounts to instill such values in his son.

Brodie couldn't understand how he was somehow being shamed for his year-long shambolic marriage—a mistake he made in his early twenties—when he was standing on a ladder asking why his dad had always looked at him like dirt. "This isn't about marriage or the band. This is about before that!" he said, trying but knowing the words would fall on stubbornly deaf ears. "This was when I was a kid. Did you ever think it wasn't a one-size-fits-all? Did you ever look at me and think, *what I'm doing isn't working?*"

"Of course I did!" Emmett snapped back, ferocious like a crocodile.

See you later, alligator.

You have a kid.

Brodie feared for a moment he might lose his balance on the ladder, his mind spun, dizzy. He looked down at the tiles for a moment to catch his breath, then he glanced at his dad and said, "So why didn't you do something different?"

But Emmett didn't answer. His head was bent again, back to the task of fixing the roof.

Brodie almost flew down the ladder he was in such a hurry to get away from his father's cold snub. Over in the driveway, he could see his car glinting in the sunshine.

His mom came out of The Silver Pantry and said, "Are you coming to have a look around? I've opened some elderflower cordial and—" She paused, taking in the expression on Brodie's face. "What happened?"

Brodie shook his head, pretended it was all fine. "Nothing."

His mom glanced up to where Emmett was banging on the roof. Brodie didn't.

Instead, he forced a smile and, putting his hand on his mom's back, said, "Love an elderflower cordial! Come on, give me the tour."

Chapter Twenty-Two

Brodie did his best to sound enthusiastic as his mom showed him hand-tied brooms, artisanal olive oil and shea butter soaps pressed with rosebuds. He drank a couple of glasses of cordial and leaned on the glossy wooden countertop, marveling at the work that had gone into the place. But when the time came to leave, he was in his car and out the gates before anyone could stop him.

It was raining again as he drove home. The clouds low and gray in the sky. He wondered if it was too late to call Caleb and reinstate himself on the sailing vacation.

His phone rang as he was thinking about it and Maeve's name flashed up on the screen. Somehow just the sight of it made up for the last couple of hours. Filled him with a fresh sense of, if not happiness, definitely interest. "To what do I owe this pleasure?" he quipped.

She was all business. "I've been called into a meeting. Carole is going to collect Zoey from school but I wondered if, erm—" She hesitated as if she'd suddenly thought through what she was going to say. "You're probably busy but—"

"I'm not busy." He cruised onto Main Street.

"Okay. I, erm … I wondered if you wanted to take over when they got home. You know, look after Zoey. Only if you want to. She's fine with Carole."

"Carole who makes her wash her face with a flannel?"

Maeve laughed.

He felt a tingle up his spine.

"She's not so bad."

Brodie found himself smiling like an idiot at the road ahead, imagining Maeve's face as she spoke, the remnants of the laugh she hadn't intended but couldn't help. Because of him. It made him feel dangerously good. A guilty pleasure that should be avoided. But Brodie was very bad at avoiding the thrill of pleasure. "Yeah, I'd love to do it."

"Sure?"

"Of course."

There was a pause.

"Thanks, Brodie."

He almost bashed the steering wheel in victory, but kept his voice deliberately cool as he said, "You're welcome, Maeve."

It was only when he hung up, stopped smiling at what had felt definitely like a flirtation, that he remembered why she would ask him to babysit. Not because he was the fun, sexy bachelor friend who was great with her kid, but because he was the kid's father.

A vision of his dad's craggy face staring at him with harsh disapproval popped up in his mind. His heart started thumping, frantic, like a mouse caught in a trap, and he wondered if he should stop driving for a moment.

He pulled over at the lights on Main Street and popped into the grocery store for a Coke. Figured he needed the sugar. Then he bought Zoey one, then put it back and bought her a diet, caffeine-free one. Were kids even allowed that? He chucked in a couple of candy bars and a big bag of popcorn.

Maeve had told him that Carole was expecting him, but when he arrived, she glared at him like a bulldog guarding her territory.

"I'm here to take over." Brodie smiled widely but it did nothing to soften her. "Relieve you of your duties." What was he talking about? He felt like he'd been hauled in front of the headmistress.

Zoey came into the hallway and started making faces and doing silly moves behind Carole's back. Brodie raised his eyebrows in warning but struggled to keep a straight face.

Carole gave him a very disgruntled once-up-and-down and, gathering her pocketbook, said, "I'll be next door if you need me."

"Yes ma'am," Brodie replied, chastened by her tone.

Zoey collapsed into giggles the moment the door was closed.

"Don't do that!" Brodie said, realizing he'd started to sweat under the scrutiny. "She thinks I'm bad enough as it is."

Zoey clearly couldn't care less and took a run and jump onto the couch. "I thought we could watch the first Harry

Potter and then watch the next ones in order every time you come over." She didn't look at him, just took it for granted that he'd be on board with her logic.

And why wouldn't he? It was a very sensible idea. But all Brodie heard was, *every time you come over*. He saw endless hours of Harry Potter stretching out ahead of him, changing at some point to whatever else kids watched. He was fine with a movie, *loved* a movie, in fact, but what he was less fine with was having plans in place, obligations in his calendar. Brodie purposely lived a very free and easy life, he wanted to be able to pick up his suitcase and hop on a plane at a moment's notice whenever he pleased.

They had tried to bind him with schedules when he was in the band and he'd coped okay with it then because his brothers were there to pick up the slack if he disappeared off. Also, being with them just made the whole time feel like hanging out with friends rather than every second timetabled. When he went solo, however, that was when the scheduling really hit him. Three hundred and sixty days all meticulously color-coded into hourly commitments. Five days' holiday. Three years that started with an explosion of excitement and promises and ended with him disillusioned, and dare he say it, lonely. But as his manager said: "At least you're rich."

"Sounds like a plan," he said as Zoey made herself comfortable, plumping up the couch cushions, trying his best to muster the same enthusiasm he'd had at the cabin.

But suddenly everything seemed a little more forced. He was more aware of himself sitting on the opposite couch, aware that she was eight and he didn't know what to say to an eight-year-old. He got out the Diet Coke and the popcorn. Zoey's eyes lit up. "Yes!" she said, cracking the ring pull then giggling guiltily as it fizzed everywhere. He laughed along with her but found it less funny than when he'd been with her before, getting up to go and get some paper towel and clear it up.

"Sorry, Brodie," she said, as if able to sense his change of mood.

That snapped him out of it, he certainly didn't want her afraid of spilling, or messing up in any way, in front of him. "Don't be silly, it's fine—not even your fault, I probably shook it up in the bag."

He imagined Maeve watching and felt himself want to step up under her gaze.

Zoey seemed appeased and snuggled back into the cushions, holding the Coke like it was a prized possession. "Ready?" she asked, finger poised on the remote.

"Ready," he agreed, forcing himself to relax, smiling back at her when she grinned gap-toothed at him. "Hey, you lost a tooth!"

"Yeah." She put her tongue in the space where the tooth had been. "I got a dollar from the tooth fairy."

"Big bucks."

"I want them all to fall out so I can get loads of money."

Brodie rolled his ideas at the reasoning.

She said, "Do you have loads of money?"

His eyes widened. "Well, I…"

He hesitated, thinking for a moment about his wealth. He looked around at the old-fashioned living room, the furnishings—barely changed, Maeve had said, since her grandma passed. The well-worn couch that enveloped Zoey like a hug, the TV half the size of his at home and probably a sixteenth of the size of the one he had in his basement cinema room. He thought of his vineyard and then of his mom's homemade elderflower cordial. His custom-built coffee table in Malibu, cut from a slab of onyx, compared to Maeve's rattan and bamboo one that had a book under one leg to keep it level. He looked at how much Zoey loved being in this room. How cozy and safe she seemed, how happy to be home. He was never home in Malibu more than a week, max. And when it came to Autumn Falls, this was already the longest he'd been back in years.

All that money, no desire to be home.

As he'd said to Maeve—nowhere's home. It had made him feel cool and carefree when he'd said it then, now however it felt a little pitiful; having nowhere he really wanted to be. He wondered if that was how Maeve had taken it when he'd said it. Had she felt sorry for him rather than being impressed? He knew instinctively that she— unlike most other people in his life—was good at reading between the lines, looking below face value. He felt suddenly uncomfortable in his seat, aware that pity was not the impression he'd been going for.

He looked at Zoey snuggled under her blankets, and finally said in answer, "You know, some things are much better than money."

She shrugged and pressed play on Harry Potter.

Brodie spent the first half of the film watching Zoey's profile engrossed in the movie. He watched her eyes widen in fright or suspense, watched her smile and laugh and say,

"Do you think wizards exist?" and "Would you prefer to fly or be invisible?"

He thought of his dad—*My job as a parent wasn't to be your friend*. Hard work. Responsibility. He looked at Zoey slurping the Coke. He didn't know how to be anything other than her friend. She'd more likely be the one teaching him responsibility.

He tried to focus on the film but he couldn't concentrate. He kept thinking about a future sitting in that living room, over and over, hours on end. He'd told Maeve he'd be there for when Zoey wanted him to be. He'd told her not to worry. But even intermittent parenting required having to be present. What was the point otherwise?

What would his own parents say if he shirked his duties now he knew about them? It was okay to be living a life free of any responsibility and obligation when it was only his own life he was wasting.

He felt a claustrophobic pressure build in his chest and found himself scratching at the neck of his T-shirt.

But then what was the point of being present, if he didn't know how to be a father. If he couldn't offer the guiding principles required of him?

Maybe he could offer Maeve a lot of money. Maybe it *was* good for something. She could replace her coffee table.

He sat forward, unable to get comfortable, elbows resting on his knees, hands clasped under his chin.

When the film ended, Zoey said, "Do you want to play Barbies?"

"Sure."

He tried to think of it like being with Willow. Growing

up, he'd battled her My Little Ponies with his Dinosaurs. He didn't have to teach Willow anything. And they always had a great time together. But then most of the time he was with Willow, he spent flirting with her dancer friends.

Zoey went off and came back with the dolls, placing the box down on the table.

Brodie sat up straighter, rolled his shoulders, gave himself a pep talk. He was being ridiculous. He could cope with a dose of domesticity. It wasn't that hard. And he didn't have to be around all the time.

Zoey handed him a plastic doll and a sparkly hairbrush. "Your one's hair needs brushing."

He sat absently brushing Barbie's hair, thoughts flying all over the place. Why did he want to help his dad fix the roof anyway? Brodie didn't want to fix a roof. He could pay someone to fix a roof. He'd offered as a favor, but it had become a test of whether he was needed. To prove that he wasn't completely useless. He thought again of everything his dad had said about being a father. The stress on his face when he said it. The burden of it. Because to do it wrong came with catastrophic consequences. It could ruin a person's life. Make them never want to come home.

"Brodie, what are you doing?"

He realized he'd been tugging so hard brushing the knots out of the doll's hair that he'd almost pulled her head off. "Sorry," he said, placing the Barbie back down on the table. He felt ill. Wondered if he might have a temperature. Felt a sheen of sweat on his forehead. "Maybe I'll just watch you." He glanced out the window at his car, felt the pull to leave. But he couldn't leave, he was trapped here looking after his kid.

"Are you my dad?"

"Whoa!" Brodie was startled back into the moment. Zoey, too, had put her Barbie down on the table and was looking at him, big wide eyes, her hands clasped neatly in her lap. Brodie swallowed, his mouth dry as dust. "What makes you think that?"

She shrugged. "I don't know. I'd like it, I guess. If you lived with my mom and were here every day and at Christmas and on my birthday and came on vacation with us and never left. I'd like it if it was the three of us, forever."

Brodie's veins ran cold with absolute, sheer, claustrophobic terror. "Yeah," he managed to laugh as if that were the dream.

Zoey didn't laugh, she just said, "Are you?"

For a moment he couldn't say anything, just felt the pounding of his pulse in his head, the clamminess of his hands, the instinctive almost primal desire to get up and flee. But then, when he managed to still his breath, he looked her straight in the eye and said, "No."

leave, but be wouldn't let us, he was trapped him, looking after his kid.

"Are you my dad?"

When Birdie was glanced back into the moment Zoey too had parked Barbie down on the table and was looking at him, the wide eyes, her hands clasped neatly in her lap, Birdie swallowed, his mouth dry as dust. "What makes you think that?"

She shrugged. "I don't know, I'd like it, I guess. If you lived with us, mom and we're here every day, and at Christmas and on my birthday and came on vacation with us and never left. I'd like it if it was the time of his forever."

Charlie's tone, rare, cold, with absolute sharp daughter logic terror. "nah," he managed to though as if that were the dream.

Zoey still, though, she just sat, "No, you?"

For a moment he couldn't say anything, just felt the pounding of his pulse in his blood, the chaos inside of his hands, the that-gritted almost panicked desire to get up and flee. But then when he managed to still be there, he looked her straight in the eye and said, "no."

Chapter Twenty-Three

Maeve drove home from the hospital strangely excited to see them both. It surprised her how relieved it made her to think of Brodie and Zoey together in the house, laughing and joking. The idea that, while it still made her very nervous, Zoey might now be able to enjoy the influence of two parents, which, Maeve assumed, could only add richness to her life. Unless Brodie messed it up. But she'd been pleasantly surprised by him at the cabin. He was different to his reputation. Seemed more reliable, less of a flake.

And none of it, absolutely nothing at all, had the slightest bit to do with the fact that when he locked eyes with her she felt a tingle through her whole body, when he smiled she could barely reply, when he looked her in the eye it was like the attention of the universe was all on her. Exactly as it had been that night at the concert. Exactly as it was sometimes when she woke up in the middle of the night having dreamt of him.

No, she was not driving home a little bit excited to see them because of anything to do with Brodie himself.

"Hi, guys, I'm home."

She saw both their shoes by the front door. Big and small.

"In here," Brodie called back, the deepness of his voice unfamiliar in their home. For a split-second, it made her think what it must be like to come home to a partner, someone happy to see you, to hear about your day. Someone who made your stomach fizz when you heard their voice. Someone who *wanted* to be there waiting for you, uptilted eyes alight.

She chucked her keys in the bowl by the front door. Brodie was not her partner.

She glanced at her reflection in the hallway mirror—tired, always tired—*pull yourself together, Maeve.*

All the same, she fluffed up her hair a bit and tried to rub a bit of color into her cheeks before she walked in to see them.

The living room was chaos. Barbies everywhere, popcorn open on the table, spilling out; a board game started but not finished, empty Coke cans … and now Zoey had clearly insisted on a beauty tutorial.

Maeve rolled her lips together to stop from laughing at the sight of them, Brodie's hair pushed back with a headband, each of their faces slathered with a green face mask, cucumber slices over their eyes.

"You're too early!" Zoey lifted a cucumber. "We're not ready for you to come back."

But Brodie jumped up off the couch, whipping the slices

of cucumber off and eating one whole. "I think we're ready," he said, and Maeve got the wary impression he'd been ready for some time.

She felt some of her excitement dissipate. "Sorry, I didn't know how long I was going to be."

Brodie grinned, cracking the mask as he said, "It's not a problem! We've had a great time, haven't we?" He glanced back at Zoey.

Maeve wondered if she was being over-cautious, aware that her hesitancy was perhaps too entrenched.

"I'm going to wash this off." He pointed to his face mask and disappeared into the downstairs cloakroom.

She started clearing up the empty packets. "You have a good time, Zo?"

"The best!" Zoey said, trying not to move her face as she spoke so that the mask didn't crack.

Maeve felt the flutter again. Nervous but excited. "Great."

She was in the kitchen, getting rid of the trash, when Brodie came to the doorway and, still with the remains of some of the clay around the sides of his face, said, "I'm going to head off."

Maeve nodded, she realized her fingers were trembling. She'd been going to offer him a drink but instead she said, "Okay, yeah, fine, I'll walk you out."

He went ahead, she tried not to be distracted by the lingering scent of him, the pull of his T-shirt across his back, the curl of blond hair at the nape of his neck. *Keep it professional, Maeve.*

He stopped by the living room. Too busy trying not to

look at him, she collided into his back. Nose pressed into the soft cotton of his T-shirt. "Sorry!" She jumped away. "Sorry."

He seemed unfazed, just turned and raised a brow. "You okay?" he said.

"Fine!" she replied brightly.

Then leaning into the living room doorway, he said, "Bye, Zoey," all Brodie-esque cool.

"Bye," she called back.

Maeve pulled herself together. Told herself it was simply that she was unused to having a man in the house. It wasn't until the door was opened and Brodie was outside on the stoop that she plucked up the courage to say what she'd been building up to. "Brodie…" she began, sounding more insistent than she'd intended.

"Yep." He turned, and for a moment she was struck silent. His hair was damp from where he'd washed his face and was half swept back, half falling forward, his eyes questioning rather than glinting, he looked boyish, maybe how he had at school or that night at the concert. She could barely find her words, but she knew she had to say what she was going to say before she changed her mind.

Pulling the door closed behind her, she stepped down so she was level with him. "Brodie, I think we should tell Zoey the truth." She was so nervous she could barely concentrate, half from being in his proximity, half from what she'd just said. But she felt the start of a smile as she warmed to the idea, her confidence in it, in him, growing as she spoke. "I think it's time to tell her you're her dad."

Silence.

She saw it in his glance to the right. In the closing of his mouth. In his swallow before he spoke. And inwardly kicked herself for believing.

"I, er—" He stalled.

She waited. Heart on pause. *Please don't say it*, she thought, seeing suddenly the image of her daughter lying innocently on the couch in her face mask and cucumber on her eyes. Maeve wanted to gather her up and press her close to her chest. Saw herself moments ago bumping into him like a flustered schoolgirl with an overactive imagination.

Brodie ran his hand through his hair. "I'm actually going away for a bit."

Maeve's hands tightened into fists, nails pressing into her palm. She felt her teeth clench. Her back ramrod straight. She knew, for Zoey's sake, she had to give him the benefit of the doubt. "Oh, right. So…?"

Brodie tipped his head side to side, did an uncertain wince. "So, I think maybe let's hold off for a bit. Maybe have a think again when I get back."

She could barely believe it. Her stomach hollowed. "When will that be?"

He sucked in a breath. "It's hard to tell with these kinds of trips. Could be a week, could be a month." He laughed like it was all just a joke.

She shook her head barely able to believe what she was hearing.

"What?" He had the audacity to feign innocence.

"Are you really doing this?" She had to confirm.

"Doing what?" Again with the innocence.

She stepped forward, closer, feeling the ire coursing through her body, seething through her muscles, just shy of pushing him with both hands, she hissed, "You're running away."

"I'm not running away, I'm going on a vacation." He said it like she was making a big deal of something.

"You're running away and you know it." She could cope with him running away from her—she'd been stupid to fall for his charm—but running from Zoey... Her lip curled. "You didn't have a vacation planned."

"I did!" He laughed.

"Don't you dare laugh at me." Her blood was pounding.

"I'm not laughing at—"

She cut him off. "This is a child's life. *Your* child. You said you wanted to be a part of it. You don't just go on holiday, Brodie, in the middle of getting to know an eight-year-old, that's not how it's done." She had to step away from him. "I knew you'd do this." She turned, pushing her hands through her hair. "It was too good to be true—the cabin, the jokes, the 'I'm great with the kids.'" She shook her head at her own naivety. "Even your darn smile. You're perfect for five minutes, but it's all just..." She searched for the words. "What is it, Brodie? An act?"

He didn't say anything. Didn't refute it. There was no hint of a smile now. The jokey claims of a vacation gone. No witty comeback. Just the silence confirming that he was going and who knew when he would be back. Maybe, at best, he might tell Zoey six months from now and swoop into her life every now and then with Taylor Swift tickets.

Maeve almost stamped her foot. "I'm so stupid!"

He pushed his hands into his pockets, wouldn't meet her eyes. "I'm sorry."

"*You're* sorry?" She laughed humorlessly, then she sighed, knowing the gates were open now and at some point she would have the task of explaining to her daughter that this restless, unreliable guy was her dad. Somehow make sure she never got too close because he would always let her down. "You'd better go."

Brodie looked down at the tired welcome mat for a second then up at her, brow furrowed, the eyes of a sad, regretful child, and nodded.

Maeve didn't want to look at him, didn't want to feel remotely sorry for him, so she turned and went inside, closing the front door without looking back.

For a second, she stood there, exactly where she'd been just quarter of an hour ago, checking her reflection in the mirror. What a fool. Who gets duped by the same guy twice? Maybe he'd send her another signed photo. She closed her eyes and felt the sudden overwhelming press of tears.

"Mom!"

She quickly wiped them away. "Coming, honey."

He opened his hands into his pockets, wondered aloud for ever, 'Tim sorry.'

'You're sorry.' She laughed humourlessly, then she sighed, knowing the gaps were open now and it came rather the world have the talk of escaping to her daughter that that useless implicable pity was her dad somehow; smile sure she never got to close because he would always let her down, 'lob'd but to go.'

Brona looked down at the street welcomed him for a second then gazed at her, brow furrowed the sides of a sad, mournful child, and nodded.

Maeve didn't want to look at him, didn't want to feel remotely sorry for him, so she turned and went inside, closing the front door without looking back.

For a second she stood there, exactly where she'd been just quarter of an hour ago, checking her reflection in the mirror. What a fool. Who yet flipped by the same guy twice. Maybe he'd said to her another, stared idiotic. She closed her eyes and felt the sudden overwhelming press of tears.

'Mom!'

She quickly wiped the tears away. 'Coming honey.'

Chapter Twenty-Four

Brodie sloped home. He felt worse than he imagined. He'd convinced himself that they'd coped admirably without him all these years and that, in a way, Zoey was probably better off without him. He simply couldn't give her what she needed. But the way Maeve had looked at him, like he had let her down in more ways than he could fathom, it had cut straight through him, made him ache to be a better person. He didn't know what was worse, disappointing Zoey or disappointing Maeve. It wasn't meant to be like that. It wasn't meant to feel this bad.

He stood by the window in his condo, staring blankly out through the dusky rain to the giant polo fields.

I knew you'd do this.

Was he that predictable? Even he hadn't realized he was going to do it up to that point. But she had seen straight through him from the start. The rain drizzled in rivulets down the window. He watched one droplet meet another and another. He turned and got his phone out of his pocket, messaged Caleb. *I'm back in. See you tomorrow.*

He got back a bicep emoji.

It felt oddly childish.

He threw his phone on the bed.

He'd made the right decision. He did not want a life where he was moping at rainy windows with an ache in his chest. He looked around the bare bedroom, no pictures on the walls, no possessions. He didn't need a home. He was a free spirit. A minimalist.

He sat down on the bed, elbows on his knees, chin resting on steepled hands.

He hadn't always been a minimalist. As a child his side of the bedroom was packed full of toys, basketballs, polo stuff, books, pens, and paper. Noah's side was all lassos and rodeo trophies and once an orphaned foal, Bumblebee, who, when his mom wasn't looking, Noah smuggled upstairs to sleep on his bed.

Brodie smiled into the darkness, lips resting against his fingers.

It was the best bedroom ever. They'd lie on their respective beds and chuck a ball to one another, forfeits for whoever dropped it.

He remembered doing the same on the tour bus when they were in Silver Sky. Or out shooting hoops with Ethan at the court near the studio. Brodie had a restless energy that meant he couldn't sit still for long, couldn't put in the unbroken hours recording. He got bored, distracted. When he was with his brothers, it was fine because they'd all come out to the court in the end, or bribe him with the promise of a game if he stuck out another recording. Then it ended, Silver Sky disbanded and suddenly Brodie was on his own. Suddenly, there was no one to chuck a ball around with, no one to tell him it was probably time to call it a night, no one to tell him that the songs he was writing were tipping into cliché.

He sighed, looking back out at the unceasing rain. He didn't like the feeling inside himself as much as he didn't like the weather. When it rained, Brodie headed somewhere hot—he didn't have the clothes for rain—and when he felt even remotely sullen he did something to cheer himself up. That, he reminded himself, was exactly why he was going to San Diego.

He got up to grab his case from the top of the wardrobe, flung it open on the bed and started to toss his clothes in. As he packed, he wondered if Maeve ever threw a ball with Zoey. He was pretty certain Carole the babysitter never did. Had anyone taught her how to shoot hoops? Had anyone taken Maeve out for dinner? Where had that come from? Of course people—men—took her out for dinner. Probably handsome, intelligent neurosurgeons who wowed her with tales of operating-theater heroism. His stomach tightened—with what? Envy?

Get over it, Brodie.

He glanced at his reflection in the bathroom mirror as he collected his toiletries and shook his head. He didn't want to think about it. His muscles were already itching to move on, his brain planning the best route to San Diego. He'd make up for it when he was back.

Brodie intended to slip away the next morning, but as he drove past the Silver Sky Ranch gates, guilt made him flick the indicator and turn in, knew his mom would be upset if he didn't say goodbye. It was still pouring, the weather, the songwriter in him concluded, was matching his mood. There were no rainbows today.

When he pulled up in the drive he saw Logan's car already there, which, while it would be nice to see his brother, meant he'd be there longer than he intended and really, he just wanted to get going.

Sprinting to the door, he was soaked by the time he pushed it open. His mom and Logan were sitting at the kitchen table. Martha made a face when she saw him all wet and said, "Brodie, why don't you have a jacket?" as if he was still Zoey's age.

"Because I'm never anywhere when it rains." He slicked his hair back and pulled his wet T-shirt from his chest. Then he looked at Logan who was watching with wry amusement because Martha had got up and, grabbing a towel from the downstairs bathroom, was now trying to pat Brodie dry as he tried to push her away. "I'm fine," he protested, pulling out a chair and taking a seat opposite his brother. "How was Napa?"

"Excellent," Logan replied without hesitation. "It's a nice place you've got there. And great wine."

His mom said, "Do you think I could stock it in the shop, Brodie?"

Brodie shrugged like he hadn't considered it before. "Of

course," he replied, feeling a tinge of pride at Logan's words of praise.

Stupidly, he glanced around to see if his dad was anywhere in the vicinity to hear as Logan started rhapsodizing about the vineyard to Martha.

"I haven't actually got that much to do with it," Brodie admitted.

"They said you were very enthusiastic."

Brodie barked a laugh. "That does not sound like a compliment."

Suddenly the door bashed open and Noah stalked in, dripping wet, long black slicker done up to his chin, a puddle already on the floor around his boots. "We're gonna need some help out there," he said by way of greeting.

"Why, what's happened?" His mom and Logan were up in an instant. Brodie felt his heart sink, this was the last thing he needed.

"The river's burst its banks." Noah was rummaging through drawers looking for things as he was talking. "The cattle are up there and the water's rising too fast."

Martha was already pulling on her boots and Logan had his jacket and hat on as Noah added, "We need to get them moved. Now."

Brodie closed his eyes. If only he'd left as soon as he'd finished packing last night. Saving cows from the river was his least favorite job. It had only happened once before in his life, and it had lodged its place right up there at the top of the list as an experience he never wanted to repeat. Trying to drag cattle back to safety was a nightmare.

But if his mom and Logan were going, Brodie knew he had to go, too.

Noah was already back out the door.

"Brodie there's a spare slicker—"

"I know—" he cut his mom off "—on the peg by the door."

He got up and reluctantly yanked on a dark green waterproof, zipping it up and pulling up the hood. He hadn't worn one of these for a while. He swapped his trainers for a pair of Noah's old boots and followed after the others into the torrential rain.

Out in the yard, it was all shouting and commotion. His dad was heading out, rope slung over his shoulder. Rocky the dog was barking, desperate to get moving. Noah pointed Brodie in the direction of the lovely palomino mare he'd seen when he was there the other day and said, "You take Dove."

Brodie saddled her up and jumped on. He couldn't deny the rush of adrenaline now that he was racing out over the pasture. This was the fun bit. Logan was slightly ahead. Brodie knew he could sense the distance between them. It wasn't the time to be messing about racing but it was innate in them all. He felt his skin prickle with every foot they gained, aware that Logan would be battling to stay ahead.

Then they got to the north pasture and the ground beneath them started to disappear into water. The grass was nothing now but a flood plain. Cattle wading, waist deep, others huddled on high ground. His dad was wading out trying to corral them away from the deeper water. One little one was trying to swim but got sucked under and away. It was impossible to tell where the edge of the river was but the current in the center was hurtling along, frothing and tumbling, debris from the mountain swept along with it. On the back of his horse, Noah lassoed the frantically flailing calf with brisk efficiency, bracing as the rope went taut against the onslaught of the river.

Brodie had memories of this as a kid. His dad snatching the lasso off him to do it himself when he fumbled a throw. *This is why you practice!* Even in emergencies there was a lesson to be learned.

"Brodie, is that your phone?" Logan shouted over the noise of the rain as he followed Martha further up the river.

Brodie hadn't heard it but could now feel it vibrating in his pocket. He fumbled with the slicker to reach his back pocket. It was raining too hard to see the screen properly, but he thought it said Maeve. "Hello?"

"Is Zoey with you?"

"No." He frowned. "Why would she be with me? Where is she?" He felt a chill run through his blood as he looked around through the cascading rain.

"I can't find her. She's not here." The panic in Maeve's voice was palpable.

"Where is she?" Brodie found himself half shouting, cupping the handset so he could hear better.

"I don't know!" Maeve shouted back. "She wanted to see you, she'd made you something. I had to tell her you were leaving. She was really upset, she went up to her room… She's not there. What am I going to do?"

"Okay, slow down." Brodie tried to think straight but couldn't handle the panic in her voice, or the million and one possible scenarios popping into his head, each one more terrifying than the next. Emergencies were not his forte. He glanced around for Logan or one of the others, but they were all further upstream now, engrossed in the cattle rescue. "So, she's looking for me. Does she know where I live?" He started to pull Dove around, thinking he'd head back to his condo.

"No, but she knows Martha's your mom—she knows the ranch."

"Well, I'm *at* the ranch," Brodie replied, looking back in the direction of the house, just a speck in the distance. He should go back. "So if she turns up here—"

Suddenly he heard a small, high voice shout, "Brodie!"

He looked across the river to see a small figure on a red bike pedaling frantically through the forest path, as if he'd conjured her up himself. "Brodie!" she shouted again, waving through the rain, hair plastered to her head, wobbly on her bike in the mud. It was definitely Zoey.

He thought his heart might pop out of his body it was suddenly beating so fast. "Stay there!" he hollered. "Don't move!" There was water everywhere, rising higher by the second, mud gushing down the mountain.

"Brodie, what's going on?" Maeve's voice was even more frantic on the other end of the line.

"She's here." He couldn't take his eyes off Zoey as he galloped downstream. So small, so unsteady. Lifting her feet off the pedals as the bike hit the mudslide. "Stay where you are!" Before his eyes, the path she was on disappeared into a mass of slippery bubbling mud. It was his fault she was here. "No, Zoey! Stop!" he hollered, turning to shout at the others, his older brother the closest to him. "Logan!"

On the other end of the phone Maeve was shouting for details. He could hardly take everything in. Zoey was trying to brake but the bike was skidding, the side of the path too steep and slippery for her to turn and cycle to higher ground. Perhaps she had an instinct to keep her shiny red bike safe because she was scrabbling after it as it got caught in the fast-flowing water.

"Leave the bike!" he shouted, urging Dove forward into the water. "Leave it!"

But Zoey didn't leave it, instead she grabbed the handlebars and the force of the current pulled her in and under.

"Please, no." He couldn't see anything except her head, chin tilted up as the undertow carried her away. "Maeve, I'll get her, I promise." He dropped the phone and without any further thought, yanked off the slicker and he threw himself into the river.

"Brodie what are you doing?" Logan shouted, unaware of what had happened on the opposite bank. "Get out the water!"

But he wasn't listening. "Grab a branch," he yelled at Zoey as she flailed in the churning torrent.

Logan was shouting for Noah.

The force of the water was brutal, so different to the peaceful swim at the cabin. There was no hope against this, Brodie was dragged through it, swimming as hard as he could, but was sucked down into eddies, bashed against logs and fallen branches and carried along by the power of the stream.

He looked up and to his utter relief saw that Zoey had managed to grab onto the branch of an overhanging tree. He fought against the powerful drag of the tide to haul himself over to where she was, kicking against the brutal force trying to wrench him on down the river.

"You were going to leave without saying goodbye," she shouted over the noise of the water, clinging on, frightened eyes wet with tears.

His departure was not Brodie's top priority right at that moment. "Just hold on tight, Zoey."

"Why weren't you going to say goodbye?" She was crying now. She looked so tiny and helpless against the force of nature, one slip and she'd be gone, sucked down and away.

"I don't know," Brodie said, all too aware of how precarious the situation was and reaching for something other than the branch she was holding onto, because it was nothing more than a fragile twig. "Because I'm stupid," he said, managing to get a foothold on the bottom and stretching to grab what looked like a tree root. "Because I don't think enough about other people's feelings."

"You only had to say goodbye," she said, voice quivering.

"I know, I know. I'm sorry!" He was so close, he just had to stretch his arm, but as his fingers found purchase on the gnarly root, a rock churned up in the murky water smacked against his leg knocking him off-balance, the river immediately dragging him away.

"Brodie!" It was one of his brothers hollering his name.

He managed to right himself, swimming as hard as he'd ever swum against the iron-clad press of the current, grasping for anything he could reach on the bank, the water pummeling against him, in his mouth, his eyes. Zoey was crying. "Brodie, help me!"

On the other side, Noah was galloping over. He flung his lasso but was too early and missed.

All Brodie knew was that he had to save this kid. *His kid.*

He stretched across, was in touching distance of her striped T-shirt. Then he heard the crack as Zoey's branch snapped and her scream as the river swept her away. All he could do was lunge and try and grab her before she disappeared into the swirling gray waves, and as he did he felt his hand connect with her thin little arm. Gripping her and holding on as tight as he'd ever held on to anything, Brodie yanked her toward him as the rushing water dragged them both downstream.

"I've got you," he said, his arm now locked around her waist. "Wrap your arms and legs around me and *do not* let go. Whatever happens, okay?"

She nodded, frightened eyes wide, and clung to him like a little monkey.

This was his daughter.

He didn't care what happened to him, he could not let anything happen to her.

Suddenly he was underwater, sucked down by the whirlpools, bashed against more debris cascading down from the mountains.

He was up and gasping for air. He just had to keep her head above water, that was all that mattered.

Where the heck were Noah and Logan? The river swept them now deeper into the forest, between the trees, his brothers would have trouble with the horses.

He could feel the weight of Zoey, of the water, of his clothes dragging him down. Deeper. He was choking, gasping. There was a burning in his lungs.

Just keep her head above water. Nothing else matters.

Suddenly he heard his name. "Brodie! Catch!" and the slap of a lasso again against the surface.

He felt it rather than saw it, but it was gone before he could scrabble for the rope.

Brodie went under. Zoey clung tighter.

He was up again, gasping. Noah threw the rope again. This time Brodie reached up his arm and felt the rough lasso loop over his hand.

Keep her head above water.

He grabbed on, winding his arm around the rope, felt the tug and drag of his brothers' combined strength against the vicious force of the river.

He couldn't see, but he could hear Zoey crying. If he could hear her crying then it meant she was breathing—and if the river didn't kill him, if anything happened to Zoey, then Maeve surely would. He felt the heave of his brothers on the rope. His head was struggling to keep above the surface. Water was in his mouth.

"I am your dad," he managed, choking on the water. "I *am* your dad." He felt Zoey's arms lock like a vice round his neck. He was calculating the time—seconds, minutes—it would take to get her out of the water and safe.

Then his world faded into nothing but the murky gray swirl of the river around him.

Chapter Twenty-Five

Brodie woke up gazing into gorgeous caramel eyes. "Is this heaven?"

Maeve's brow arched wryly. "You'd be lucky to make it there."

His mouth quirked. It hurt his head, he winced. More so when he tried to sit up. Looking around he saw the stark white walls, electric strip lighting and the various machines and charts. Everything ached.

Maeve wore pale blue scrubs and a stethoscope round her neck. "How are you feeling?"

"Dreadful."

He watched her try not to smile. Then she checked all his vitals and said, "I think you're going to live."

It was his turn to laugh. Again, it hurt, burned in his throat. "Is Zoey okay?"

Maeve nodded. "Yes, she's fine." Then she swallowed. "Thanks to you."

Brodie managed a little proud smirk as if it were

nothing, but then Maeve added, "Except if you hadn't decided to leave in the first place...."

Brodie shook his head, immediately hissing in discomfort, he really had to stop moving. "I think I'd prefer it if you stuck with the 'she's fine, thanks to you' line."

Maeve looked at him for a second, pierced him with the sudden seriousness of her gaze, and then nodded. "You're her hero," she admitted.

Brodie felt a warmth in his chest.

"You're lucky, Brodie, this could have been much worse."

"At least I would have died a hero."

Maeve shook her head. "I'm serious."

"So am I," he quipped, a bit unnerved, then added, "Would you have been sad?"

She paused and looked at him for a moment, unblinking. Brodie wondered if his pulse reading was going up. Then she shrugged and said nonchalantly, "Devastated."

He could only laugh. It hurt his lungs.

A male nurse came in to take his blood pressure and moving past Maeve said, "How are you feeling, Mr. Carter?"

"Like a hero," he said, eyes still on Maeve, who could only roll hers in response—but did he notice a tiny hint of relief under that mask of professionalism?

Brodie fell back to sleep with a smile on his face, thinking of Zoey with her arms wrapped tight around his neck, imagining her being hauled to safety by his brothers. Then he thought of Maeve, as he was wheeled into hospital, clasping her chest in despair, wringing her hands, weeping at the sight of him fighting for his life. Her hero.

No, he remembered wrongly. *Zoey's* hero.

Maeve had only thanked him. It was almost worth it just for that.

He woke up in a different ward. Sunshine streaming in through the window. Logan and Noah there.

Noah folded as best he could into a too-small chair, chin propped in his hand, eyes shut. Logan standing by the window, hands in his pockets looking down at whatever was going on below them. He turned when he heard Brodie move and his tired face cracked a smile.

"Hey."

Brodie yawned. "Hey."

Noah's eyes opened. Without moving, he said, "That was quite some rescue."

Brodie shuffled himself to sit up in the bed, everything still ached. "I thought you said you could lasso anything."

Noah laughed, sitting up straight, he shrugged and said, "I'll admit it wasn't my best."

Brodie raised his brows like that was an understatement. "Three tries! It was like you were me."

Noah sat forward, elbows on his knees. "What can I say, panic set in."

Brodie feigned being unimpressed for a moment then smiled and said, "Thanks for getting there in the end."

Noah shook his head, half-smile on his lips, clearly incredulous he was getting chewed out for not being quick enough on the lifesaving. Then he raised his chin toward the open door and said, "So she's your kid, huh?"

Sucking in a breath, still more terrified by the knowledge than the near-drowning, Brodie nodded. "Yeah."

Noah nodded back. "Nice."

Brodie let out a breath. He'd weirdly expected something more, maybe some shock or admonishment. The ease of Noah's reply made his heart slow to a more manageable rate. He found himself glancing guiltily at Logan, wondering if that was where his reprimand would come from.

But Logan simply came over and, standing by the side of the bed, said, "You're a lucky guy, she's a great kid. And Noah's right, that was an impressive rescue mission, Brodie. I honestly didn't know you had it in you."

Brodie glanced down at the bed sheet, this time the pride infusing him felt more boyish, more bashful, even. He looked back up, shrugged a shoulder and said casually, "One day when you're a father you'll understand."

Logan narrowed his eyes, gave a slow shake of his head. "You're still full of crap."

"That's a dollar in the swear jar," came a small voice.

They all turned to see Zoey standing in the doorway. She was wearing red leggings and the Jackson General Hospital sweater that seemed so favored by her family.

Logan stood up straighter. "Apologies, ma'am."

"That's okay," Zoey said, but looking very seriously at Logan added, "You can give my mom the money. We're collecting for the new children's wing."

Logan nodded. "Will do."

Noah stood behind him trying to keep a straight face at

his brother being kept in check by an eight-year-old. "We'll leave you to it," he said.

Brodie nodded, but as Noah walked away, he added, "I am really grateful that you did your lasso practice."

Noah snorted a surprised laugh. Then he looked his twin in the eye and said, "Me, too."

The men filed out. Logan still suitably abashed at having been caught cursing.

Zoey stood where she was in the doorway and said, "Is it okay to come in?"

Brodie nodded. "Always."

She walked across the room and stopped by the bed. Her hair was brushed off her face in a hastily tied ponytail, her eyes were tired and still red-rimmed, there were a few scratches and bruises on her neck.

He didn't need to glance at the monitor next to his bed to know his pulse was going through the roof.

"Thank you very much for saving me," she said solemnly, hands clasped in front of her, fingers fidgeting. "It was silly of me to put us in that position. I won't do it again."

Brodie resisted a smile. Zoey's words were straight out of her mom's mouth.

"If you did, I wouldn't hesitate to save you again," he said, with equal solemnity.

She looked at him, her big brown, heartbreaking eyes just like her mom's.

Brodie sat up a bit more, tried to ignore the pain of the bruises on his chest. "I'm sorry, Zoey. I'm sorry I didn't accept your offer to be part of your family." He was about to smile, but it was like his features took over and his mouth went very serious and he felt the odd sensation of—was it tears?!—press against the back of his eyes. "It was by far the dumbest thing I've ever done. I'm sorry."

"That's okay."

"No, it's not." He breathed in through his nose, tried to clamp down the emotion. "I'd like to be your dad, Zoey. More than anything." He stopped, rephrased. "It would be an honor to be your dad. To see you grow up. To be there for you. To listen. To make you laugh—hopefully. To beat up any boys who dare to try and kiss you."

Zoey made a face. "Ew."

"Well, you wait." Brodie raised a brow, knowingly. "I'll be there." He held up his hands in a boxing pose and did a mock-punch. His injured shoulder screeched in his head.

Zoey giggled. Then she went serious. "What about my mom?"

Brodie didn't really know what she was implying, but he thought it best whatever it was that he circumvent the issue. "What you have won't change, Zoey." He didn't know how he was going to go about what he was offering, but he knew, as she stood there chewing nervously on her bottom lip, hands twisting, trying to look super grown-up, that he was offering it all the same. "This is about you and me. This is extra to what you have. And I'm telling you now, that I want to—no—I *will* be there for you." He felt himself get stronger as he said it, felt the unfamiliar tingle of pride—stature—solidify his muscles, tauten his features, make his breath controlled and purposeful. Like he suddenly knew how Clark Kent felt the first time he became

Superman. Knew suddenly what all those comics were about. This. Responsibility. Manning up, saving—or, not saving, but putting others first. Selflessness. It was a new skin and it felt good. Unfamiliar but good. Comfortable, like a great new suit.

"I will be there, Zoey. Whether you decide you want me to be or not. And if you don't, that's fine, too—but I'll always be waiting in the wings, ready for whenever you are."

Don't cry, Brodie. Don't cry. Superman never wept.

Zoey nodded, eyes earnest. "I think I should think about it."

He nodded back. "You do that. Take your time," he added, "I'm not going anywhere."

Zoey turned and walked to the door, where Maeve, who'd been waiting all along he realized, stepped into the frame to greet her. Of course she had been there, Brodie thought—a bit embarrassed now by all his Superman stuff—who let their eight-year-old go visiting in hospitals alone.

Maeve had her arm wrapped around Zoey's shoulders. She glanced up at Brodie in the room and when he caught her eye he chanced a smile, unexpectedly nervous in its delivery.

Maeve just nodded, exactly like her daughter, giving nothing away. What had he expected? That she would have melted, doe-eyed at his speech? Yes, quite frankly. But then again, arm's length was a good distance. He wasn't Superman after all. He was just a fallible, good-time guy who happened to have a kid.

With a very pretty mom.

Without another glance, Maeve put her hand on Zoey's back and steered her away down the corridor.

Brodie sunk back on the pillows and closed his eyes. "Wow," he breathed, uncertain quite how he was feeling.

"Tough gig, eh?" Logan swaggered back in the room, hands in his pockets, smirk on his face.

Brodie shook his head. "You wouldn't believe." He checked his pulse on the monitor, somehow it was ticking along normally.

Noah came in, too, holding a coffee. He flopped down in the chair, legs apart, elbows on his knees. "If all else fails maybe you could serenade them."

Brodie raised a brow. "That's what got me into this mess."

Chapter Twenty-Six

The laughter stopped abruptly when Martha and Emmett walked into the hospital room.

Martha angled her head in relief the moment she saw Brodie sitting up in bed. She walked straight over to envelop him in a hug.

"I'm *so* happy you're all right. Urgh. Never do that again. Or do if it's to save someone. But don't. I don't know what I would've done Brodie if anything—"

"I'm fine, Mom," he lifted his hand to place it reassuringly on hers, even though everything ached from the hug.

His dad came over and offered a curt nod.

Brodie said, "How are you doing, Dad?"

But Emmett just said, "So you've got a daughter, have you?"

Behind his father, Brodie saw Noah wince, and he and Logan again made themselves scarce.

"Not now, Emmett!" Martha scolded. "He's been through enough."

"He's fine." Emmett gestured roughly to Brodie. "What are you planning to do?" There was an accusation in his tone.

Brodie tried to find the words, shrank a little. "Be a dad."

"Right." Emmett nodded, contemplating dubiously. "So I take it you'll be moving back?"

"Well, I mean, not, you know…"

"No, Brodie, I don't know."

"Of course he's moving back," Martha said. "Zoey's his daughter. I still can't believe it. All those times I looked after her and I didn't see it. Now I know, all I can see is you in her. Just the dimples should've been enough. She was such a sweet little baby, Brodie. She had these fat, squidgy legs like the Michelin Man. And her feet were like little wedges of cheese. Just adorable."

"Shame you missed it," Emmett said, matter-of-factly.

Brodie could feel his panic rising again. "Like you spent hours with us as babies!"

"An hour more than you did, Brodie."

"Emmett!"

"Well, it's just typical," Emmett sighed. "It's so frustrating. It's always the same, Brodie. This is exactly what I was talking about—responsibility, good decisions. But you're always just running off ahead, not caring what you leave behind." He rubbed his hand over his face. "Maybe now you'll *have* to grow up."

"*Maybe*," Brodie shot back, regretfully childish.

Martha said, "Stop it. It's enough." Then more gently, "When are we going to see them?"

Brodie gladly turned away from his dad who had moved to look out the window. "Give me a bit of time to smooth things over, then maybe we could have lunch or something?"

Martha squeezed his hand. "Lunch would be lovely. Take all the time you need. We'll be here." Then she added with a grinning whisper, "*Very* excited!" And shook her clenched fists like a kid on Christmas Day.

Chapter Twenty-Seven

It was a couple of days later. Brodie was out of hospital and back at his condo. It was the longest he'd ever lived in the apartment, he even had milk in the fridge. His body had recovered. His mind, however, was still catching up, fighting off the sense of being totally overwhelmed by trying to stick to his life motto of *one day at a time*.

The sparseness of his condo meant there were no distractions. He'd spent too much time on Instagram, following the San Diego trip, zooming in on photos of Caleb's yacht crashing through the waves. It looked so fun. He was contemplating whether he should buy a PlayStation for something to do, when Maeve's number flashed up on his phone. He found himself smiling as he answered. "Hi."

"Hi, Brodie, it's Zoey."

He felt a perplexing twinge of both disappointment and pleasure. "Hey, what can I do for you?" he asked, sipping his coffee, hand wrapped round the mug.

"Would you like to do something together?"

It felt like a punch to the gut, so exquisite it was painful. Better than sailing, he realized. "Yes," he replied, trying to keep it cool, emotion doing funny things to him, the lump in his throat making it difficult to speak. "What d'you have in mind?"

"I was thinking Disneyland."

"Zoey!" He heard the warning from Maeve in the background.

"Ok-ay," she relented.

Brodie said, "How about we start with going to the park? Play a bit of basketball?"

"Can we go for a Cookies and Cream Dream?"

Brodie had lived in Autumn Falls long enough to know every flavor of milkshake in the diner. He heard Maeve again say, "Zoey…"

Zoey said, "We don't have to get a milkshake, I can bring water."

Brodie smiled inside. "I'd love to get a Cookies and Cream Dream with you."

"Yeah?"

"Yeah."

Quarter of an hour later, Brodie rapped on the door of Maeve's house, his nerves on edge, smoothing back his hair in the reflection, pulling at his T-shirt. It was worse than any date. The fear of rejection was acute.

Maeve opened the door looking unbelievably lovely in a white shirt and jean shorts. Still with the ugly mushroom shoes, but he'd grown quite fond of them. Her hair swept over one eye, like she hadn't had time to do anything with it. He felt his unaccustomed nerves get stronger.

"You look better," she said.

"I feel better," he replied. "Totally fine." Which belied the constant knot that had appeared in his stomach.

She seemed to sense his nervousness and smiled up at him through dark lashes. "That's good."

He had rarely been around a woman he was this attracted to for this long without at least kissing her. It made him unfamiliarly awkward in his movements, like all of a sudden he'd forgotten how to stand still.

"You all right about this?" Maeve asked.

Brodie nodded, although he felt increasingly terrified.

Maeve seemed totally unaffected. "What are you going to do if there's photographers or anything like that? Will you just make sure that Zoey is safe, please?"

"Maeve, I'm old news. People don't take photos of me anymore. I'm boring."

She raised her eyebrows in disbelief. "I don't think that's strictly true."

Did that mean she didn't think he was boring?

Focus, Brodie!

"Look, we're going to have to deal with it sooner or later," he said. "If I see a photographer or someone takes a picture on their phone, I tend to just smile and wave. It's the best way to deal with it."

Maeve nodded uncertainly.

Brodie wanted to ask her to come with them. But before he could say anything more, Zoey came bounding down the stairs in dungarees and a yellow top.

"Hey, you look like a Minion," he said.

Zoey paused, looked down at herself and immediately

turned around and went back up the stairs. "I have to get changed."

"I didn't mean—" he called but Maeve shook her head and said, "You've done it now, day's ruined."

"You serious?" He could feel himself start to sweat.

"No!" Maeve laughed, incredulous. "Brodie, she changes her outfit about five times a day. It's fine." She seemed to realize then that he *was* actually nervous. "You'll be fine."

"You wanna come too?" he asked, not the suave invite he'd been intending, but half desperate, half hopeful.

Her expression softened but she still shook her head. "No. You two just have fun together."

"You sure?" Brodie asked. He'd like to sit opposite her having a milkshake, he'd even found himself wondering what flavor she'd get. He'd pipped her for a Strawberry Serenade kinda person. It was Willow's favorite, too. "The more the merrier."

Maeve said, "Brodie, you don't need me there, you'll be fine."

He wanted to say that she'd read it wrong. He didn't need her—although she would be useful—he *wanted* her there.

Zoey came back then in a purple top under her dungarees.

Before Brodie could ask her to join them again, Maeve said, "Bye, guys, have fun."

"Bye, Mom."

He found himself momentarily reluctant to step off the porch, felt the unfamiliar tug of the warm, easy sense of family created when these two were together, but he tore his gaze away from Maeve's doting smile and turned to his daughter. "Right, you're teaching me to shoot hoops, yeah?"

"Oh, yeah!"

Chapter Twenty-Eight

Zoey left giggling. That was good. It was a good thing, Maeve told herself, leaning against the wall in her hallway.

She closed her eyes. Could she do this? Every day, forever? Answer the door to his radiant smile, endure his easy flirtation, his refreshing happy-go-lucky take on life? Look across at him at Zoey's birthdays, her graduation, her wedding. Him and his many girlfriends. Could she chat and laugh and be normal?

Yes, she told herself, walking back down the corridor, because she had to. Because this was a good thing.

It had been a long time since Maeve had a Saturday free with no work and no Zoey.

She made herself a coffee and sat in the garden, tried to relax looking at the birds but kept checking her phone in case something had happened. She thought about them together drinking Cookies and Cream Dreams. Him saying his silly jokes and making Zoey laugh. She felt a squeeze of something inside her—envy, sadness?—but it wasn't because of Brodie's time with her daughter, she realized, it was wishing she was there with them. Wishing she'd said yes to Brodie's invite. She'd order a Strawberry Serenade and Zoey would tell Brodie how gross strawberries were. What would Brodie have, she wondered? Probably a Cookies and Cream Dream to make Zoey happy. But if he were to choose for himself ... the triple-chocolate Mudslide.

Why on earth was she thinking about Brodie's milkshake choices?

She stood up too quickly. *Don't be ridiculous, Maeve.*

To keep busy, she cleaned the house from top to bottom. There wasn't a speck of dust by the time she finished. No random Cheerios under the kitchen table. Then she made a pie.

When the screen door banged to show they were back, she heard Zoey say, "Wow, Mom, you baked something?" Then to Brodie, "Mom *never* bakes."

Maeve rushed to the kitchen doorway to defend herself. "I bake!"

Brodie was kicking off his sneakers, basketball under one arm; so at home. She had to get a grip.

Zoey scrunched up her nose. "When?"

Maeve looked around her as if the answer might present itself. "Now," she replied in the end.

She saw Brodie smirk, as if she'd been caught out doing something to impress him.

Had she been trying to impress him? Or was she just bored? And if she was trying to impress him, what made her think that her distinctly average attempts at baking would do the trick?

Zoey stared at her like something weird was going on, then she leaned over to Brodie and whispered, "I've literally *never* seen my mom bake anything, ever."

Maeve knew she was blushing. That she'd overdone it by baking an apple pie. That in some bizarre homespun dream, she had indeed been trying to impress him. To show him the delights of small-town life. Was she insane? Not only had he grown up here—this was not her normal life! He'd seen the chaos she lived in.

"Good basketball?" she asked, busying herself cutting the pie so she didn't have to look at Brodie.

"Brodie didn't know I was on the team," Zoey said, pulling out a chair at the table. "Yum!" she grinned, taking the slice that Maeve had cut her.

"She's good," Brodie said, leaning against the doorway, arms folded.

"Mom's good, too," Zoey's voice was mumbled from the pie she'd crammed in her mouth.

"I was okay at school." Maeve tucked her hair behind her ear, far too aware of Brodie in her house—all sparkly and clean and smelling of warm sugar. It was safer before, when she was wary of him. "And I do bake, by the way. Sometimes," she added, wishing immediately that she hadn't.

"I didn't say you didn't." Was that a hidden grin? Could he tell she was awkward? Why was she suddenly awkward around him?

It felt like everything had changed. Now that the truth of

Zoey's parentage was out in the open, it felt different from before. There was no covert truth to edge around, no accusatory whisperings. The conversation was no longer all explanations and a desire to be understood. This was it—he was the missing father—it was happening. He and Zoey could build their own relationship, he didn't even have to be in the house. But here he was. All six foot of him, with his dimples and his shaggy blond hair and his surfer tan. She fumbled the pie as she plated it up. "You want some or have you overdosed on sugar already at the diner?"

Brodie took the plate from her, sauntering to the table with his broken, crumbling slice. "Oh, I'll most definitely have some pie. I wouldn't pass up such a rare treat."

Maeve rolled her eyes, had never had more cause to do so than with this man.

Was he teasing her? She couldn't read any signals, she was too overly aware of him in her house, sitting at her table. She thought about how she'd wanted to be with them playing basketball and having shakes. Wanted to be part of the giggling and the easy asides.

Her and all the other women in the world.

She took in a calming breath. *He's the father of your kid. That's it.*

Suddenly, as if her mind had been suppressing it until the issue was resolved, the image of her night with him flashed into her mind. She remembered, as she sat across from him, exactly what the touch of his lips felt like, his hand tracing down her arm to lace his fingers with hers and lift them above her head. She remembered the weight of his body. The smell of his skin. The crease of his smiling eyes when he was mere inches away from hers.

"This is great pie," he said, mouth full.

"Yeah, Mom, you're good at this."

For a second, Maeve forgot what they were talking about.

Brodie said, "I think your mom's good at everything."

"Me, too."

She couldn't bear it. Her palms were clammy. She didn't want to sit, she didn't want to stand. She could just feel the thrum through her body of having Brodie wrap his arms tight around her waist and kiss her with a careless laugh on his lips.

"Coffee?" she asked.

Zoey scraped her chair back. "Can I go and watch TV?"

Maeve nodded.

Brodie twisted round in his seat. He looked too big for the kitchen. She imagined her grandma making eyes at her behind his back, giving her a cheeky thumbs-up. Grandma would have loved Brodie with all his slick charm and compliments.

"Have I done something?" he asked, elbow on the table, chin propped on his fist as he studied her. "I feel like I'm making you nervous."

Maeve shook her head, nonplussed. "No not at all."

Brodie narrowed his eyes like he could tell she was lying. Before he could say anything, she said, "What milkshake did you have?"

His lip quirked as if he hadn't expected the question

from her. "Same as always. The Mudslide—triple chocolate."

She swallowed. She'd guessed correctly.

"What's your favorite?" he asked.

"Strawberry Serenade."

"Willow's favorite, too," he said, a little smile on his lips. Had he been guessing hers? No, of course not, because he wasn't behaving like a pathetic teenager.

Zoey burst back in and said, "You want to play *Mario Kart*?"

"I *always* want to play *Mario Kart*," Brodie replied, getting up and following Zoey into the living room, just one amused backward glance at Maeve.

Maeve blew out a breath and slumped against the kitchen counter. She looked at the remains of her pie and, torn between wanting to throw it in the bin and have a taste of it, she got a fork and scooped up some of the sweet apple and sugared crust. It wasn't half bad, maybe Brodie had been impressed, she thought, then as quickly, frowning at herself, she muttered, "Get a grip, Maeve."

Chapter Twenty-Nine

Brodie came back the following afternoon and they all went to the park. Zoey walking between them, holding both their hands. Maeve glanced at the connection, loving it, hating it, fearing it. She found herself looking round self-consciously and warily for anyone watching, waiting to take a picture. She feared it all becoming bigger than the three of them, whatever Brodie said to the contrary.

She could still see so clearly Zoey's face when she'd told her, before the river accident, that Brodie was leaving, that his lifestyle was calling him away, her daughter's heartbreaking crumple into tears. But now they were all playing ball and she forgot about it, was back in the moment, dodging Brodie's tackle, batting him away, their skin glistening with sweat, competitive, laughing, too close. Pausing to take a step back, relieved to watch as he picked Zoey up so she could score a basket. Panting on the sideline and sharing a bottle of water. Internally flinching with awareness when his hand touched hers as he took it from her. Far too aware every time his eyes met hers and pulled his well-practiced, slow, crooked smile.

This isn't real, she had to keep reminding herself. It was the honeymoon period before real life intervened.

Then they went home and, of course Zoey insisted they play *Mario Kart* again, but that time Brodie had to have time penalties because he was too good. "Weren't you quite good at this?" he said, eyes alight, and Maeve knew he was talking about their night together—had assumed he'd forgotten. She had visions of his hotel room with his Nintendo Switch connected to the TV. Remembered his mouth dropping down to hers, his fingers gently tucking her hair behind her ear, his palm cool against her back. Her skin got hot again. Zoey said, "Mom, you crashed out!" She looked at the screen and saw poor Princess Peach overturned on the tarmac. Brodie smiling slyly next to her as his Mario cruised over the finish line.

When Maeve made dinner, Brodie and Zoey went out the back and ran races. She watched them out of the kitchen window and had visions of him forever in her backyard, all sweaty and laughing. She would never be able to relax.

When Zoey ate dinner, Brodie asked her questions about school and boys she fancied, which made Zoey pull faces of horror.

Later, they all made name bracelets. "Who's yours for?" Zoey asked, leaning over the table to look at which letters Brodie had threaded onto his bracelet. Then she said delightedly, "Mom, Brodie's made one for you!"

Maeve looked up from her own—which had Zoey's

name on it—and saw Brodie holding up a bracelet with Maeve spelt out with two little stars on either side. "Oh, lovely, thanks," she said, aware of Zoey grinning widely beside him.

"Put it on!" Zoey pleaded, and Maeve found herself reluctantly holding her arm out for Brodie to tie the bracelet on her wrist. She knew she was blushing and hated it.

Brodie, however, seemed to be thoroughly enjoying the whole process. "There you go," he said, tying the knot tight. "Looks great."

Maeve couldn't cope with the attention—the two of them grinning at her with their matching dimples. "Okay, it's bedtime," she said, standing up.

"Can Brodie read my story?"

"He probably has to—"

"I'd love to." Brodie cut her off.

Maeve wondered if she'd ever be able to relax in her house again.

When Zoey had cleaned her teeth and got into her pajamas, Brodie came upstairs and said, "So what are we reading?"

Zoey reached up to her bookshelf and her Harry Potter collection. "I thought we could read number five—from where you've got up to."

It was such a sweet gesture that Maeve found herself pausing in the doorway to watch as Brodie took the book and said, "Great idea!"

Zoey climbed under the covers and he sat down on the rocking chair beside the bed. But he didn't open the book straight away, instead he looked at the cover for a second, then, after a moment's thought, said, "Zoey, I've got a confession to make."

Maeve froze. Was he leaving again? Please don't let him leave. Even though moments ago all she wanted was for him to leave, she only meant leave the house. She almost crossed her fingers. Please don't let her down.

He swallowed and looked up, Zoey watching with her wide, wary eyes. "I'm not a Gryffindor."

Maeve almost collapsed against the doorframe with relief.

He looked down again, took another moment's pause before, clearly bracing himself, added, "I'm a Hufflepuff."

Zoey clutched the quilt for a second then, hands relaxing, shoulders dropping, she said, "Me, too."

Brodie flinched in surprise. "What?!" He shot a look at Maeve who nodded.

He turned back to Zoey, open-mouthed, then to Maeve again. "But you—" He seemed to be recalling his teasing of her being a Ravenclaw. The two of them united in their superior Gryffindorness. She watched the gradual softening of his expression as he realized that she had simply done it for them, for him and Zoey to unite.

She shrugged, like anyone would have done the same.

He laughed, totally taken aback, then returned his attention to Zoey and said, "I think Hufflepuffs are the best, anyway."

Zoey nodded in very serious agreement. Then added, "And Ravenclaws."

Brodie glanced over at Maeve with a smile on his face that had none of its usual mischievous flirtation, but instead just genuine warmth. "And Ravenclaws," he agreed.

Maeve wanted to run to her own bedroom and lock the door. Why couldn't she have been on shift tonight? Bring on the patients, the stress, and the overtime. Anything was better than dealing with that smile.

She left Brodie sitting in the chair by Zoey's bed, reading in various voices that made her daughter snort with laughter, and busied herself downstairs, determined to put a stop to her wandering, wayward thoughts.

All of a sudden, a voice right close behind her said, "Okay?"

She jumped.

Brodie was grinning at the fact he'd managed to startle her.

Maeve found herself pinned between the kitchen counter and the six-foot, broad-chested Brodie, smiling like life was all one big, hilarious, flirtatious joke.

Maeve chucked the cloth she'd been using to wipe the surfaces over by the sink, then raising her chin, said steadfastly, "I just want to make clear that we're not doing *this*."

He reached to pick an apple from the bowl on the counter behind her, his arm almost but not quite brushing against her. "Doing what?"

"This. Us," she said, pointing between them.

He half smiled as he took a bite. "I know," he said, chewing and smiling at the same time. Then he turned and sauntered away to get his sweater that he'd thrown over a chair.

Maeve breathed out, aware of the fine line between relief and embarrassment. Was it all in her head? He was so cool and collected, it was difficult to tell.

Brodie started to walk to the front door but paused in the hallway and came back into the room. "By the way," he said, taking another bite of apple, "Logan invited you to lunch on Sunday."

It was her turn to frown. "Why?"

Brodie cocked his head, chewing with slow amusement. "My mom wants to see you and Zoey. We thought it was better in more neutral territory."

Maeve's eyes widened in horror. "Oh, Brodie—"

"Don't worry, she's okay. And anyway, I'll look out for you." He paused, eyes glinting, as he added, "But not in any, *this*, *us*, kinda way."

Before Maeve could respond, he chucked his sweater over his shoulder and wandered out, that wicked, cheeky grin back in place.

Chapter Thirty

Logan and Bella's house was out of town, surrounded by acres of lush grass and trees that shivered in the breeze, pines as high as the eye could see, pointing like arrows up to the sky. The house was pretty traditional on the outside, but inside—Maeve gasped out loud when she saw the view out the wall of windows of the rolling, unadulterated landscape. It was nice to have a distraction from the nerves. "This is a beautiful house," she gushed.

"Better now it's got some furnishings," Bella replied, looking archly at Logan who shrugged as if he'd never really got the hang of home decorating.

Then Martha came in through the open bifold doors, glass of lemonade in her hand, and said, "Maybe you'll buy some furniture soon, Brodie?"

Maeve felt her whole body tighten with trepidation at the sight of Martha, statuesque and beautiful in wide olive-green pants and a wraparound black shirt. Brodie went, "Ha-ha, very funny." Then, placing his hand gently on

Maeve's back in a quiet gesture to say that it was going to be okay, he added, "Maybe I already have."

Martha seemed surprised at that and said, "Really? What have you bought?"

Brodie dropped his hand, reached for a glass that Logan offered him, Maeve felt both the loss of the supportive touch, and more able to breathe with it gone. "Okay. I haven't actually bought anything, but I do acknowledge that some pictures on the walls might be good."

The others laughed. Martha raised her brows in fond disapproval, then turned to Maeve and said, "Hello, Maeve, sweetheart? How are you?" With a big wide smile, a little like her son's and in turn a little like Zoey's, that made Maeve instantly relax a fraction.

"I'm good, thank you, Martha."

Martha nodded, still with her welcoming smile, and as they moved outside, turned to Zoey and said, "And you, I hear you had quite an adventure in the river."

"Oh, I wasn't scared at all," Zoey replied and Martha shook her head and said, "Well, aren't you brave, I would have been terrified."

Zoey said, "Should I call you Grandma?"

"You can call me what you like, darling."

They walked outside, Martha with her hand gently on Zoey's shoulder, to where Emmett was talking to Logan.

Zoey said, "Okay, I will. And I'll call Emmett Grandpa."

Emmett was mid-sentence and simply stopped talking, turning to stare at Zoey, momentarily lost for words.

Maeve watched his hand reach for the back of one of the chairs—possibly, to steady himself from the shock.

Martha said, "I'm sure he'd like that very much."

They all looked to Emmett who managed to find his voice to say, "It would be a privilege."

Zoey beamed.

There followed an odd moment of silence. A glance from Emmett to Brodie, Martha smiling. Maeve aware of undercurrents she knew nothing about.

Then Logan said, "Hey, Zoey, you want to come and see the horses?"

Brodie made a face. "What horses have you got here?"

Bella rolled her eyes. "There's two. One is injured and the other is here so it doesn't get lonely."

Brodie laughed, "Steady, Logan, you're turning into Noah."

They all went outside, all except Maeve and Martha, who knew they'd been given this opportunity to connect in private.

Maeve glanced down at the wooden floor for a second then said, "I'm sorry I didn't tell you."

Martha sighed, the fine lines at the sides of her eyes creasing with a sad softness, and she took a couple of steps forward. "I'm not angry, Maeve. Well, I am a bit," she relented. "It's my grandchild. I guess I'm more disappointed—not in you, but in missed opportunity. I could have looked after her, I could have helped more."

"You did help," Maeve cut in quickly, feeling the guilt heavy like stones.

Martha shook her head. "I could have done more." Then she reached forward and placed her hand gently on Maeve's arm and said, "I am very familiar, though, with the concept of *could have done*. And the thing is, Maeve, I understand." She gave her arm a squeeze and then took her hand away. "I'm upset, but I understand." She tucked her jet-black hair behind her ear, little gold horseshoe studs in the lobes. "I understand what a mother will do to protect her child. Would it have been me, I'd have found it very difficult to trust Brodie at that time of his life; especially with his—" she paused, then said less warmly "—marriage." It was the only time Maeve had seen even a hint of disdain on Martha Carter's face.

Maeve nodded, she felt too overcome for a second to say anything. That this woman could be so nice to her after everything, could be so understanding. It made her think of her own parents, made her realize that compassion was a gift, not a given. "Thank you, Martha."

Martha smiled, her eyes glinting just like Brodie's. "Thank *you*, Maeve. Zoey is my first grandchild, and I am absolutely thrilled to have her—and you—in the family. Now come on, let's head out and join the others."

They went through the house and out the back where most of the men had gone with Zoey and Logan to see the horses. Even Emmett was out there with them. Maeve watched as the older man got a packet of Polo mints out of his shirt pocket and gave Zoey a couple to feed the two inquisitive horses.

Noah and his girlfriend, Ren, had been left in charge of the barbecue.

"I think it's ready, Noah," Ren was saying, hands in the pockets of her shorts as she looked pointedly at the coals.

Noah was shaking his head. "That is *not* ready."

Ren shook her head. "I don't know why you can't just have gas? Oh, hi, Maeve!"

"No one who wants to cook a steak properly has gas," Noah replied. "Hi, Maeve."

Maeve raised a hand in greeting, grateful for the ease with which they welcomed her. She knew Ren from the diner, Zoey said she made better milkshakes than the owner, Loriana, but Ren had sworn them to secrecy on that fact.

"You good, Maeve?" Ren asked, sipping on her lemonade. "You know, your Zoey can get through a Cookies and Cream Dream faster than I've ever seen anyone."

Maeve laughed. "She'll be very proud of that fact."

Ren winked and went back to insisting that Noah start grilling.

Bella came out with the steaks and when he saw her, Logan jogged over to help, then Martha took over and told Bella that she should give Maeve a tour of the place. Over in the paddock, Emmett was helping Zoey up on one of the horses while Brodie stayed guard.

This was her daughter with her grandparents, Maeve thought, with a pang of regret that it hadn't happened sooner.

Bella picked up her glass and gestured for Maeve to walk with her. They strolled down one of the paths on the property, this one led to a small stream with a bridge.

Once they were out of earshot, Bella said, "So, how are you doing?"

While Maeve and Bella had vaguely known each other from school, they had become friends through Bella's mom,

Heather, who was a nurse at the hospital. They often carpooled because Maeve lived next door to the orchard and had become friends with Bella as a result.

Maeve took a sip of lemonade, the ice clinking. "I'm okay."

Bella raised a brow like she knew she was lying.

"I am," Maeve insisted. "It's all a bit weird, but in a good way, for Zoey." She nodded toward where a horse was being slowly led round the paddock by Emmett. "He seems taken with her."

Bella agreed. "I think Emmett can be quite a softie underneath it all."

It was a warm day, white clouds drifting lazily on the pale blue sky. Bella stopped walking for a second to tie up her hair, then she looked at Maeve and said, "And what about Brodie?"

Maeve narrowed her eyes, she could see the sparkle in Bella's expression. "What about Brodie?"

Bella shrugged and they kept walking, but when Maeve glanced sideways, she saw Bella was watching her. She looked the picture of innocence in her crisp white T-shirt, pale blue jeans and sandals, but Maeve recognized the shrewdness behind her eyes.

Maeve sighed. "Honestly, nothing's happening between us. Of course there isn't, we've gotta focus on Zoey, but—"

"But?" They'd stopped on the little bridge and Bella turned and leaned against it.

Maeve leaned against the other side of the bridge. "But sometimes it feels like there's something there. Then, as soon as I say that, I think, every woman Brodie meets must say that."

Bella laughed.

Maeve widened her eyes. "See, no one bothers denying it!"

Bella scuffed the bridge slats with her sandal. "What if it was different with you and him? He's older now, maybe he's ready for a change?"

"You think he's bored of gorgeous supermodels?" Maeve asked wryly.

Bella shrugged. "You're gorgeous."

"I am not!" Maeve waved away the compliment, embarrassed. "It's silly, I don't know why I'm even talking about it. It would never work."

"It might work."

Maeve looked down at the ice cubes and lemon in her drink. "And what if it didn't? What if it all went wrong? Then what? It's bad for Zoey. Bad for me. And we're back where we started."

"Not entirely," Bella replied, hoisting herself up so she was sitting on the side of the bridge. "He'd still be her dad."

Maeve raised her brows in question.

"You don't trust him to stick around if things went wrong?"

"He hasn't exactly got the best track record."

"True," Bella admitted.

"That's comforting."

Bella laughed. "But people do change, Maeve."

Maeve looked over to where Brodie had climbed up behind Zoey on the horse and was picking up the pace, riding them faster and faster round the paddock. "You think?" she said, nodding in Brodie's direction.

Bella turned to look and laughed again.

Then they watched Emmett whistle through his teeth and Brodie immediately slow the horse down to a trot. Zoey whooped, asking to do it again, but Brodie shook his head, drawing them up level with Emmett and jumping down, handing the reins back to his dad so he could teach her properly.

Bella turned back to Maeve. "I've always had a soft spot for Brodie. I think he had a rough deal with Emmett growing up."

"What kind of rough deal?" Maeve frowned. She did not want to add sympathy to her already complex feelings about Brodie.

"Steaks ready!" Noah hollered and everyone moved back toward the table. Brodie standing by the horse so Zoey could get down onto his shoulders.

"Why don't you try asking him?" Bella smiled, jumped down off the bridge and started to walk back toward the barbecue.

Chapter Thirty-One

They all sat around the big long table on Logan and Bella's deck. It was plain to anyone there that this kind of gathering didn't happen often in the Carter family. Emmett, awkward, and often punctuating conversations with something that made at least one person shift uncomfortably in their seat. It was people like Ren who kept the conversation light—she could win awards for glossing over awkward subjects with new facts or conversation starters. Maeve asked Martha about The Silver Pantry, as the town was abuzz with news of it opening soon.

"Ren has agreed to run the coffee shop for me," Martha said proudly, and Ren smiled bashfully at the news.

"That's amazing," Bella said. "Congratulations, both of you."

"Thanks," Ren replied, resting her head on Noah's shoulder because she was embarrassed by the attention.

Bella topped up everyone's water. "Did you hear John-Luke wants to sell the orchard?"

Martha gasped. "I did not."

"Yeah," Bella nodded. "My mom wants to travel. Go back to the UK for a bit. I think they just feel like they're getting older and want a change of pace."

Emmett reached forward for his glass. "It's a beautiful orchard."

"Isn't it vines as well?" Logan sat back in his chair. "Brodie, maybe you should buy it?"

Without missing a beat, Emmett said, "Would be a shame if those trees died."

Everyone round the table shifted this time. Maeve caught Bella giving her wide eyes across the table.

Brodie put his fork down and said, "Are you kidding me?"

"Brodie." It was Noah, his tone a friendly warning not to rise to it.

But Brodie ignored him. "You know I *own* a very healthy vineyard, yeah?" he said to his dad.

Emmett wiped his hands on his napkin and, without looking Brodie's way, said, "I'm sure you do, I'm just saying that's an age-old orchard and it needs proper care. It is not something that should be bought on a whim."

"And you think that's what I would do?"

Emmett fixed him with a hard stare and said, "I know that's what you would do."

Brodie was all set to reply when Noah cut in with, "Zoey, how'd you like to be taught how to throw a rope?"

Zoey had already scraped her chair back. "Yes, sir."

Noah laughed. "C'mon, then." He stood up, taking a quick drink of water before leaving the table. "You got a rope in that barn, Logan?"

Logan stood up, too. "Yeah, I'll get it for you."

Noah glanced warily at Brodie, who sat visibly seething, and then at his dad and said, "You wanna help?"

Emmett shook his head. "I'm fine where I am."

Noah narrowed his eyes a second, once again looked at Brodie all fired up and tight-lipped. "Fine," he said to Emmett, "but I don't want you telling her later that I taught her wrong."

Emmett huffed at that idea, but it seemed to do the trick because, throwing his napkin on the table, he got up to follow Noah. Then he paused, as if remembering his manners, and said, "Thank you, Logan, Bella, for a very nice lunch."

No one could quite meet anyone else's eye.

"Yeah, thanks, guys," Brodie muttered, getting up and stalking into the house.

Again, Bella made eyes at Maeve across the table and then nodded for her to follow Brodie inside.

Maeve thought that maybe someone else should do that and luckily Martha said, "I'll go have a word with him."

But to Maeve's horror, Bella said, "Maybe Maeve should go, she's a doctor, right? She's good at talking to people, solving their problems."

"I'm not that kind of—" Maeve began, with a glare at Bella, who shrugged, biting down on what was clearly a mischievous smile.

219

"Always good to get a fresh take on things, don't you think?" she said.

"Absolutely, be my guest." Brodie's mom stood back willingly. "I think he's heard everything I have to say."

At the end of the table, Ren sat forward, watching, intrigued at the turn of events. Maeve felt herself blush at the undercurrents and, not wanting to draw any more attention to the situation, pushed back her chair and said, "Sure. I'll see what I can do."

Inside, crossing the palatial living room, she took a breath, tried not to think of what she knew would be covert looks between the women at the table behind her back, and went in search of Brodie.

She found him upstairs, where there was a second living room with a higher aspect, so the view was even more incredible. They could see Zoey getting her lasso lesson.

Brodie was standing in front of the window with his back to her, but he glanced over his shoulder when he heard someone approach and seemed momentarily surprised to see it was Maeve. "Sorry," he said, "I just needed a break."

Maeve nodded. She walked across the room, glancing around as she went at the stylish furniture, the large abstract canvases, the warm, muted tones of the walls that seemed to somehow accentuate the view. "This is a really nice room," she said, coming to stand next to him. "Makes me think I should have done *way* more with my house!"

Brodie shook his head. "I like your house."

It was funny to hear him say it with such honesty, her house still with her grandma's furnishings was not somewhere she would envisage Brodie enjoying. "That's kind of you to say," she said, "but it definitely needs a bit of a TLC."

They fell into silence, both watching Zoey out in the back yard, Noah showing her how to hold the rope, making her laugh. Emmett watching, leaning against the paddock fence.

Maeve said, "Bella was saying that you and your dad don't get along so well."

"You been talking to Bella about me?" Brodie's eyes lit up at the idea.

Maeve shook her head and looked frustratedly down at the floor. "Can you ever just have a conversation?"

"Not when there's a pretty girl around." He moved so that he was leaning against the back of the couch, legs stretched out in front of him, tanned arms crossed.

"Okay, I'm going." She turned to walk away.

Brodie laughed, jumping up and reaching out a hand to stop her. "Sorry, sorry. I'll focus, I promise."

All Maeve could think about was the touch of his hand on her arm. It was the guilty feeling of being a hypocrite that made her stay put.

She perched beside him on the back of the couch. He rested his hands either side of him, legs stretched out again, then he screwed his face up and said, "My dad. Okay." He thought about it. "I guess I just annoy him." He paused. "He's very serious, always has been. I like music and people and enjoying life. He likes cattle and being alone, and I have no idea if he enjoys life or not." Brodie shrugged. "I disappoint him because he thinks I lack purpose."

"You do lack purpose," she said without really thinking.

"Whoa. Don't hold back." He laughed, lines fanning the sides of his eyes, dimples in his cheeks from the grin that always took the edge off a situation.

It was her turn to shrug. "Well, it's true."

"Maybe so," he relented, "but even when I *did* have purpose, when I was in the band, when I was making it on my own, I still disappointed him, because I wasn't doing it his way. We're just too different."

Out the window, Emmett had stepped in to correct Zoey's hold on the rope, and Brodie said, "I might buy that orchard just to prove him wrong."

"Then the trees really will die."

He frowned. "Why do you say that?"

She turned to look at him, at his mouth tight with irritation, a bit like his dad's. "Because you can't live a certain way to spite someone. It never ends well. You buy that orchard because you *want* to buy it—whether the trees die or not—not because your dad told you that you can't."

He weighed up the argument, then said, "Aren't you working so hard all the time to spite your parents?"

Maeve went to speak, to defend herself, and then stopped and thought about it for a second and laughed that he'd caught her out. "I think my problem is that I'm trying to make them see that they made a mistake."

"Interesting," he replied, head tilted in encouragement for her to carry on.

She shrugged. "Being a doctor was all I ever wanted to be. Of course, I wanted to help people but I just knew that I'd be good at it. I enjoyed it, I like the science of it and the work, and it felt right." She paused, glanced out at Zoey getting all tangled in the rope as she tried to throw it. "I think what I realized when I fell pregnant, was that for them, me going to study medicine at Stanford was more about the prestige. The kudos, you know? It wasn't about me."

She was surprised by how easy she found it to talk to Brodie. How, when he looked at her, it made her feel like he didn't want to be talking to anyone else, like what she had to say was somehow precious. And it made her say things that were precious, that she didn't say to many people. "I didn't work so hard to spite them, I think I worked so hard in the hope that they might notice me!"

Brodie nodded in understanding. She imagined him with his platinum discs and number-one albums just craving a *well done*.

Maeve shifted so she was sitting facing the window rather than Brodie's profile, the sun catching his hair as it flopped messily over his forehead, highlighting the sharp slices of his cheekbones. It was easier to talk to him if she didn't look at him. And she found she wanted to talk to him, she liked talking to him. She watched Zoey outside attempt a throw of the rope again and miss wildly. "Do you know one day, a couple of years ago, they turned up on my doorstep? Said they were just passing through." She paused at the memory of it, the surprise of seeing her parents in their fancy clothes standing there. They'd been back in town meeting old friends at the club, they said. She had frozen at the sight of them, thought it might be her imagination, like a mirage. "My grandma used to say that the test of a person is whether they can admit their mistakes. Whether they're willing to change. I think that's part of why she was so frustrated with my parents—she didn't just think they'd let me down but they—my dad—let her down, too. She wanted him to be better."

"Did you let them in?" Brodie asked, clearly intrigued by that turn of events.

"Oh, yeah," she said, amused at the idea of her not doing, because seeing them had made her realize how long she'd been out in the cold. "We had coffee. They met Zoey. They asked a few questions about my work, and then they left. That was it, no mention of what had happened. No real acknowledgment of the fact we hadn't seen each other for years. I like to tell myself that they were too proud to say they were sorry. Or at least too proud to say well done for getting there in the end, but who knows."

"I bet they were proud," he said with certainty. "I'd be proud of you if you were my kid."

She turned and smiled in grateful surprise. "Thanks, Brodie."

"It's true," he said, holding her gaze. She felt the look shiver over her skin even after he looked away, out at Zoey and Emmett in the back yard, and added, "So are you saying that my dad's secretly super proud of me?" He glanced back, corner of his mouth raised like he knew that was a lie.

"I guess I'm saying that you must have worked really hard once upon a time. Not everyone becomes a superstar. Your songs are loved by people…"

He grinned at the compliment.

"Brodie, I'm not saying this to fan your ego."

"No, I know." He tried to stop smiling. "It's good to hear, though. I appreciate it."

She rolled her eyes. That made him laugh again.

"Do you despair of me?"

"Yes," she replied but her lips twitched with a smile.

He made her laugh, she realized. Apart from with Zoey, there hadn't been that much laughter in her life over the last few years, there hadn't been time or reason. But something about Brodie, he could switch a moment and lighten it and make you realize that life could be funnier than you thought.

"I don't know, Brodie," she said, trying to be serious for a second, "do you ever think your dad was just wrong and can't admit it? It must be pretty galling to be telling your kid one thing every day and then they go off and prove you wrong. Maybe you make him feel like a fool. Maybe that's why he gets at you, because being any other way would admit he was wrong. Maybe it's pride."

Brodie raised his brows and seemed to think about it for a moment, nodding his head from side to side. "That's an interesting way of looking at it."

"I'm not saying that's definitely what it is, but it's a possibility. Or at least, it might be part of the reason." She shrugged. "Pride's a very powerful thing. It's hard to admit our mistakes."

Brodie nodded again, then he nudged her on the shoulder and said, "Do you think you make your parents feel foolish?"

"All the time," she replied with a smile that told him it was an out-and-out lie. "I wish I did think that way. I still feel their judgment in everything. I worry sometimes that everything I do is trying to prove I'm not a failure." She paused, running her hand through her hair, surprising herself that she was saying this much to him, but there was that look again like he wanted to hear what she had to say, like he was genuinely interested in her. "They made the thing I love the most—Zoey—out to be my biggest failing. And I look at her and I struggle to see how that could be true."

"If Zoey's your biggest failing, then believe me, you're doing more than okay!"

Again, he caught her off-guard with his sincerity. She smiled more bashfully than she thought she was capable of, shy under his praise.

Brodie seemed surprised himself by the genuineness of her reaction. Without seeming to think about it, he reached up and very gently swept a lock of hair that had fallen over her eye out the way. "I think your parents are fools."

Maeve quickly re-tucked her hair, hyperaware of where his fingers had touched her skin. "Well, maybe your dad is, too," she said, trying to gloss over the moment. "Maybe he's more embarrassed than he is angry."

"Maybe." Brodie sat up straighter, rolled his shoulders back. "See, this is what I need—someone sensible in my life."

"Sensible?" Maeve said it before she could think about it. "That's like the worst thing!"

"No, it's not!" Brodie frowned, almost perplexed.

"Sensible is great. It's a compliment. Sensible and beautiful and—" He stopped.

There was that tension again, that crackle.

The air between them changed. Suddenly heavy and laden. She felt like time stilled. The noises outside receded. She could just hear her breathing, feel their hands side by side on the couch, almost touching. The sunlight streaming in through the window.

This time she couldn't tear her gaze away, found herself caught by the realization—the hope—that he was going to lean in. He *was* leaning in, just a fraction at a time, his fingers hooking over hers on the couch. She swallowed. Felt the touch ricochet like a shock. But already his other hand came round, slipping under her hair, cupping the back of her head, drawing her closer. Every touch igniting something inside her that had been waiting. And she found she wanted him to do it, wanted to be close enough to feel the brush of his lips, the smell of his skin, the kiss, the release of everything bubbling under between them. She could feel the relief of giving into the moment, wrapping her hands round his neck, letting herself be pulled closer, tighter, feel in the smile of victory on his lips as he kissed her, remember the crackle and the flame of their connection. Of that night. Of letting go completely.

Her eyes drifted closed, her hand reached to his shoulder, the softness of his shirt, her thumb brushing the bare skin at his neck, her stomach knotting, reason abandoned for just that millisecond to have this one beautiful moment—

Reason. The word immediately made her rationality kick

in. Her sensibleness drew her back, made her say, "We should go downstairs, join the others."

"Yep." Brodie dropped his hand in an instant. His eyes shone with mischief as he nodded, though, seeing exactly what was warring inside her.

Maeve's heart was in meltdown. Her legs carried her on autopilot. She feared she looked as disheveled and ragged as she felt. This was *not* her.

When they got to the bottom of the staircase, walking through the downstairs living room to the deck, Brodie said, super casual, in a way only Brodie could, "Do you think you might want to have dinner with me sometime?"

Maeve stopped up short in shock at the question. "No," she replied quickly. Then, "I mean, I don't think that's a good idea."

Brodie put his hands in his pockets, strolling slowly, cool as ever, to the open doors. "Why not? What's the worst that can happen?"

"Zoey gets hurt."

He stopped and turned to face her, his eyes glinting playfully. "Zoey's not coming for dinner."

"You know what I mean."

"Okay, take Zoey out of it," he said. "She's separate, ring-fenced. You're stuck with me on that count. What then?"

I might get hurt.

Maeve knew the answer was a no however much her irrational mind might want to say yes, however hard he tried to persuade her.

"I'm not right for you, Brodie. Look at me." She pointed down to her dress that was somehow crumpled already and her scuffed boots. "I'm scruffy, my house is a mess, I'm busy all the time. I don't fit your lifestyle. Stop doing that face!"

"What face?"

"That one! That smug look, like everything I'm saying is just making you feel better."

"It's just my normal face," he laughed.

She stopped and covered her eyes, her cheeks flaming. "I can't live up to *this*." She waved her hand up and down him.

"What are you talking about?"

"You," she said, mortified that she was even saying it. "You're too much for me."

Brodie's mouth spread into an even bigger grin.

Maeve tried not to look right at him. Looked at the dip of his neck instead, which itself was a bad idea, the hollow of caramel-tanned skin. "I'm not very good at things like this, Brodie. I understand my life as it is. I can only cope with so much. And I don't want anything to upset that."

"What if it made it better?" he asked, his upturned eyes half smiling, half beseeching.

There was an earnestness in the way he held her gaze, like she was different to any other woman he'd met, that she could trust him with anything. She could feel it inside her, the temptation to nod, to let herself fall and believe he would be there to catch her. She was so close. The risk within sight.

Then suddenly Zoey came bolting in from outside

waving a framed photograph. "Brodie, why didn't you tell me you were famous!"

Maeve's heart sank.

Brodie, however, switched immediately back into his fun-dad persona and strolling over to Zoey, said, "I'm not famous."

But she was brandishing a photograph of him and his brothers in the band.

At the table, Logan looked over at them apologetically, as if he hadn't thought to hide any evidence of Silver Sky.

"Looks like you are!" Zoey said, pointing to him in the picture. "Looks like you're as famous as Taylor Swift."

Brodie scoffed. "No one's as famous as Taylor Swift." Then he pulled out a chair, real casual, and sat down, hoisting Zoey onto his lap. Holding the other side of the photograph with her, he said, "I *was* famous. We all were." He gestured to his brothers. "But we're not now. Some people know who I am, but that's just a bigger version of people at your school knowing who you are."

Zoey thought for a second, everyone watching, braced like they could all see her mind working. Then she looked at Brodie and said, "Is that why when I told people about you being my dad at school, Suki Watson said that her mom said that you had a *reputation*?"

Maeve spluttered.

Noah laughed.

Emmett, at the other end of the table, raised his bushy eyebrows.

But Brodie said, without pause, "A reputation for making *very* good music."

Zoey grinned, clearly delighted to hear that her dad was once a pop star.

Maeve, however, felt the weight of the comment in the pit of her stomach. Glad of the reminder that Brodie Carter wasn't the man to trust your heart to.

Chapter Thirty-Two

It was the first week of school vacation and Maeve had to work. But for the first time, rather than scrabbling around for childcare, she had Brodie. He would saunter up the path five minutes before she was due to leave, never early but never late, although she would say he was cutting it close, with his sunglasses on, baggy pants, expensively disheveled T-shirt, ready for his day.

Maeve would say, "There's a list of—"

"Emergency numbers on the fridge," he'd cut in. "I know." Then Zoey would bound to the door dressed in whatever took her fancy that day, huge smile on her face about what was to come.

Throughout her shift at the hospital, Maeve would be updated with pictures of Zoey eating ice cream, Zoey feeding penguins at the zoo, Zoey climbing Starlight Mountain. Sometimes, Brodie would be in the shot, too, and Maeve would try hard not to look at his smiling face and his perfect white teeth and the way clothes just hung beautifully off him. He had a knack for making life seem so effortless.

When she came home, sometimes he stayed for a while, sometimes he left right away. She hated to admit that those times, she felt a pang to see him walk off down the path. During the tiny snatches of downtime she had at work she realized she felt a warmth in her chest about going home, about Brodie being there. Sometimes she wondered if he left on purpose to make her feel exactly that, but no one could be that calculating, that adept at reeling a person in, could they?

A couple of weeks into Zoey's vacation, when Maeve came home, Zoey was bursting to tell her, "Someone asked for Dad's autograph! Isn't that amazing!"

Maeve hardly heard past the word *Dad*. "Yeah, isn't it?" she agreed, less convinced. It was a reminder that the guy she could see sitting casually at her kitchen table making models out of air-dry clay was actually still a celebrity. That one day he would have another lavish wedding and live in a beautiful, expensive house like his brother, and her daughter would go off and stay with *Dad*.

She swallowed, felt suddenly, unexpectedly, like she wanted to cry.

"He was so cool, Mom, he just took the pen and he signed and they took a selfie, I was just like wow!" Zoey couldn't get enough of the topic.

Maeve followed her through to the kitchen. "That sounds very exciting."

Brodie glanced up, the corner of his mouth tilted in a wry smile as if he knew she thought it was anything but.

"Can I just say the whole thing lasted less than a minute! The rest of our day was spent doing very educational things, wasn't it, Zoey?" It seemed important to him that Maeve knew this. Because of course, she was *sensible*.

Oh, for goodness' sake! What was wrong with her? She didn't want him unsettling her life, but then she wanted him to be there when she got home. She didn't want his flirtatious attention, but then she didn't want to be seen as sensible. He was driving her crazy.

She went to make herself a cup of coffee just to calm herself down.

Brodie stood up from his chair.

He was leaving?

"We went to the museum, didn't we? And we went to the library—"

Zoey wasn't having any of it. "And then when we were in the park the lady came right over with her piece of paper and a pen, it was *super* cool."

Maeve switched the coffee maker on and turned back to face them. Brodie was waiting, watching with his hands in his pockets. "Did *you* have a good day, Maeve?"

No one ever asked her that, not that she needed it, but it threw her off-balance. "I did, thanks for asking."

He shrugged a shoulder like it was no big deal. Then he said, "Okay, kiddo, I've gotta go."

For a second, Maeve thought about asking him if he wanted to stay for dinner. Then she thought if this was all an elaborate plan, it was working.

Zoey had gone back to her clay modeling. "Bye, I'll see you at the weekend."

Maeve frowned. Her shifts at the hospital were so frantic at the moment, she barely knew what day it was. "What's happening at the weekend?" she asked, puzzled.

"It's the Redemption River Fair."

Maeve went to look at the calendar on the fridge. "Is that this weekend?"

"Yes, Mom!" Zoey said, exasperated by Maeve's inability to keep track of such deeply important events. Then she pointed at Brodie and said, "Brodie's running it."

To which Brodie waved a hand modestly and said, "I'm not running it, Zoey, I'm emceeing it. I'm the ringmaster—I introduce stuff."

Maeve laughed at the idea. "You are not!"

"Such little faith." Brodie raised a brow. "I'll have you know that Mrs. Hernandez asked me very politely the other day and I, of course, agreed."

Maeve tried to keep a straight face. "It seems very un-you."

"And what, pray tell, is *me*?" he asked dryly.

"Not emceeing the Redemption River Summer Fair! I just can't see you introducing the jelly competition and the costume parade. More likely running a mile the other way."

Brodie kept his eyes on Maeve, a flicker of amusement in his deep blue gaze. "I find that very insulting. I'll have you know that I love nothing more than the Redemption River Summer Fair."

Maeve tried her hardest not to smile back. Not to let it radiate out her eyes. The casual banter in her kitchen with this man feeling more and more natural every day.

"I'm going to go as a duck," Zoey piped up.

"What an excellent idea," Brodie replied, still with half an eye on Maeve.

As they walked down the hallway, Maeve plucked up the courage to say, "Did you want to stay for dinner? It's only fish sticks but…"

"Love a fish stick," he said, "but—" he winced "—I've got plans."

"Oh, okay," she said, quickly covering up both the disappointment and embarrassment at having asked and been turned down.

"Truthfully," he said, clearly able to sense the change in her, "I would have totally stayed, but—" he glanced at his watch "—I, er … I'm running late as it is."

"Going anywhere nice?" she asked, imagining him meeting one of his brothers at the Firestone. Or maybe he was going on a date…

Don't Maeve.

"I'm actually meeting some friends in Vegas."

Maeve spluttered. "I'm sorry, you're what? Going to Vegas? But you're going to the fair on Saturday?"

"Yeah, it's just one night." He shrugged like it was no big deal.

Maeve's last vacation had been driving upstate to a theme park for the weekend. Naively—wishfully?—she had pictured Brodie settled in Autumn Falls. Zoey—maybe even Maeve herself—keeping him tethered. But no, of course he'd been jetting off on the days she didn't see him. Carrying on his free-spirited, very untethered existence. The news, while obvious, made her feel foolish. To think they—she—had been worth staying for.

"That sounds fun," she said as nonchalantly as she could. "Anytime you need to go away for longer, Brodie, feel free. I can always get Carole. There's no obligation to be here all the time."

He narrowed his twinkly blue eyes so knowingly that she feared for a moment she had inadvertently said some of her thoughts out loud. "It's no obligation, Maeve. I'm enjoying it."

That was the problem, she thought. It was fun for him. He hadn't dealt yet with the tantrums or the drudgery.

She was aware always of the intransience behind his being here. That they were still a novelty, still shiny. She didn't want to think that of him but it was impossible not to, especially with the notifications that came through constantly on his phone that made him smile as he read them, giving the impression there was always more excitement to be had somewhere else in his world. What would happen when the fun of the park and the milkshakes wore thin? Where would Brodie go then?

Chapter Thirty-Three

Since Zoey had been tiny, the Redemption River Summer Fair was one of her favorite days of the year. Maeve never had time to make her a costume and always ordered it online. Now, however, she was part of the Carter family and Martha Carter was a whiz at running up a kid's costume.

When Martha stopped by to drop it off, Zoey was wide-eyed with excitement.

"I don't know if it's duck-like enough," Martha said, holding up the suit made of white terry cloth with big orange feet and a padded bill. "I'm afraid you might look more like a goose."

"I'm happy with either," Zoey said, and took it from her like it was treasure. "It's awesome. Thank you so much."

"You're welcome, Zoey." The fondness in Martha's eyes was unmistakable. When she ran off to get changed, Martha looked at Maeve and said, "She's so cute, I just want to eat her up."

"Now that would be a waste of a good costume," Maeve replied with a half-smile.

Martha chuckled, giving her a playful pat on the arm. "I'm glad this has all happened, Maeve, I truly am. I think it's been really good for Brodie."

Maeve nodded, tucking her hair behind her ears—aware of how easily she blushed at the mention of Brodie—imagining him jetting off to Vegas and wondering if Martha knew.

"I know he acts like he doesn't take anything seriously or care too deeply, but I can see that this is real important to him. I just wanted to say thank you, for telling him—for trusting him."

Maeve didn't know what to say. She'd never, in all of Zoey's life, thought that Martha Carter would be on her doorstep thanking her with such warmth and kindness. She thought fleetingly of her own parents standing there all formal, stiff like statues, seeing only the negatives of the situation. No matter her increasingly complicated feelings for Brodie, it made her suddenly less fearful for who Zoey now had in her life. Grateful, in fact.

The Redemption River Summer Fair was held at the fairground on the outskirts of Autumn Falls, where the river looped around the land like a horseshoe. There was always a full schedule of events from the kids' costume parade and Pee Wee animal showmanship to flower and plant judging and a carnival.

The Silver Pantry had a stall selling snacks and coffee, and a selection of beautiful homewares. Word had spread that Martha's infamous coconut cake was for sale and there was already a queue snaking almost to the Ferris Wheel.

"Let's go and see Brodie. I mean, Dad." Zoey, in her white duck costume with its big yellow feet and beak, pulled Maeve by the hand to where they could hear Brodie on the microphone calling out the competitors for the dog show.

Logan was nearby with his horse, Jojo, who he was getting ready to show at the next event. When they went past he said, "Hey, Maeve, where's Zoey?"

Zoey said, "I'm right here!"

Logan looked confused. "I can only see a giant duck."

Zoey giggled, "It's me!" while Logan shook his head and said, "You had me fooled!"

They wished Logan luck and carried on to watch Brodie, Maeve again reminded what it meant to have all that family around for Zoey, all that support. To know that she wasn't quite so alone anymore.

She wondered momentarily what it would be like to be part of it herself, if her and Brodie were together. But she shut that thought down right away. Especially when she saw him up on stage.

Brodie was a natural. Putting nervous contestants at ease and cracking jokes when the animals did something unexpected. The audience loved him. He'd dressed up for the role, wore navy pants and a tie, the sleeves of his white shirt rolled up to his elbow, his hair slicked to the side like some old-fashioned movie star.

Zoey said, "He looks so handsome."

Maeve could only agree. He was totally out of her league. Jetting off to Vegas! She rolled her eyes. Her life was so pitifully small-town in comparison.

When he saw them, he smiled and raised a hand in greeting, without even pausing his commentary.

Maeve leaned on the railing that surrounded the ring and watched him in his element. Unfazed by the attention, effortlessly self-assured, he had the adoring crowd in the palm of his hand. He was just so charismatic, it was hard to look away.

When it came to the kids' costume parade, Brodie was very professional—Zoey didn't get any special treatment—but Maeve didn't miss the little wink he threw her as she waddled past where he was standing with the mic. The tenderness made her heart lurch.

She was in *so* much trouble.

The judges placed Zoey third, which she was very happy with because usually she didn't come anywhere close. She went and got changed but kept her rosette pinned to her T-shirt. After the Pee Wee Rabbit Showmanship, Maeve suggested they go and look at the craft and food stalls and go on the carnival rides, just to get away from the fluttering longing in her chest when she watched Brodie on stage. The mortifying term *starstruck fan* came to mind again.

Zoey, however, just wanted to be where Brodie was. After Maeve had tried to distract her with carnival rides and cake, they headed straight back to the main arena. The fencing for the events had been removed and everyone was milling around now in front of the stage. Ren was there with Noah, who had a first-place rosette for roping tucked into his shirt pocket. When he saw Zoey he said, "You see your Grandma Carter up there?" and pointed to where the Autumn Falls band were warming up on stage. Martha tuning up her Dobro guitar. One of Maeve's friends, Claudette, who worked with Bella at the theater, was on vocals, dressed in a gold mini dress, the sequins catching the light like a disco ball. She was trying to coax Brodie to join her. But he just grinned into the mic and said, "I'm here to dance not sing."

Claudette threw up her hands in good-natured disappointment.

Maeve found herself wondering if there had ever been anything between the pair of them, they had sung together a couple of times at town events. Was she jealous? She quickly berated herself for even thinking about it. Who Brodie chose to fraternize with was none of her business.

John-Luke, Bella's stepfather and leader of the band, gave Brodie the nod that they were about to begin, and Brodie called out, "Grab your partners, people. There's dancing to be done!"

Ren immediately pulled a very reluctant Noah onto what was now a dance floor, flashing with colorful spotlights from the stage, along with lots of other familiar faces from town. Zoey ran to join some of her schoolfriends who had made a little group at the front.

On the mic, Brodie scanned the crowd and said, "Now, I just need to find myself a partner." His eyes found Maeve and that familiar crooked grin started to spread on his face.

Maeve shook her head.

Brodie's smile only got wider. He raised his brows.

She couldn't do this. She wasn't the practiced flirt he was. She did things seriously, sensibly, things meant things when she did them. He, however, was the master of easy fun. She shook her head again, trying to convey absolute finality by crossing her arms as well.

Brodie seemed to take the hint and his gaze traveled further across the crowd, landing eventually on a tiny woman with a white bun, wearing a long floral dress. "How about it, Mrs. Hernandez?"

"Oh, you don't want to dance with me, Brodie Carter," she called out, waving away the offer. "Dance with someone your own age."

Brodie shrugged, feigning dejection and said, "I'm trying to dance with Maeve Dixon but she won't have me."

All eyes turned to find Maeve at the edge of the crowd. She felt her face go beacon-red. "Oh, no, not me, I don't dance." She glared at Brodie who just grinned wider.

Mrs. Hernandez called, "Go on, dance with Brodie, Maeve! My knee is not up to it."

Maeve held up a hand to protest.

"I don't dance, either," Noah shouted, from where he was being forced into it by Ren, "And look at me!"

"Have some fun, Doctor Dixon!" someone shouted. Maeve looked and saw Old Mr. Zimmerman, whose life she'd saved from a heart attack over New Year. "If anyone deserves some fun, it's you, darlin'!"

Brodie stood there innocently up on stage, head cocked in increasingly smug amusement as Maeve came under pressure from the townsfolk—all desperate for their hard-working doctor to enjoy herself.

"Go on, Mom!" Zoey shouted. And the whole place seemed to smile indulgently.

Maeve sighed, knowing that refusal again would just cause more of a furor, and took a reluctant step forward.

When he saw it, Brodie docked the mic and jumped down off the stage to meet her, eyes glinting in triumph.

"Don't," Maeve warned.

"I never would," he replied, any attempt to rein in his self-satisfied smile clearly failing.

"I'm only doing it because there would be too much attention otherwise."

"Of course," he replied, wrapping his arm round her waist and drawing her close toward him. She put her hand reluctantly on his shoulder and he laughed at her obvious hesitancy. "It's only dancing, Maeve."

He took her other hand and clasped it with his, their cool palms together, their bodies a whisper away, his head dipping just a little bit to look her in the eye.

Maeve feared her cheeks were apple-red and her heart might literally be thumping out of her body. It wasn't *only dancing*.

Brodie looked down at her with that satisfied, cat-that-got-the-cream look still on his face.

The band played on behind them. "How was Vegas?" she asked.

"Same as Vegas always is."

"Is that good or bad?"

"To be honest," he said, "I spent most of the time thinking about coming back here to see you and Zoey."

"You did not!" She bashed his chest. He caught her hand, clamped it in his, held it flat against his shirt. "I did," he said, seriously.

Maeve suddenly felt like she was somewhere miles away from the Redemption River Fair, maybe back at the cabin, or further back than that, maybe in that front row at Stanford Stadium, knowing the exact moment his eyes locked on hers as he was performing. The same lazy grin on his face as when she and Piper went with Ethan backstage and Brodie was standing drinking a bottle of water, his eyes clocking her as she came in. The unhurried way he screwed the cap back on the bottle, wiped his mouth with the back of his hand and, swiping the sweat off his face with a towel, sauntered over like he had all the time in the world. Seeming to know in that moment, that Maeve would be going with him that night.

Being in his arms again so close, so aware of everywhere their bodies touched, the glint in his eye, the dip of his mouth, was a dangerous reminder of the last time.

"You smell the same," he said, quietly in her ear.

She tried to keep her face neutral.

"Like warm evenings." He paused. "Maybe jasmine?"

She kept her eyes fixed on the knot in his tie, the fine gray line of thread in the black fabric. "I think it's probably just shampoo."

He laughed at her attempts to make it all very normal. "I can still picture those silver boots, you know? And a little black top?" He asked it as a question, but he seemed certain.

"I don't remember," she lied.

"Your hair was different, though," he went on regardless, letting go of her hand for a moment to touch where the end of her braid rested on her collarbone. "Shorter like a little pixie."

Maeve swallowed. She couldn't fall for this again.

"I won't lie, Maeve, I don't remember everyone," he said. "But I remember quite a few. I remember the ones I wish I'd seen again."

"Brodie, I know you say that to everyone."

He shook his head, said plainly, "No."

She kept telling herself not to look at him. Not to meet his eyes.

"I bet you remember what I was wearing," he said. She heard the jokey smile in his voice.

Blue jeans, navy T-shirt, white and red Nikes.

"No," she said.

He laughed. "You're lying. I think you remember."

She shook her head, focusing on the top button of his shirt, undone, just above the knot in the tie. She worried he could hear her heartbeat.

"It wouldn't have ended well if we'd got together then," he said, almost musing to himself.

"No, it wouldn't," she said, her eyes still on the button, thinking about a long-distance relationship with him when he was at the height of his solo success. She thought about her arduous journey to graduating medical school. Would she have finished it if, by some chance, they had got together? Would she have followed him round the world with her baby or would she have stayed and slogged her guts out to achieve her own dream and get qualified? She couldn't say for sure but thinking about it then, she immediately saw herself on a tour bus, feeding a baby, alone.

"I was not ready then by any stretch of the imagination," he said, blowing out a breath.

She thought about herself back then, all idealistic ambition. "No, me neither," she admitted, grateful for the first time that their paths had diverged. It hit her unexpectedly hard, the idea that she would have almost definitely given up her own dream. How deep their resentment would be now.

She watched him smile down at her, his straight white teeth and the smattering of freckles over his nose. His hand held a bit tighter. The song changed. She found herself relaxing, allowing herself finally to keep looking at him.

"I know what you were wearing," she relented.

He grinned. "I *knew* you did."

She bashed him on the arm. "You're so arrogant."

He laughed, she felt the vibration in her chest, found they were dancing closer now than she'd thought. "One of my many charms," he replied.

She had to look away again because, when he looked at her like that, it made her worry not about when he might leave again, but what might happen if he stayed.

More than anything, though, in that moment, she wanted them to be alone. Back in Logan's house or at the cabin. She wanted him to pull her closer, wanted to reach up herself, rest her palm on his cheek and draw his lips to hers. To disappear into a moment that was just for them.

Older, wiser, yet still with the same crackling, searing energy between them. Looking at his lips, she could almost taste him.

"Brodie Carter, can I have this dance?" a voice cut in next to them. It was Janette, Suki Rogers's mom from Zoey's class, the one who was so clued up about Brodie's reputation.

"Certainly," he said, because of course it would be impolite to say anything else, but Maeve felt the icy chill of stepping out of his embrace. The loss of his hand in hers.

Up on the stage, she was sure she saw Brodie's mom narrow her eyes at Janette, like she was messing up the plan.

When Maeve turned, she was struck by the sight of Zoey watching gleefully, sitting on the edge of the stage with Logan and Bella, a toffee-apple in her hand, kicking her legs against the side.

She realized then that her and Brodie *were* the show, and that, of course, it wasn't just the two of them. It was all much more complicated than that. Maeve wanted to melt into the crowd and disappear.

Chapter Thirty-Four

The band took a break, which gave Brodie the opportunity to thank Janette Rogers for the many dances—she just wouldn't let him go—and slip away. She wanted a quick selfie before he did, pressing their cheeks together as she beamed for the camera. He caught Zoey doing an impression of Janette behind them, which made him struggle to keep a straight face. When he went over to join her he said, "You gotta stop doing things like that, you'll get me into trouble."

"Please don't marry Suki's mom. I don't want to have to go to their house for Christmas," Zoey said with a scowl.

Brodie frowned, and turned to lean against the stage where Zoey was sitting. "Zoey, I danced with her, I'm not marrying her. You don't need to worry about spending Christmas anywhere other than at your home with your mom."

"And you," she said, without hesitation.

Brodie remembered the rising claustrophobia when

she'd said it the first time, when she'd asked him if he was her dad and he'd denied it. He may have managed to leap the dad hurdle but judging by the clamping of his lungs and the immediate denial on his lips, the instinct to say that he spent Christmas in St. Moritz every year, he clearly hadn't made peace with the idea of being tied to Autumn Falls for the holiday season and beyond.

He was saved from having to answer by the band leader, John-Luke, who'd been drinking a paper cup of coffee while the band took their break, coming over and tapping him on the shoulder.

Zoey jumped down from the stage to dance with her friends because there was now a DJ playing loads of their favorite songs.

"Your dad tells me you might be interested in buying the orchard?" John-Luke said as he sipped his coffee.

Caught off-guard, Brodie smiled. "Oh... No we were just messing around."

John-Luke seemed unperturbed, he said, "I did think it was a little weird. Can't really picture you settling down and looking after apple trees."

Brodie laughed along, but as he stood there, the notion that his dad had actually taken the comment seriously enough to mention it to John-Luke made him suddenly want to defend the idea. "Though I am interested in the vines," he said. "I own a vineyard in Napa."

John-Luke chuckled. "We're small fry compared to that, Brodie." The older man's eyes twinkled at the idea of someone like Brodie tending his ancient orchard.

Again, Brodie laughed along, but in his mind he

suddenly saw his life ahead of him split in two. On one side was him on his yacht, bobbing in the waves, or careening down off-piste slopes in Switzerland with a bit of tinsel round his neck, waltzing in and out of his vineyard whenever he felt like it. And on the other side, he was up a ladder pruning apple trees and tending a tiny plot of vines, picking Zoey up from school at three on the dot every day, maybe finally breaking down Maeve's barriers and getting her to have dinner with him, go on a date even, but to what end? He never looked to the future, and suddenly it dawned on him that he was currently chipping away at something that he was yet to envisage. Yes, he was attracted to Maeve. Yes, she made him laugh. Yes, she challenged him to try harder. But he couldn't see her fitting in with his life, with the St. Moritz ski crowd, for example. Or maybe that was unfair. Maybe he just wouldn't want to inflict his skiing buddies on her and Zoey. It all suddenly seemed very juvenile with Maeve there watching. If he went skiing with Maeve and Zoey, he'd want fondues and mulled wine in a little alpine chalet. Evening sledding, lit with twinkling lights, plaid blankets and thick hot chocolate round a roaring fire. Maybe if he carried on down the path he was currently on, he wouldn't just be going around to Maeve's house at Christmas in a novelty holiday sweater but he'd be there every day.

Every. Single. Day.

Brodie swallowed down an almost suffocating panic at the idea, felt his throat close and his palms sweat, but before he could think much more about it, his dad was there, walking over with his own rosette for the Horse

Showmanship, shaking John-Luke's hand, reaching up to hand Martha a soda that she'd obviously asked him to go and get for her.

John-Luke said, "Brodie doesn't want my orchard, Emmett."

Brodie winced, feeling immediately his dad's judgment.

Emmett's only reaction was a raise of a brow but it was enough to shrink Brodie down to size. For a second, he even wondered if his dad had told John-Luke he might be in the market for the orchard just for this moment, to prove that Brodie would never have the staying power to make such a move.

He thought of Maeve saying that maybe he made his dad feel like a fool, that it was pride that provoked him to say certain things, to cut Brodie down to size. He tried to stay calm and rational, but he was already too on edge and couldn't help himself reverting to type. Itching to defy his dad, to provoke for the sake of provocation. He shrugged a shoulder, a smirk on his lips, and said casually, "I just don't think apples are my thing."

And just as Zoey came skipping back over, his dad scoffed, like Brodie was a child himself, and muttered, "Might be about time you made up your mind what *your thing* is."

In that moment, Brodie thought there might have been many times when his dad said stuff because of pride, but he knew deep down inside that this wasn't one of those times. That was a look, father to father, questioning whether Brodie had it in him to step up.

Chapter Thirty-Five

Maeve lay in bed thinking about the previous day at the fair. Dancing with Brodie in front of everyone, Old Mr. Zimmerman encouraging her to let her hair down and have some fun. It made her roll her eyes up at the ceiling. Then she remembered the feeling of being pressed so close to Brodie, his hand wrapped around hers, the angle of his jaw as she looked up at him, the feel of his laugh vibrating through her chest. She pulled the quilt up over her head to try and hide from both the tingling excitement and the cringing mortification at having been watched by the Carters and Zoey.

She took a calming breath and let the quilt come down a fraction so she could see again, and looked up at the ceiling rose as she remembered him giving them a ride home. It made her wonder if Martha had planned the offer of a ride to the fair for exactly that reason.

Brodie had walked them up the path to her front door.

Zoey ran off inside to display her third-place rosette in her bedroom, and Maeve said, "I think she had a great day."

Brodie leaned against the veranda post and with a tilt of his head, said, "See, you gotta love the fair."

Then there was a pause, both awkward and expectant, hanging between them like ripe fruit.

Maeve found herself suddenly shy, smiling but trying not to. She glanced back into the house and, thinking that it suddenly looked a little dark and lonely compared to the zinging, almost unbearable tension out there on the veranda, found herself saying, "Did you want to come in for a cup of coffee or something?"

Brodie seemed uncharacteristically hesitant at the suggestion, which made her say, "You don't have to!"

As quickly as she'd glimpsed it, the reticence vanished, and she wondered if she'd just been paranoid as she watched the corner of Brodie's mouth tip up and he said, "I appreciate the offer but—" he paused, with a slow smile "—I wouldn't want you to think I had a reputation."

Maeve bit her lip, looked down at the scuffed wooden floor and smiled at the shared joke, aware however of an underlying shiver of disappointment.

Then Brodie had reached forward, lifted her hand and kissed the back of it, looking up as he did, back to his normal flirtatious self. "Goodnight, Maeve."

When he'd let go, she could still feel his lips on her skin. "Goodnight, Brodie."

Now, as she lay in bed, Maeve caught herself grinning like an idiot. She got up, shaking her head at herself in despair but not without stealing a glance at the back of her hand, running her thumb over the skin.

Zoey was still snoring. Brodie was coming to take her to a basketball game. Maeve had to be in work in an hour and a half.

She'd had a shower, was changed and putting the coffee on when she checked her phone.

There was message after message, piling up from all her friends, people she hadn't spoken to in years, including moms at Zoey's school. There was one from Janette Rogers that just read, *OMG, Maeve!* with a shocked-face emoji and a link to a gossip website.

Maeve hardly dared let her thumb press on the link. Her skin was on fire, her mind racing. She felt the shot of adrenaline as the story loaded and then a sudden cold shiver at the picture itself and the headline:

PLAIN JANE SNARES BRODIE CARTER WITH LOVE CHILD!

Like a fortress locking down, she felt every barrier she had click firmly into place.

The main photograph was of her and Brodie walking to the park, Zoey holding both their hands. Zoey's face was blurred out, but she'd obviously said something funny because Maeve and Brodie were both laughing, looking dotingly down at their daughter.

They'd clearly waited to run the story until they got the other money shot—Brodie and Maeve dancing face to face at the Summer Fair, her cheeks flushed, hair mussed from the carnival rides, Brodie looking as slick as a movie star in his shirt and tie, Zoey's grinning face in the background.

Maeve thought she might be sick.

The doorbell went.

She went to open it, fearful it might be reporters, but it was Brodie, early for a change, back to his normal casual self in blue jeans and a white T-shirt.

"Have you seen it?" she said, her hand trembling on the door lock.

Brodie shrugged. "I've seen it." He walked inside like nothing had happened.

"Are there photographers out there?" she asked, peeking her head out before she shut the door.

Brodie paused. "Maeve, have you seen who published the pictures? We are not headlines news! If there's anyone out there, it'll just be one or two max."

"That's one or two too many!" she replied, unable to believe how casual he was being. "This is my life," she hissed. "Zoey's life!"

"You'll get used to it."

She shook her head. "I don't want to get used to it."

"Well..." He held his hands out like it was too late for that. Then he said, "Is there coffee?"

She followed him into the kitchen.

"Where's Zoey?" he asked.

"She's still asleep."

"Man, I wish I could still sleep like her," he said, getting a mug from the cupboard. "When I'm awake nowadays, I just have to get up."

"Brodie!"

He stopped pouring coffee for a second. "Sorry, did you want one? I figured you already had one." He opened the cupboard to get another cup.

"Brodie! Our photograph is online. I have moms from the school messaging me! People from the hospital! You're saying there might be one or two reporters outside, like that's nothing. Well, it's not nothing to me. I don't want them there." She pulled out a chair and sat down with a sigh.

Brodie placed a mug of coffee in front of her, made, she had to note, just as she liked it, then went and sat down in the chair opposite her.

"Just smile, Maeve," he said. "That's all you gotta do. Smile and say hi and keep walking. It's only if they think you're hiding something that they're real interested, that's when they get excited. That's why they like the picture of Zoey." He took a slug of his coffee then sat back, arm looped round the back of the chair. "And, well, that's done now, so…"

Maeve sat with her hands at her temples. How could he be so relaxed? Was it the photograph or was it that she was hiding something? That her heart beat way too fast around him. That she dreamt about him. That she wanted him not to jet off to Vegas at weekends but be content to sit with her in her grandma's house while their daughter made bracelets or slept soundly upstairs.

It was a simple fact that she would never be enough for him—a cliché to think she might be—but she feared the camera wouldn't fail to miss that longing in her eyes.

More messages came through on her phone on the table.

One from Bella. *I know how you must feel but don't worry. It'll be old news tomorrow, I promise x.* Then immediately afterwards she sent another. *BTW, you're DEFINITLEY not a Plain Jane!*

Brodie read them upside down as they came up on the screen, her phone lying between them.

"This is a nightmare." Maeve put her head on the table.

Brodie just laughed. "Come on, it's funny."

"*Plain Jane, Love Child.*" Maeve sat up straight again and shook her head. "Brodie, I'm a doctor! I'm a normal person. This cannot happen to me."

Brodie raised his hands either side of him and said, "Well, it has happened." He picked up his coffee again and seemed to quite enjoy watching her freak out.

Suddenly Maeve felt her whole body run icy cold. "My parents are going to read this."

"So?"

Her vision went a little blurred at the idea. Her heart was in overdrive. She sat forward, hands at her temples again trying to rationalize, trying to steady her breathing.

Brodie leaned forward, too, arms crossed, elbows on the table. "They kicked you out, Maeve. You don't owe them anything. Remember, it's just pride stopping them admitting they were wrong."

"Oh, I only said that to make you feel better." Maeve waved a hand in dismissal. "I don't actually think that. They don't think they're wrong, not for one millisecond."

Brodie seemed surprised, hurt even, but then he smiled and said, "Well, I thought it made sense."

She picked up her phone and looked at the picture again

then she tipped her head back in despair. More messages flooded in. She put it on silent.

"Maeve," Brodie said, firm but gentle. "This is going to happen. I can't help what I am, but it won't happen much. Not like it would have done eight years ago. I'm old news. So, I've got a daughter, who cares? It's only there 'cause it's a slow news day. You've got to shake it off. It's just a photo."

He didn't understand. "I don't want to be in the news with you," she said. "I don't want Zoey in the news! I don't want this attention for either of us."

Brodie narrowed his eyes. "Are you ashamed of me?" He sat back in the chair and studied her.

She spluttered. *"What?"*

He tipped his head, eyes still assessing. "I think you are. You're this top doctor and you fell for me."

"Don't be stupid." She brushed it off. She'd literally just been yearning after him!

But Brodie seemed to be warming to the idea. "I'm not who you want to be the father of your child. That's the failing, isn't it?" he raised his chin as he said it, as if he'd clocked now exactly how she worked. "At least, that's what you don't want your parents to know."

She looked away, couldn't reply. Felt her cheeks flame with the possible truth. Her parents would be appalled.

"I'm not as clever as you, we know that, but you don't have to be ashamed, Maeve. I can work hard. I worked hard when I was in that band and afterward. I just choose not to now."

"Yeah, and look at you, you're bored out your mind!"

she replied, before she could stop herself, knowing she was attacking him as a defense mechanism. Yes, she was ashamed of her parents finding out, but she was more ashamed of him finding out that every time she saw him she was secretly fantasizing about him leaning over and kissing her. Declaring that he'd love nothing more than to ditch his glamorous life and settle in Autumn Falls with her and Zoey.

"I'm not bored!"

"Brodie, you just hosted the Redemption River Summer Fair! You're bored!"

He rolled his shoulders, uncomfortable with the comment. Neither of them said anything. She could hear the noise of the second hand making its way round the clock.

She was being unfair, juvenile. She was better than that.

She looked down at the table, at her rapidly cooling coffee. "Maybe I am embarrassed by it," she admitted. "I had a one-night stand with pop star. It's embarrassing!" She looked up at him, all beautiful and perfect. "I look like one of your screaming fans. I'm not embarrassed of *you*, Brodie —I mean who *could* be embarrassed of you? I'm the Plain darn Jane!"

That made Brodie smirk despite himself.

She sighed, reaching forward to take a sip of the coffee just for a breather.

Then, as if feeling he owed her equal honesty, he said, "Maybe I am a bit bored. I've never really thought about it too much before."

Maeve looked into his guileless blue eyes and said, "That's what I'm afraid of, Brodie. That boredom is why we're so interesting to you. We're a novelty." She glanced pointedly at her phone. "We get you in the news."

"That's unfair!" He sat back, arms folded, and blew out an incredulous breath. Even annoyed, he was handsome. It was *so* unfair. But then, in a way, it was good—reminded her who he was, how different they were.

"Maybe." She shrugged but wasn't so sure. "I worry about what you're going to do when the novelty wears off." She looked him in the eye, uncertain what she wanted him to say.

He narrowed his eyes. "Now *that's* unfair."

"What?"

"You turning this round on me. I know how your brain works." He shook his head like he wasn't having any of it. "You think you can twist it back on me. It's like you *want* me to go. You *want* me to prove you right so you don't have to lighten up and take a risk."

"That's ridiculous." She bristled defensively.

"Have I given you any reason to think I'm going to leave?" He cocked his head as he stared right back at her.

There was a pause. The air suddenly pumping with tension again but a different kind from the previous evening. This seemed more fragile, like a line spun from silk that was already stretched as taut as it could go.

Maeve swallowed as she looked into his bright accusing eyes and wondered briefly what it would be like not to worry, to trust him at face value and willingly take that first step on the tightrope.

But she was too certain of the drop.

With a sharp shake of her head, she said, "No, but you

haven't given me any reason why you're going to stay, either."

The clock ticked in the background, marking out the fading of time. It felt suddenly more like the fading of what they'd had. She could almost see it receding into the distance. "Are you going to stay, Brodie? Live in Autumn Falls? In your condo? Here with your family—your dad—right here?" She pointed to the table like it marked the whole town itself.

It was Brodie's turn to be silent. To let the clock tick on.

Maeve smiled weakly, however much she'd expected it, still crushed by foolish disappointment. "There's your reason, Brodie."

Chapter Thirty-Six

Noah's house was three-quarters built. Noah liked to do everything perfectly, and do it all himself—with Ren's help, of course—so it took longer than it might most people who'd bring in tradespeople. The house was situated by the side of Halfmoon Lake where the brothers used to camp as kids; building dens, sparring, fishing, making fires. It was on the opposite side of the land to the main ranch house and sat underneath the towering pines of the forest and the shadow of Starlight Mountain.

Brodie was quite jealous of the peace. As he sat on a plastic lawn chair on the grass out the front, he gazed up at the peak of the mountain, thought about the many treks they'd made up those craggy rocks, backpacks on, sandwiches in plastic wrap, trudging on with the purpose of getting as high as they could. There was that word again: purpose.

Brodie sat back, hands behind his head and stared at the shadows of clouds drifting over the mountain.

Noah came out with two Dr Peppers and sat in a lawn chair next to him. It was new and cheap and creaked when he sat down, like it might break under the weight.

Noah and Ren hadn't bought proper outdoor furniture yet, they had barely bought anything for inside, the place was still all ladders and workbenches and sawdust. But it was getting there. When it was done, Brodie could see it would be awesome. It was all very Noah. Nothing too big or flashy but precisely made and exacting. The timber cladding was black and cleverly insulated, the roof was lined with solar panels, the wraparound deck had been angled so that each room got the sun at the right time of day. It was impressive.

As Noah handed Brodie a soda, Ren came out with a pot of paint in her hand. Zoey followed behind her, in coveralls rolled up at the sleeves and ankles, brandishing a paintbrush.

When Ren had opened the door to Brodie earlier she'd taken one look and said, "Oh, dear." While Zoey had walked inside poking her nose into various half-built rooms exclaiming how fun the place was, he'd checked himself out in the mirror and said, "What? I don't look that bad, do I?"

Ren stuck out her bottom lip in pity and said, "You look like a sad puppy, Brodie."

He'd laughed it off, but she'd ushered him outside, telling Noah to stop working and go talk to his brother while she taught Zoey how to paint. Now she was leaving them to it, while she and Zoey got to work on the window frames. They looked cute together, both in matching bandanas to protect their hair from paint, with their brushes in their hands.

"So, what's going on?" Noah asked, taking a long gulp of his drink. He'd been working on the house since finishing for the day at the ranch and his clothes were all sweaty, his face smeared with dust.

Brodie sat forward, hands clasped around his can, and said, "I don't know." Then he proceeded to fill him in on what had happened the previous day, what had been said.

He'd spent the day with Zoey, trying not to think too much about the earlier conversation with Maeve. He kept seeing her face when she said, "There's your reason." Big eyes full of disappointment. She thought she was a closed book, didn't have any idea how visible her emotions were—something he both adored and couldn't bear. It wracked him with an unfamiliar guilt, played on his ingrained desire for no-strings, carefree attachment. He didn't suit family life, relationships, commitment. He liked to move on at will, not be tied down. He itched for new adventure. Or he always had.

He had taken Zoey to play basketball, had lunch, gone to the diner, for a milkshake—if there was a reporter there, he hadn't seen them. A couple of people had snapped covert pictures on their phones, and when that happened, he tended to smile and wave and encourage them to come over and take a proper one. He'd chat for a little while, pose with them—if they liked him, they were less likely to try and take photos on the sly. And he liked people, liked talking to them, smiling with them, he didn't see much of a problem with having his picture taken, but he didn't *need* it, didn't crave it, like Maeve had accused him of. He was almost glad for feeling a sense of injustice at some of the things she'd said—accusing him of wanting the media attention, and then there was the lie … the advice she'd given him about her parents—it allowed him to take the high ground, nurse the feeling of being wronged, rather than dwell too long on what else had been said about his future in Autumn Falls. But it was still there, sitting in his stomach, making him confused and uncharacteristically on edge, which in turn had led him here—to Noah's house.

"*Are* you staying?" Noah asked.

"I don't know!"

His brother shook his head, the movement made his jaw-length hair fall forward and he pushed it back with his hand, holding it there for a second as he looked at Brodie despairingly and said, "You're real annoying, you know that?"

Brodie sat back, throwing his arms wide, defensively. "I can't say if I'm going to stay or not."

Ren walked over to where they were sitting and said, "Noah, have you got the measuring tape?"

He dug in his pocket to get it, while saying to Brodie, "I don't see why not."

"Because I might say I am, and then wake one day and just have to leave. I can't help it. I get restless."

As Ren took the measuring tape, she didn't say anything but Brodie was pretty sure he saw her arch a brow knowingly.

"You got something to say about that, Ren?" he asked.

She paused, turning his way, eyes beady like a little

bird's, but she feigned being nonplussed by the question. "No, Brodie, I got nothing to say."

He turned back to his brother, narrowed his eyes and said, "Why'd your girlfriend just raise her eyebrow at what I said?"

Noah laughed and shook his head. "Don't ask me. Ren, you certain you've got nothing to add?"

She started to walk back to the veranda. "I didn't do anything. I'm not even here. You brothers just get on with your talking."

Brodie sat back, arms crossed, legs outstretched. "I've never known you not to have an opinion, Ren," he called over.

She turned and rolled her eyes like he was being paranoid.

Noah said, "Don't worry, if she has got one, she won't be able to hold it in for long."

"I heard that."

"I know." Then he gave Brodie a look like, *just wait*.

So Brodie sipped his drink. Noah put his hands behind his head. They talked a bit about fishing.

Then when Zoey said, "I gotta use your bathroom," and skipped inside, Ren came jogging over to where the brothers were sitting.

"Okay, fine," she said.

Noah smirked.

She wiped her hands on a rag. "I don't think people run from a place, Brodie," she said, slipping the rag into the pocket of her dungarees. "I think they're running from what's inside."

"What the heck does that mean?" Noah asked.

Ren kept her gaze fixed on Brodie, smiling at him a little sadly. "It means, you gotta find peace with who you are—maybe with your dad…" She paused, letting the words sink in. "With who you wanna be. Maybe then you won't feel so restless."

Noah, silent, glanced at him, eyes curious as to whether that struck a chord.

But Brodie just shook his head none the wiser. "How am I meant to do that?" he asked, hands spread wide in question.

Ren glanced over her shoulder to check that Zoey wasn't back yet. She tilted her head, those beady eyes now all sympathy as she looked at him. "I think maybe you gotta sit with the feeling, Brodie, rather than run from it."

It was Brodie's turn to be silent.

He felt a building horror in his chest at the idea of being forced to sit still rather than jetting off to someplace new, some new island, some new ski slope, some new beach with towering surf. The very thought of having to wait and see what it was that was inside of him was beyond imaginable. Made him struggle to draw breath. Made him laugh and say, "Sounds a little too deep for me, Ren!"

Before she could say more, Zoey came back out and called, "Hey, Ren, I thought we were painting?"

Chapter Thirty-Seven

Being at work that day was odd. A little like being a mini celebrity. Maeve wasn't sure exactly what she was expecting, but her imagination heavily featured the cool judgment she knew she would get from her parents on the faces of everyone.

Instead, when she walked in, Barbara on reception clicked her tongue and said, "They're devils, those reporters, sell their soul for a quick buck. It's disgusting."

When she went into a handover meeting, fellow resident Henry cracked a joke with a good-natured smirk, which prompted the head of department to say, "Are we here to do our jobs or gossip about Doctor Dixon's love life?" and one of the nurses, Georgia, to reply, "Gossip about Doctor Dixon's love life!" Which made everyone snigger.

It was all harmless fun that somehow made Maeve feel more fondly of her colleagues—even relax a little and be more accepting of them as friends. They seemed pleased to be able to rib her a little, see her relax and laugh. Maybe in every aspect of her life she needed, as Brodie put it, to lighten up.

Maybe she owed him an apology? Had she been too defensive and overly protective? That, of course, was her job as a mother but the fallout from the photos wasn't too bad. She got a few requests for interviews, but politely declined. Barbara thankfully fielded any other requests that came through the hospital switchboard, and had the same advice as Bella: "Don't worry, dear, tomorrow you'll be yesterday's news."

It was this kindness, this newfound sense of camaraderie, of allowing herself to relax, that made the phone call catch Maeve off-guard.

It came as she was walking to get a coffee in her break.

Dad flashed up on her screen as she was standing waiting for the machine to fill the cup.

Suddenly, every muscle in her body tensed. She was back at nineteen again. Terrified. Her fingers trembled as she took a moment to steel herself and pressed answer. "Hello."

"Maeve," came her dad's voice, so familiar yet equally that of a stranger. "We've seen the photographs."

No, *How are you*. No, *How's Zoey*. No, *Is this a good time to talk*.

She pulled out a chair and sat down. The view from the break room was of the gray concrete car park.

"I'm going to be honest, we're more than a little disappointed," her dad said.

Maeve wondered if that was what he'd said when he found out about Zoey—it was all a bit of a blur.

She heard her mom in the background saying, "Very surprised." Which her dad relayed. "We're very surprised that you didn't think to tell us yourself and we had to find out like we did."

Maeve saw herself sitting in the living room of her parents' house, perched on the couch. She could picture the golf clubs by the door, the two dogs wagging their tails excitedly that she was back, feel the tearstains on her cheeks. She remembered the drowning terror at having discovered she was pregnant, the nerves of having to tell them. Not knowing what to do, what was best, and wishing someone would support her, put their arm round her and say, "It's okay, Maeve, we'll help you." But instead, they said the very same things they were saying now...

Embarrassed. Shocked. Lack of judgment. Daughter of ours. The words went in like an IV line.

But this time, as they spoke, she found that the words didn't hit quite as powerfully as they once might. She looked up and saw her reflection in the window—professional, scrubs, hair neatly tied back, nametag, stethoscope. This person wasn't a pregnant teenager. This person had survived. More than survived—she'd thrived.

She heard her own words—her grandma's words—about pride, and admitting one's mistakes, drown out her father's.

She heard Brodie at Logan's house as he'd leaned across and tucked her hair behind her ear and said, "I think your parents are fools." It made her do a little snort of unexpected laughter.

On the other end of the phone, her dad paused for a second, "Did you just laugh, Maeve?"

"No," she lied.

Her mom said, "Is she laughing?"

"No," said her dad and carried on. Always talking, never listening.

Maeve thought how far away they seemed. Not just in distance, but in everything. Especially when compared to Martha—even Emmett—embracing Zoey into their family, no questions asked. "You're missing out," she said, cutting her father off.

"Excuse me?"

"I said, you're missing out. You have a grandchild. Do you not see?"

"That's not the issue here, Maeve."

"Of course that's the issue!" It came out louder than she intended.

"Please don't get hysterical."

She almost laughed. She could never win.

Suddenly the shrill sound of the pre-alert call came from the ER which meant a critically ill patient was on their way. It meant, all-hands-on-deck.

Maeve opened her mouth to say that she had to go, that she'd call her dad back, but then, instead, she took the phone away from her ear and looked at it, heard his voice like a tiny mouse coming through the speaker.

Out in the hallway she could hear people rushing. It occurred to her in that moment that she had already won. She had Zoey. She looked around her, she had this, she had the Carters. She had people in her life who *wanted* her to succeed, who were on her side.

Without a word, she placed her phone down on the table, the mouse's voice still squeaking, and went out to join her colleagues; her friends; her life.

Before the controlled chaos kicked in of the ambulance arriving, she allowed herself a moment to think about what she'd just done. All that pride. All that harm it had caused. She didn't have to be bound by it. Whatever she did, her parents would be like that. Whatever success, whatever failure. There was no pot of acceptance waiting at the end of the rainbow.

Why did she need it, anyway?

As Brodie said, "If Zoey's your biggest failing, then believe me, you're doing more than okay!"

As Brodie said, "I'd be proud of you if you were my kid."

As Brodie said—

The doors to the ambulance bay flew open and it was go, go, go. She didn't have time to think more about the fact she was quoting all the things Brodie had said.

Chapter Thirty-Eight

Back at Maeve's house, Brodie couldn't sit still, hemmed in by the floral wallpaper in the living room, the bright primary colors of the family kitchen, the color-changing bubble bath in the bathroom. Out the window, he could see the orchard and the mountains behind, the epic landscape making the rooms feel like cages. Even the view was loaded now with expectation and decision. There was no escape. At the ranch there would be questions from his mom. At the polo club, Logan would corner him, having almost definitely spoken to Noah. In the diner, Ren would tip her head knowingly.

Anywhere he went in this town there would be questions from someone.

He sat at Maeve's kitchen table, fingers pushed into his hair.

You gotta sit with it.

No, he didn't.

He stood up. He was too hot. His legs were restless. He couldn't breathe.

"You okay, Dad?" Zoey asked.

"Fine!"

Dad.

They were making Slime at the kitchen table. Zoey had a zip-lock bag full of glue and some magic liquid, glitter and food coloring that she'd had to pull up a chair to reach at the back of a cupboard. Brodie had been sitting next to her, he'd poured glasses of OJ, opened a packet of Oreos; it was easy, mundane, everyday stuff.

Now that he was standing up, however, he surveyed the scene wondering if he should be doing more. Should he be guiding Zoey with more life lessons? Should they be studying? Watching educational documentaries? Should he be somehow imparting fatherly wisdom? What did he know that he could tell her?

He thought of earlier, when he'd asked Maeve if she was ashamed of him. Why wouldn't she be ashamed? He'd never had to justify his existence to a woman before and when it came down to it, what did he have to offer?

What if he ruined Zoey's life?

His mom rang, interrupting his spiraling thoughts, to see if he wanted to drop by for dinner. Relieved for the reprieve, Brodie took the phone call in the hallway.

"I can't," he said. "I'm with Zoey."

"Bring her with you."

He didn't want to see his dad, face more denigration.

"No, it's okay, thanks."

His mom didn't push it. "Okay, well, I'll leave you to it."

He was about to hang up when he found himself saying, "Mom?"

"Yes."

Brodie paused, tracing his finger over one of the lines in the hallway wallpaper. "How did you know how to be a parent?"

"I didn't," she replied without hesitation.

He rolled his eyes. "Yes, you did. You always knew what to do with us." He thought of her keeping all six kids in check.

She laughed. "No, Brodie, no one knows what to do. You just go with what feels right."

That was no help at all. He turned and leaned against the wall, stared at the struts of the staircase. "What if it's wrong?"

There was a pause. He could imagine his mom thinking for a moment what to say, maybe sitting down at the big kitchen table, a cup of coffee in her hand.

"Brodie," she said, "children aren't yours to own. They are in your life for a certain amount of time and it's your job to be there for them." He could hear the smile in her voice when she carried on. "They are their own people. Usually interesting, clever, sweet, funny people who you may actually find yourself enjoying spending time with. All you have to do, Brodie, is be there, shepherd them. That's enough."

Brodie listened, nodding.

"It's just practice," she added. "Like everything."

He thought of the hours with the band in the rehearsal room where he was terrible at sitting still. "Okay," he said, trying to sound casual.

He imagined her eyes narrowing. "You okay?"

"Yeah, yeah, totally fine." He waved a hand in dismissal.

They said goodbye. Brodie slipped the phone in his pocket feeling no better. He went back into the kitchen. There was Slime everywhere. Like an explosion of goo. One of the food-coloring bottles had tipped over and bright red liquid dripped onto the floor where Zoey was on her hands and knees trying to catch it with a dishcloth, the scarlet dye bleeding into the fabric. When she saw him, she looked up guiltily.

"What the heck's happened here!" Brodie's voice came out loud with horror. His eyes widened, his hands raised. Where Zoey had tried hastily to wipe it up, the spilled Slime had taken the top layer of varnish off the table. He felt the infusion of adrenaline and panic, what would Maeve say? He'd left Zoey alone for five minutes and this happened. He watched the cascade of food coloring sloshing onto the floor. He stood open-mouthed for a second, then said more despairingly, "What have you *done*!"

"Please don't be mad!" Zoey looked like she was about to cry, big eyes blinking back tears as she tried to contain the food dye chaos.

He could feel his heart beating in his head. He felt the urge to shout, to rant and rave, to throw his hands up, but then he looked at those huge watery eyes and he heard himself in his head and said, "It's okay, Zoey. It's fine." He grabbed the roll of paper towel and lay a mountain of it under the dripping coloring, then tried his best to swipe up the varnish-stripping glop. "We can clear it up."

Zoey nodded, bottom lip trembling.

"Hey." He put his hand on her shoulder. "I didn't mean to shout. I'm sorry."

Practice was not making perfect. Brodie felt worse than ever.

Chapter Thirty-Nine

When Maeve came home, she expected they'd have a conversation, but Brodie kept his distance. She had wanted to apologize. Say that she'd been too defensive, overreacted about the photos—that it wasn't his fault—that instead of taking a step forward, she'd taken one, maybe three, steps back.

But before she could say anything he said, "I'm really sorry, your table's ruined. And the floor. There was Slime everywhere and—"

"Zoey!" Maeve interrupted him, frowning at her daughter. "I told you not to play with that stuff! You know what it does. It's a nightmare!"

Zoey looked like she was about to burst into tears.

Maeve said, "No. Don't turn on the waterworks, because you know it was wrong." She turned to Brodie. "I'm sorry."

He shook his head, looked a little like a rabbit in headlamps. "It's okay. We cleared it up," he said. "And I can get you a new table." He pointed again to where all the varnish had been eaten away.

Maeve waved away his concern, it was a really old table and had probably suffered worse. "Thanks, but don't worry. I don't need a new table. Zoey, that stuff was hidden at the back of the cupboard for a reason!"

Zoey nodded, putting on her best wide-eyed worried face. Maeve shook her head, silently telling her to knock it off.

Brodie looked equally terrified, but she was pretty certain his expression wasn't an act.

"Well, anyway," he said, "I gotta go. Bye, Zoey!"

She waved, chastened. "Sorry about the Slime."

"It's not a problem," he replied.

Maeve walked with him out to the hallway. When they got to the front door, she said, "Brodie, I wanted to say—"

"Really sorry, Maeve." He cut her off as he looked at his watch. "I've really gotta run. I'm late. And I, er ... don't want to draw attention, you know..." He gestured to the road where there might be someone waiting to take a photo of him leaving the house, though Maeve didn't believe that was the reason for his hesitation, especially not given his attitude to the press coverage. "We can talk tomorrow."

"Sure." She nodded, watching, a little disappointed as he jogged away down the path.

Back in the house, Zoey was unusually quiet. Maeve went and sat next to her, stroked her hair away from her face and said, "Are you okay, Zo?"

Zoey nodded, but her big brown eyes said different.

Then she bit her lip for a second and it almost made Maeve smile, because she knew Zoey had learned the gesture from her. "I didn't want to make him mad."

"Well, Slime is a nightmare, Zo." Maeve wondered how Brodie was feeling about it. "And it can't always be fun and games. He's your dad. Sometimes he's going to tell you off."

Zoey looked up, bottom lip trembling a little with worry.

Maeve smiled gently. "That's what moms and dads do. Sometimes, when you've done something wrong, they get mad. Doesn't mean they don't love you. I get mad all the time and I love you."

"I guess."

Maeve wasn't sure her little speech reflected that well on her but it seemed to do the trick where Brodie was concerned. "Come on," she said, "It's bedtime."

Zoey did her normal reluctant routine about going to bed, but once she was tucked up, it became apparent that she'd been saving another topic for discussion and said, with the utmost seriousness, "By the way, if you and Brodie got together, I'd be okay with that."

Maeve was so taken aback she said quickly, "We're not going to get together, Zoey."

Zoey frowned, pulling her stuffed monkey closer under her arm. "I'm just saying, I'd be fine with it if you did."

Maeve had managed to compose herself and said, "Well, that's good to know, thank you."

"So you're *never* going to?" Zoey persisted.

"No!" Maeve shook her head. "And even if we wanted to, which we don't," she said, "there are so many things to take into account."

"Like what?"

Maeve was kicking herself for not being better prepared. "Like what if we got together and then broke up? You'd be very upset."

"So you're saying we shouldn't do things if they might make us upset?" Zoey wriggled up the bed so she was sitting upright.

"No, I'm not saying that." Maeve felt herself getting flustered under the scrutiny of the eight-year-old. "No, I'm saying I don't want to do anything—willingly—that might make you upset."

"You not doing things you want to do makes me upset," Zoey said with a mischievous grin. She looked dangerously like her dad.

"Oh, for goodness' sake." Maeve clamped her hand to her forehead in despair. "You're too clever for your own good!"

Zoey giggled. Maeve shooed her back down the bed, so her head was back on the pillow and giving her a big kiss said, "Goodnight, Zo."

Zoey was still grinning when she said, "Night, Mom."

Strangely, Maeve found herself smiling as she went back down the stairs. She allowed herself to question her own logic. To take the advice of her eight-year-old and wonder if maybe she was being too cautious, finding problems where maybe she could be finding happiness.

She paused on the bottom step, looking out the window

by the front door to the wire fence and the road beyond, she thought how liberating it had felt walking away from her dad on the phone. Then everything Zoey had just said. Brodie or no Brodie, she realized how much she'd let fear have control of her life.

Chapter Forty

Back in his condo Brodie stood with his forehead pressed against the glass, staring down at the view of the dusky polo field.

Why had he instinctively believed that the Slime debacle was his fault? It hadn't occurred to him that Zoey was taking advantage of the fact he didn't know she wasn't allowed to play with the stuff. He should have handled it better. Instead, he'd caved in the moment there was the slightest hint of tears. Whereas Maeve just stood firm at the sight of the crumbling emotion on her daughter's face. It wasn't even that big of a deal, but he'd been frozen by his own reaction, terrified that he'd upset her. He squeezed his eyes shut. That was surely just a miniscule fragment of what parenting entailed but he'd panicked, then gone into apologetic mode—even offering to buy Maeve a new table.

He kept picturing her standing on the doorstep about to say something important. He could tell it was important from the seriousness in her eyes. It would be something honest and well-considered that would leave him more conflicted.

She wasn't like the others. Everything with her was real. If she said something, she meant it. If she laughed, then the joke really was a good one.

Kiss her and it was real.

Don't think about kissing Maeve, Brodie.

It wasn't a game.

In his mind's eye, he saw the moment their lips almost met upstairs at Logan's house, the sweet, subtle scent of her perfume, the softness of her skin, the wildness of her eyes; the exquisite, satisfying moment her guard dropped. When her hand reached up tentatively and her fingers touched his neck. When they had danced at the Summer Fair and he could see where the tiny gold heart she wore dipped beneath the neckline of her dress, and where the loose tendrils of hair, fallen from her braid, brushed her pale skin. And in contrast, the endearing blush on her cheeks, which he knew she'd hate but which he relished—tried as hard as he could whenever he saw her to make that telltale blush break past her stony façade.

What was he thinking?

He moved away from the window. Walked aimlessly around the condo.

Brodie, you idiot.

He had been playing with treasure, not realizing it was real, underestimating its value, everything that it meant. You didn't walk away from someone like Maeve, but that meant you didn't walk away from Autumn Falls.

He thought of his stifling life there before the band. No sense of self, no value. He thought of staying there and being gradually ground down again. He thought of the orchard for sale, of his dad's open disdain—always in the background, judging.

Brodie blew out a breath, standing back at the window, this time in his bedroom, he stared out at the wide navy sky, the endless blanket of stars. This wasn't the place for him. He couldn't breathe here. He couldn't be himself.

Or maybe he could. Maybe this was exactly where he *could* breathe. Maybe when he was with Zoey and Maeve that was exactly who he was. Who he was meant to be.

But what if it went wrong? What if he couldn't hack it? What happened when there were problems bigger than Slime? What if he messed it up—which was more than likely—what then?

He could feel the urge to flee rising up inside him.

You gotta sit with it.

He sat on the side of the bed, hands either side of him, staring at the bland pale gray carpet. Voices started crowding in his head.

You're bored.

You lack purpose.

You run from what's inside.

He stood up again and went to the window.

Of course he's staying. Such a cute baby. Shame you missed it.

He turned, leaned with his back against the glass, the four walls getting closer, tighter.

All you have to do is be there, shepherd them.

Maybe now you'll have to grow up.

Before the thoughts could engulf him, Brodie's suitcase was packed, the top was down on his car and he was hurtling along the highway out of Autumn Falls.

Chapter Forty-One

The next morning, Brodie was late coming over.

Maeve called him but it went straight to voicemail. Zoey sat eating Cheerios, checking her watch saying, "He'll be here in a minute."

Maeve stood for a moment in the hallway, phone clutched to her chest, remembering his awkwardness the evening before, knowing this was it. Knowing he wasn't coming.

"Where do you think he is?" Zoey asked, getting up to go look out the window to see if there was any sign of his car.

Maeve couldn't bear it. He'd proved her right. But she didn't feel victorious, she felt awful. "He's probably just got held up."

Online, there was a photo of Maeve covering her face with her hand as she walked to her car in the hospital parking lot. And one of Brodie with Zoey in the diner,

Brodie was grinning and waving welcomingly at the camera, it was just the back of Zoey's head. There were a few more details in the follow-up article, but nothing shocking. Brodie's broad smile seemed to undercut the whole story, made it so that having a daughter was no big deal. It made Maeve wish she'd stood up straight and let the camera have her whole face.

She called Carole to come over and look after Zoey.

Throughout the day, Maeve kept checking her phone at work but there was nothing from Brodie. The messages she sent him remained unread. The sick feeling that he wasn't coming back remained in her belly.

She took Zoey to the diner when she got home, as a treat, because she knew she was disappointed about Brodie.

Ren was serving. "Hey, guys, what can I get you?"

Maeve pointed to Zoey and said, "One Cookies and Cream Dream and—" She thought for a minute about getting a milkshake just for the fun of it, but then said, "A coffee."

Zoey said, "Try a Mudslide, Mom, Brodie has it."

The mention of Brodie having milkshakes made her remember the conversation where he asked her favorite flavor and how she'd wondered if he'd secretly been guessing. She thought about him telling her to lighten up. "Okay, a Mudslide, it is."

"Great choice," Ren said, ruffling Zoey's hair fondly before heading back to the counter.

Bella came in then to get two coffees to take away. She caught sight of them after she'd ordered and came over to their booth. "Hey, Maeve. Hey, Zoey. How are you? Brodie here?"

"We don't know where he is," Zoey said matter-of-factly.

Bella's forehead creased. "Oh. Really?" She threw a covert glance Maeve's way.

Zoey nodded.

"I think he had to go away for a couple of days," Maeve replied vaguely.

"You're making that up," Zoey said back. "I can tell."

"I'm not making it up," Maeve lied.

Zoey narrowed her eyes. Then she turned to Bella and said, "I think it's because we made Slime and it went everywhere and ruined the table."

"What? I don't believe that!" Bella shook her head. "There's no way Brodie would go away because of Slime. I would think Slime was right up his alley. Nah. He's always got to go to different places, don't worry about it."

Maeve looked at her daughter and said seriously, "Zoey, it's definitely *not* because of the Slime."

Suddenly Martha was there carrying bags of groceries. She came over, placing the bags on one of the tables next to them and said, "You okay, Zoey?" She laughed when she saw her. "You look very annoyed about something."

"Brodie's gone away."

"Oh."

Martha glanced from Zoey to Maeve to Bella and raised her brows. Maeve winced, knowing Zoey would read the subtext behind the expression.

Emmett came in then, looking around for Martha.

All Maeve needed now was Logan and Noah and the whole Carter contingent would know Brodie had disappeared.

The bell over the door rang and Maeve looked up. There was Logan. He sauntered over in his grass-stained polo kit. "I was driving past, saw you through the window," he said to Bella. "Came in to say hi!"

Bella rolled her eyes. "I'll be home in an hour!"

"I know." He grinned and slid his arm around her to kiss her on the cheek.

Emmett, who had no truck for public displays of affection, looked at Martha and said, "Did you order?"

"Not yet, I saw Maeve and she said that Brodie—" Martha stopped herself, realizing too late who she was talking to.

"Brodie what?" Emmett frowned.

"He's gone away," Zoey filled him in.

"Cookies and Cream Dream and a Mudslide!" Ren came back carrying huge milkshakes that Maeve suddenly didn't have the stomach for.

Logan narrowed his eyes in confusion. "Where's Brodie gone? We're meant to be playing golf tomorrow."

Zoey shrugged, sipping her Cookies and Cream Dream through the curly straw.

Emmett had to sit down.

Ren said, "You all right, Emmett?"

He took his hat off and blew out a long breath. "I'm fine," he muttered. Then shaking his head, added tight-lipped, "That darn boy!"

To which Maeve said sharply, "Emmett!" and made big warning eyes in Zoey's direction.

That made Emmett pause, and for a moment, Maeve understood Brodie's fear of the man. But then, as if realizing his actions, Emmett sat up straighter and said vaguely, "I'm sure he'll—"

Logan cut in. "He'll be back soon. I'll give him a call."

Zoey was overly focused on her milkshake.

Martha made apologetic eyes at Maeve and then said, "I'll go order at the counter." She tapped Emmett on the shoulder as she went and he heaved himself out of the chair, picking up the grocery bags as he followed her.

Logan seemed to be assessing the situation, watching his dad walk away.

Bella hovered. "Do you need any help or anything, Maeve? I'm off tomorrow, if Zoey wants to come and hang out with me and the horses?"

"Oh, yeah!" Zoey perked up.

Maeve smiled. "That would be awesome. Thanks, Bella."

Logan turned back to the table. "So you're coming to us tomorrow, Zoey?"

Zoey nodded, eyes smiling.

"We'll have to think of some pretty special things to do, won't we?" Logan said to Bella.

"Absolutely," Bella agreed. "We'll have a great day. But for now we'll leave you to your milkshakes."

Logan gazed at the Mudslide longingly and said, "I might have to get one of my own!"

When they were alone again, Zoey said, "Mom, is Brodie gonna come back?"

Maeve had taken a sugary sip of her triple-chocolate milkshake. She wiped her mouth and said, "He'll be back."

"Do you promise?"

Maeve looked across at her daughter who was staring at her, big brown eyes unblinking.

She saw Brodie so clearly in Zoey's face. In the trusting, openness of her expression, in the hint of the dimples when she was being serious that made her look like she was still trying not to laugh, in the way she tilted her head to one side with a question and her messy brown hair fell forward over her eye.

Maeve thought of being ashamed of the picture of the three of them, of her parents seeing it. Of what they would think. Of what people would think. Seeing it had taken her back to believing that her night with Brodie was a mistake, when actually, from that one time she'd let go of control, had come the most wonderful, precious thing in her life.

But she'd been so busy thinking of it as a failure, something to be atoned for, that she couldn't see that. In the same way, Brodie was so fearful of his own father's opinion of him, that he failed to see what he had here. All these people—this family—looking out for him.

She knew now that she had become so afraid of stepping out of her comfort zone into the unknown, that she was blinded to all the good things in her life.

Like her grandma said, *you gotta to be able admit your mistakes.* Maeve couldn't control if Brodie was going to stay or leave, but she could be open to the possibility that he might stay. That if they did ever get together, it might not work, but on the other hand it might. She had seen enough life and death at work to know that right now was all they could guarantee, and maybe what Brodie needed most of all was someone to believe in him.

Pride and fear had stopped her from giving him a chance.

She owed him a chance.

"I promise, Zoey."

Chapter Forty-Two

Brodie paced his Malibu home. Up and down like a panther. He'd done everything he normally did when he was there. He'd gone to a friend's beach club for a party, where he'd stayed till the sunrise glowed like copper on the water. He'd fine-dined at his usual table at Nobu. He'd driven out to the State Park to do his favorite run. But none of it hooked him the way it usually did. It felt like he was killing time rather than living.

His house was right on the beach with direct access to the sand. He looked out at the paltry surf, waves too small to tempt him. He crossed his arms on the balcony and rested his head on his forearms. He didn't know what he was doing, couldn't think straight.

A message came through on his phone. He'd had it mainly on silent—ignoring calls from Maeve, from his brothers, from his mom. He checked it now, it was a message from Maeve. It would surely be something telling him not to bother coming back, how he'd sadly lived up to her expectations of him, how upset Zoey was. He didn't want to read it. He only did because it felt like a punishment he deserved for skipping town. He hated his own actions as much as Maeve did.

He clicked on the message, braced himself.

Not sure where you are or what's happened, but – and this may sound stupid, especially if you're in Vegas – I just want you to know that I believe in you. As a dad, as a person, as a friend. Maeve x

Brodie frowned. He closed the message then opened it again to check he'd read it right, hadn't conjured up an illusion. He had to go and sit down on his couch, read it again.

As a dad, as a person, as a friend.

He realized he was welling up, and dabbed the tears away with the back of his hand.

He flopped against the cushions, perplexed. *Why? Why* did she believe in him? He didn't even believe in himself. He chucked the phone on the couch cushion.

He didn't want her to believe in him; it was much easier, he realized, to be self-indulgently morose.

"Darn it!" he said, out loud.

He sighed, raking his hands through his hair. What now? He stood up, needed some air. The waves might suck but they'd have to do.

He got his board out and ran down to the water. He rode a few mediocre waves but there was no decent break, nothing to distract him.

In the end, he gave in, paddled right out past the wave line and lay on his board staring out at the horizon.

I believe in you.

He felt a swell of pride—courage, even—flow through him at the idea of her typing the words.

Courage.

You gotta sit with it.

Sit with what?

The sky out ahead built from blue, through orange, up to dusky pink like a rainbow. Clouds drifted in wisps. Gulls floated lazily on the warm air currents.

Images, memories, flowed through Brodie's mind like a baggage carousel. Shooting hoops with Zoey and Maeve, the scent of Maeve's perfume when they danced, watching Harry Potter under a blanket. All of that made him smile, resting his chin on his hands, the water bobbing beneath him, lulling him like a cradle.

He thought further back. Saw Logan carrying him home as a kid on his shoulders when he twisted his ankle. Making his sister Willow laugh so hard when she was eating her cereal that milk came out her nose. Sitting next to his mom at the piano, singing a song they wrote together.

Seeing his mom cry at his brother Jack's funeral.

Drinking hot chocolate with Maeve that fateful night. Playing on his PlayStation with Ethan, laughing at the smell of the tour bus after a week on the road. Playing practical jokes on Jack because he always got the maddest and there was a nerve-racking thrill that came from making him lose his temper. Waiting under a trap door beneath the stage, listening to the growing crescendo of screaming applause, the ground beneath him shaking. Rising up, ears ringing as the noise got louder and louder, arms spread wide, drinking it all in like a superpower. Looking across and just seeing his brothers, all together on stage. Like being out in the wild together. Same thing, different place. Just them, having a good time. Together.

He loved being in that band. Writing those songs. Sixty thousand screaming fans shouting his name, wanting to touch him, worship him, adore him. Number-one albums, world tours, platinum discs. All from lyrics he wrote with Ethan, lyrics he sang, melodies played by his brothers. It was magic. He would give anything to have that back. *Anything*.

That was the problem: he'd reached the pinnacle of life at sixteen.

How could anything ever live up to that?

Who was he without it? Who did he *want* to be without it?

The questions and the thoughts kept coming, rippling through him like the waves. He saw his dad when they left, turning his back as they packed into the old truck, Logan at the wheel. Their decrepit labrador, Duke, at his heels. He remembered the bubbling freedom inside himself, the bursting of sheer joy to be leaving, to be on the journey toward his dream, so strong that it made his fingers tingle. His notebook of songs, snippets on his phone, ideas just coming at him as plentiful as rainfall. So young, so free. It felt as if chains were literally falling from him as they turned out the Silver Sky Ranch gates. He had sat back, turned his head to see the mountains retreat in the distance, and seen the reflection in the window of his own beaming smile.

Lying on his surfboard in the ocean, came a cascade of memories he simply couldn't hold back, Brodie's muscles twitched with the urge to move, to flee, to turn around paddle back to shore.

I believe in you.

He forced himself to feel it, to let it roll over him. All that excitement, that hope, that fun. Best darn days of his life. Then it had vanished, quick as that. And there was nothing, just an empty void beneath him, the dream shattered. All that regret and frustration. He'd wake up in the night sweating, lie staring up in the darkness trying to find who he was. His sense of self. His purpose. His pride. His brothers. Jack. Ethan.

Brodie shut his eyes and rested his face down on the board. He could taste the salt water on his lips and wondered if he was crying again.

The waves lapped gently around him like soothing hands where his skin touched the water, the sun beat down on his back. He couldn't say how long he lay there but it felt like he'd seen his whole life before his eyes, every painful memory, every delicious one. Everything. Unfettered. Shameful, exhilarating, terrifying, loving. A cacophony of experiences held back as he raced forward.

He propped his chin on his hands and gazed at the swathes of blue. *I believe in you.* He smiled.

It was then that he heard a whistle. Sharp and quick, like summoning a dog.

Brodie narrowed his eyes, felt like there was something familiar in that whistle.

Then it came again. Louder this time.

He sat up, straddling the board, and glanced over his shoulder to see where it was coming from. Looking across the water to the beach, he saw two incongruous figures standing side by side, one with his hands in his pockets, the other with his finger and thumb in his mouth ready to whistle again.

Logan and Noah.

Brodie laughed out loud.

Logan raised a hand when he saw that Brodie'd noticed them.

Brodie shook his head in disbelief, then he turned his board around and started paddling, smooth long strokes, back in to shore.

"What the heck are you two doing here?" he called when he was knee-deep, scooping his board up under his arm and striding through the shallows.

"What the heck do you think we're doing here?" Logan lobbed him his beach towel.

Noah answered for him, "Come to find you, you idiot!"

Chapter Forty-Three

Brodie took his brothers to a bar up the beach from his house that played reggae music and served cold beer. They sat at a round table, the sun streaking in lines across them through a wooden-slatted awning, the ocean behind them, almost turquoise in the late-afternoon sunlight.

Brodie traced his thumb down the condensation on his glass. "I think Ren's right," he said, looking up to meet both pairs of enquiring eyes. "I'm just running. I don't know who I am anymore. Who I want to be." He sat up and stretched his arms above his head, let them flop in his lap. He'd stopped off at his house long enough to have a shower and change, now he sat in dry board-shorts and a T-shirt. "I feel like my best version of me was in the band. When I was up on stage. Everything since then, well—" he shrugged, hated to admit it "—it's nothing."

Neither Logan nor Noah said anything, just waited. No one bothered trying to deny it.

Brodie drank his beer, glanced away from them out to

the water, wished for a second that he was still back out there on his board. He hung his head for a moment, then turned back to the table. "When I go back to the ranch, it makes me feel like I'm nothing. Like no time has passed. I'm back to being that kid who doesn't know what he wants to do." He paused, watched the bubbles in his drink rising to the surface. "I just remember liking writing songs and knowing there was no real place for that there."

Logan leaned forward, rested his chin on his knuckles as he listened.

"I guess it's kinda terrifying to wonder what my life is if it's not that. If it's not the band, if it's not making music." Brodie lifted his drink half-heartedly. "I guess maybe I don't want to know."

Noah batted a wasp out the way of his glass. "Okay, so let's say you could have anything, what is it that you want?"

Brodie thought for a moment. To his surprise, the first picture that flashed into his mind, was of Maeve and Zoey at the cabin. He saw Zoey bringing him cereal and Maeve doing her yoga upstairs. But he wasn't going to say that to his brothers.

What *did* he want?

"For Ethan to come back," he said, without really thinking about it, just saying what came to mind after Maeve and Zoey. "To write songs together again."

"Really? Are you sure about that?" Logan reclined back, narrowed his eyes at him as if he were in a boardroom. "Brodie, you can look back on it rose-tinted and all, but you'd had enough by the time your solo career ended."

"Yeah, I'd had enough solo." Brodie heard the defensive edge to his voice. "Not in the band."

Noah almost choked on his beer. "Don't go getting any ideas about reforming the band."

Brodie thought he would reform in a heartbeat.

Logan, however, scratched his head. "You ever think that it's not the fame or the band, that it was the music? It was having people listen to what you wrote, to what you could sing?" He reached forward for his drink, took a sip, then added, "All the other stuff, Brodie, that's just fame. None of that's real. There's nothing to say you can't form another band, you can't write more songs—you don't even need Ethan to do that—but maybe it doesn't have to be quite so huge."

"But then what is it, if it's not huge?" Brodie asked, uncertain by the prospect. "If it's not like the success of Silver Sky, then wouldn't it just feel like failure?"

"Or a real good time?" Noah suggested. He'd never been a fan of the trappings of fame.

"Or it would be a success," Logan chimed in. "Just a different kind of success. It depends how you look at it, Brodie. Would you say Silver Sky was a success? Sure, we made a lot of money, but it didn't do us any good as a family, as brothers. There were times when we became people who I don't think any of us would want to be again." He let the comment linger for a moment, before adding, "I mean, I like you, Brodie, but you could be a pain in the butt when you were famous."

That made Noah laugh.

Logan softened it, adding, "But then I think we all could."

Brodie nodded slowly, only half listening, his mind had wandered off on a tangent as he considered what it might be like to pick up a pen again. To do something small but committed. Not the odd guest appearance with the Autumn Falls band, but something proper, that meant something. Something that gave him reason to write something. Something with *purpose*. That word made him imagine his dad saying, *I told you so*. But then he imagined writing songs for Zoey. Maybe about being a dad. About Maeve. He thought of Maeve rolling her eyes at his love songs—they'd have to be darn good to impress her. He felt a tingle of excitement over his skin at the prospect. "It would be nice to be a writer again, and be a little more in control," he mused.

Noah raised both brows and nodded as if that was a given.

"Do stuff I'm proud of rather than—" He thought back to some of the dismal records he'd put out nearing the end of his solo career, bad decisions made by both him and his manager. But then, without the fame and the success, would there ever be the same rush, the same impetus to continue? And like Logan said, did he even want that? "I don't know. I'm older now. Maybe I need to do something different."

"Maybe," Logan agreed. "I know you don't like to have to sit and think too much about things, Brodie, but you don't have to decide everything right this second." He laughed fondly, like a big brother. Then he leaned forward, forearms crossed on the table, and looked at him more seriously as he said, "You got a kid now. You got something worth staying for. You've got a reason to stop running right there in front of your face."

Brodie felt a bolt of trepidation shoot through him and he almost flinched. But then came something else, something gentler yet also more powerful, that it dawned on him was longing. Maybe even nerve-shredding, stomach-clenching love.

"You got an orchard of trees to buy," Noah added over the rim of his glass. "May they rest in peace."

Brodie snorted into his beer.

Logan stifled a laugh. Then he raised his hand to order another round of drinks.

Out on the ocean, the sun glittered on the gentle waves, winking and sparkling like diamonds. People were taking afternoon strolls, coming down to the beach after work to catch the late sun, stretching out on loungers.

Noah looked around and said, "Don't you get bored here?"

Brodie turned to take in the view, then back to his brother. "It's pretty easy doing nothing."

Noah rolled his eyes, incredulous at the idea.

Fresh drinks arrived. Brodie looked back out at the rolling ocean, the line of the horizon, the bathers stretched out on the golden sand, then he took a deep breath and said, "What if I can't hack it? What if I leave?"

"I'll come and drag you back," Logan replied without hesitation.

Noah smiled as he drank his beer. "You won't leave."

"How d'you know?" Brodie asked, sitting back, folding his arms.

Noah put his glass down on the table. "Because I trust you. And every time anyone's really needed you, Brodie, and I mean *really* needed you, you've been there. For Logan, after Jack died—" Noah glanced at Logan who nodded in agreement. "For me, all the time in the band. You're more of a support than you give yourself credit for. And I truly don't think you'd walk away from what you believe is right. You left a number-one solo career because it wasn't right for you anymore, not because you couldn't be bothered. Maybe you're here because you needed some space, but I get the feeling you would have come back on your own."

Brodie listened as Noah spoke. "Yeah," he said. "Yeah, I think you're right." Then he smiled, leaned forward and bashed Noah on the arm. "Thanks, man," he said, grinning. "That means … well, something."

Logan laughed. "I thought my plan was better."

Someone came over to the table, a woman in her thirties with her phone. "Hey, guys, sorry to interrupt, but do you think I could take a picture?"

Logan shook his head. "I'm sorry, we're actually—"

But Brodie jumped up out his seat and said, "Sure!" He went round to stand between where his brothers were sitting, threw his arms around them and said, "Smile, everyone."

Noah's was more of a grimace.

The woman giggled with excitement. "Thanks so much!" she gushed. Then Brodie posed for another shot with just her and her cheeks flushed red as she thanked him again.

"You're welcome, anytime," he replied, and went and sat back down.

Logan raised a brow.

Brodie shrugged. "It's done and there's no bad feeling. Didn't kill ya, did it?"

Noah muttered, "I have a bad feeling."

Brodie barked a laugh. "You just said you wanted to be more like me."

Noah almost reared back. "I never said—"

But Brodie cut him off. "It's okay, Noah, everyone wants to be a bit more Brodie."

"You're *so* annoying." Noah shook his head.

Brodie just grinned.

Chapter Forty-Four

Brodie arrived back in Autumn Falls the following afternoon. Driving along the road back to his condo, he passed the turning to the Silver Sky Ranch and the big metal gates. He slowed to a crawl, thought about driving on, but found himself flicking the blinker and taking the turn.

It felt as if, before he did anything else, he needed to talk to his dad. Needed to tell him that in some ways he was right but in others he was wrong. Just needed to be honest.

The lights were on in The Silver Pantry. But this time, Brodie parked up at the far end of the drive nearer the main ranch. He got out the car, slammed the door and, bracing himself, crossed the yard.

The chickens were scratching in the dirt, squabbling over food. Brodie had never been a big fan of chickens and circled them as he walked toward the horse barn and the paddock.

A couple of the horses were out. The dog, Rocky, came

out to greet him, jumping up with his paws on Brodie's sweater, which would have earned him a scolding from Noah. Then he bounded back into the barn.

Brodie followed. "Hello?" he called out as he reached the entrance. The radio was playing. The evening sun warming the wood. Noah's horse Blue's inquisitive head stretched over a stall. But no sign of his dad.

Then the dog barked again, and Brodie looked down the end of the path and there was his dad, lying prostrate on the ground, hand to his chest.

"Dad!" Brodie shouted, sprinting over to where he lay, pale-faced, sweating, barely breathing. "It's okay, Dad, I'm here, I've got you." Mind racing with panic, Brodie got his phone out and dialed 911. "Yes, the Silver Sky Ranch. You need to get here fast!"

He pulled off his sweater and folded it under his dad's head. Then he rang his mom who went from bright and breezy to panting as she ran to the barn.

Brodie sat on the concrete floor, holding his dad's cool hand in his, praying for him not to die. Just thinking that he wanted to be able to talk to him, to understand him, to know him. His eyes kept straying to Emmett's old, much-darned shirt, one he used to wear when they were kids, faded now with age, scattered with burn marks from bonfire sparks. He stared at his craggy face, softer in what looked like sleep, and had to squeeze away tears. "Oh, Dad, come on, please! Please!"

The dog was outside barking.

"I'm sorry, Dad." He pressed his hand over his face—thought of all his defensive, sarcastic retorts. Thought of them winding each other up, bashing heads. But saw suddenly a glimpse of some moments of laughter. A loud, unplanned cheer from Emmett the time Brodie scored a long-range, game-winning shot in polo. His smile of relief when, standing on the edge of the Halfmoon Lake, Brodie finally mastered fly casting. Emmett's toast to them all when branding was done.

Not every good moment held an absence of his father, he could see that now.

He thought of mistakes he had and would make with Zoey; understood how hard it all was. Realized that his mom was right. No one knows what they're doing.

Be there, shepherd them, that's enough.

It was Brodie's turn now, to do it his way.

Looking down at his dad, he felt an overriding passion to protect this man, to make him feel safe and loved and unafraid, at a time when terror flooded icy through his own veins. "It's okay," he kept saying, holding his dad's hand tight in his. He could hear his mom's running footsteps approaching. "An ambulance is coming. It'll be okay," he said, whether he believed it or not. And as he said it, calm and gentle, fatherly, trying to keep his own panic at bay, he felt his dad's hand squeeze lightly back.

Chapter Forty-Five

"Maeve!" Brodie jumped out of his plastic hospital chair when he saw her. He looked dreadful. Tired, stressed, hair all over the place, eyes dark. "What's going on? What's happening."

"I can't tell you anything you don't already know, Brodie," she said, as she came out of the ER.

It had been a shock when Emmett Carter was brought in with a heart attack. He wasn't Maeve's patient, but she'd kept an eye on what was happening, making extra special sure that he was given the best care.

The first opportunity she had, she went out to see the Carters, uncertain who would be there waiting. Surprised when the first person she saw was Brodie. It meant he must have been nearby when it happened, back in Autumn Falls. The thought occurred to her, but she filed it away for later, not appropriate right then to be thinking about what—if anything—was going on between them. Her message had been read but remained unanswered. If it wasn't for the current circumstances, she might feel foolish in front of him for sending it. Logan was there, too, and Noah. Martha was in her Silver Pantry apron, clutching a Kleenex in her hands, trembling lips pressed together.

Maeve hated it, seeing them all like this, not being able to say anything to make it better. "The next twenty-four hours are critical."

Brodie nodded, eyes alert like they were absorbing every little detail, every scrap of knowledge. She found herself wanting to touch him, put her hand on his arm, maybe round his neck, hold him close.

It was Logan who said, "Is he going to be okay, Maeve?"

"I can't tell you that, Logan, I'm sorry."

Martha let out a small sob and Noah put his arm around her.

"All I can say is that they're doing everything they can. He's in the best hands." Maeve could picture Emmett, ghostly pale. Suddenly a shadow of a man.

"Thanks, Maeve," Brodie said, looking at her gratefully. "We really appreciate it."

"I'm sorry that I can't give you any more news than that."

Brodie shook his head. "Just you being here is a relief."

Maeve smiled. He looked so pained and tired. "I'm sorry, Brodie."

He put his hand on her arm and steered her away from the others. "It's me that's sorry," he said, when they were out of earshot. "I'm sorry I left. I got spooked. I panicked. I'm sorry—"

Maeve cut him off. "Don't, Brodie, you don't have to say

any of this now." She tilted her head as she looked at him, ashen-faced and distracted. She had been mad with him for disappearing, but all she could see was his fear for his father. The futility of life right there in front of them made it almost impossible to look at him with anything other than tenderness. "Just concentrate on your dad. Don't worry about me or Zoey, we're okay."

He took in a shaky breath, then he smiled appreciatively and she saw a little of the old Brodie. "Thanks."

She smiled softly back. "Stay with your family," she said, before returning to the ER.

The next time Maeve saw Brodie, she was on a break. Emmett was in surgery.

All the family were sitting in the waiting room, with various expressions of concern. Ren was there now, sitting with Noah, wearing her paint-splattered dungarees.

When Maeve appeared, all their heads shot up when she came out like she could give them some golden-ticket answer when all she could say was, "The surgeon doing the operation, he's one of the best there is at what he does. Emmett couldn't be in better care, I promise."

It wasn't much, but even just those words seemed to give them a little of the reassurance they craved.

She was about to go back, but instead, a little apprehensive, she went and took a seat next to Brodie. "You okay?"

It was weird not seeing him all smiles. "I would like to

talk to him, you know? I don't want what we had to be it," he said.

She nodded. "I know."

They sat side by side for a moment, then Maeve plucked up all her courage and reached across and took hold of his hand. Threaded her fingers through his, palms touching, skin against skin.

She saw him glance at her and then look down at their entwined fingers. For a second, she feared he would pull away, that it was the wrong move; too close, too intimate. Then she felt him grip tighter, holding on like it meant everything.

Time ticked by. She sat beside him for as long as her break would allow. His brothers kept getting up, Logan pacing, Noah going outside for fresh air. Martha sat with her hands clasped, resting her forehead against them.

Suddenly, the door flew open and their little sister, Willow, rushed in. A cloud of wild chestnut curls, wearing leggings, cropped T-shirt, and an oversize green cardigan, she'd obviously been crying, her face was all red, eyes puffy. "Is he alive?"

Logan stalked over to greet her. "He's in surgery, Willow."

She covered her face with her hands and sobbed. Logan wrapped his arms protectively around her.

"I came as soon as I heard." Willow gasped for breath as she spoke, moving away from Logan when she saw her mom, going over to sit by her side, hold her close. "Are you okay, Mom?"

"I'm okay. I knew he was working too hard. I knew I

should have made him slow down. I knew something wasn't right."

"Mom," Willow said, "no one can tell Dad what to do."

That made Martha laugh sadly. "I know, I know. Why does he have to be so stubborn?" She wiped a tear away.

"Maybe he'll slow down after this," Willow comforted.

Martha patted her hand. "Maybe." But they all seemed to know how precarious *after this* was.

Brodie covered his eyes with his hand.

Maeve gave his other hand a squeeze. He glanced her way and smiled. "Thanks for being here."

"It's kinda my job," she joked.

He smiled again. "You know what I mean."

She nodded, looking into those beautiful, sad eyes and felt like she was one step on the dangerous tightrope between them, desperately hoping she wasn't about to fall.

Chapter Forty-Six

Emmett came out of surgery. It was all still pretty touch-and-go. Maeve knew well enough how precarious the situation was and didn't dare offer any false hope. She popped in to check on him in the ICU at one point. Looking at him lying there, eyes closed, machines bleeping, the oxygen mask obscuring his face, the slow, steady rise and fall of his chest, it was hard to see the great Emmett Carter looking so gray and helpless.

She stood at the end of the bed, hands on the bed frame, and said quietly, "You can do it, Emmett." She swallowed, felt a lump in her throat, thought of him teaching Zoey to throw a rope. "You got a granddaughter to get to know," she added with a sigh, fingers crossed that he could hear, because a lot was down to hope now—and Emmett's will to fight on.

Then Martha and Logan came in and Maeve made herself scarce.

She stuck her head around the door again later when she

was walking by, but stopped up short when she saw Brodie in there. He was sitting in a hospital chair, his back to the door, holding his dad's hand. His head slightly bent.

Maeve watched, knowing that she should make her presence known, but then he started to speak.

"Come on, Dad," he said, "You can do it. You're too stubborn to die." He laughed then wiped his eyes.

She leaned her head against the doorframe.

He sat back and folded his arms, seemed to be watching the rise and fall of Emmett's chest. The room was quiet. Maeve was about to leave them to it but then Brodie said, "I know what you meant now about growing up, taking responsibility. I understand." He shifted so he was leaning closer to where his dad lay. "I know who I am—or maybe not quite who I am, but who I could be, would like to be. I'm getting there," he said, laughing a little at himself and his own jumbled explanation. "I don't know why I'm telling you this now. I suppose it's because, while I want you to get better—one hundred percent, believe me—I want you to know, just in case you can't hold on, just in case … I want you to know that it's all in safe hands. We've got it. We'll look after everything—the ranch, Mom, each other." He clutched his dad's hand in both of his. "I'll look after Zoey. I'll be her dad. As good as I can be. I promise. I won't mess it up. You can trust me," he said. "I promise you. I've got it. You don't have to worry."

Maeve stood in the doorway, watching Brodie's broad back, his hands wrapped around his dad's, too stunned by what he'd said to move away quick enough. As if sensing he was being watched, Brodie turned and their eyes met, silently, wordlessly. She felt everything he had said in that gaze. Without looking away he nodded, as if confirming it to her.

She nodded back. Then stepped away, both ashamed she'd been caught listening and entranced by what she'd heard.

Chapter Forty-Seven

Emmett Carter woke up at 7 a.m. the next morning.

Brodie, Noah and Logan all slept in hospital chairs. Brodie had his head propped up against the window ledge, his neck cricked, his back aching, but he had never been happier to hear his dad's voice.

"Where the heck am I?"

"Jackson General," Logan said.

Emmett made a disgruntled face then closed his eyes again.

They'd sent their mom home to rest but when Emmett woke up she came straight back, bustling in and taking over —making the boys go home and sleep.

Brodie went back to the hospital after Emmett had had his dinner. He was sitting up in bed, wearing his gown, looking pale and fragile but like he wanted to be anywhere but that hospital room.

"How's the food?" Brodie asked.

"Passable."

Brodie nodded. He felt weirdly nervous going into the room and sitting down now the bulk of the fear had receded. Martha had brought in magazines and books that sat in a pile on the bedside cabinet. Brodie picked up a tractor catalogue, turned it over and put it back down again.

The machine Emmett was hooked up to, the one charting the steady beat of his heart, Brodie remembered being hooked up to himself after jumping in the river. "This is a better room than I got," he said, just for something to say, nerves making him edgy.

Emmett looked at the machine and then at Brodie and said, "That's two lives you've saved now."

Brodie smiled, he hadn't thought about it like that. "I guess so." Then he said, "You're going to have to thank Rocky, too, he was a regular Lassie, led me right to you."

Emmett snorted affectionately. "I'll bet he did. I always knew that dog was special."

There was a moment of silence. Brodie focused on his dad's hand, thought how he'd held it, would never dare hold it now he was awake.

"I wouldn't be here now if it wasn't for you," Emmett said.

Brodie, lost for words, could only nod. He felt like a little boy.

"I appreciate it."

To his horror, Brodie felt his cheeks color. "Thanks," he said, embarrassed and awkward, "but it could have been anyone who found you."

"But it was you," Emmett said frankly, looking him in the eye.

Brodie swallowed under the hard gaze. "Yeah."

Emmett nodded.

Brodie had to look away, back at his dad's work-worn hand again, the fingernails familiar in their shortness, the blisters, the deep mahogany tan.

Outside the room was a constant flurry of hospital activity. Inside, it felt like their own small world, all white, neutral.

"I heard you, Brodie," his dad's voice cut into the quiet.

Brodie's head shot up. "When?"

"All the time," he said, his turn to look away, awkward. "I heard you when you found me, and I heard you in here."

Brodie felt his heart skyrocket, was thankful he wasn't hooked up to that machine. "I was just talking," he said, cringing now at his outpouring, "saying anything, so you knew someone was there."

Emmett nodded. "I was grateful for what you said about you all taking care of the ranch and your mom."

Brodie found he'd lost his voice.

It was silent again. A painful, pulsing silence that he wasn't sure he could bear filled the space between them. His muscles urged movement. He thought about saying he'd go find Mom for him. But he made himself stay, wait it out, endure the silence.

You gotta sit with it.

Then, seemingly finding it all as torturous as Brodie, his dad said stiffly, "I'm glad you feel like you're taking responsibility for Zoey, and for yourself."

This was not the kind of conversation Brodie and his dad had. Brodie was not practiced in how to respond. He feared he'd regress to his childhood self. No. That was over. This was man to man. Father to son.

Brodie watched the older man reach for a glass of water and got up and passed it to him. Emmett took a sip and passed it back. "Thank you."

"You're welcome."

Another silence. Then Emmett cleared his throat and said, not without obvious trepidation. "I think all this—" he gestured to the machines and the tubes "—it makes you question things. Makes you think about your life and the people in it." He paused, took a breath. "You asked me why, when you were a kid, I didn't do something different."

Brodie froze, heart suddenly thumping. *Please don't cut me down.*

"I didn't know how, Brodie." His dad locked him with his big watery eyes. "I knew I was doing a bad job and I would think to myself that next time it happened I would do it differently but I'd get frustrated and, well—" he sighed "—now you know what it's like to be a father…"

As he spoke, Brodie felt the words like a weight in his stomach, his whole body, his breath, paused as he waited, listened. He saw himself Zoey's age with a basketball under his arm, imagined if his dad had sat down next to him then and said this.

"I was busy and stressed, and there were six of you!" Emmett huffed a laugh. He took another sip of water.

Brodie imagined himself with six Zoeys, all different. Six different types of Slime chaos. He could barely fathom it.

Emmett sighed and, looking more seriously at his son, said, "I know that's a poor excuse, but it's the truth. I could have done better. I know I could. And you were right to tell me so." He inhaled deep and looked away. When he looked back, he said, "I'm sorry, Brodie."

Brodie felt the same press of tears behind his eyes that he'd felt when he was Zoey's age. He swallowed them away, same as he used to, and bent his head, looking down at where his hands were clasped resting on the side of the bed, the tips of his fingers white he was pressing them together so tight. He imagined himself in his Nike high tops with his basketball vest on, hearing this. He'd want to give that kid the same hug—or have his dad give that kid the same protective hug—as he felt the instinct to give Zoey, to make everything better. To make sure, above all else, that she was happy.

He watched, almost in slow motion, as his dad's hand, a canula in its back, veined and work-tanned, reached over and rested on his own, gripping for a moment before releasing it. Brodie wondered if Emmett had ever touched him like that before, with such apparent affection. It was like an elixir going into his blood, coursing through his body. Taken away too quickly.

"I don't know you, Brodie," Emmett said, matter-of-factly.

Brodie shook his head. "No."

Emmett nodded in regretful agreement. Then gesturing to the monitor to his right where his pulse beat steadily, said, "I appear to have been given a second chance."

Brodie laughed. "Looks like it."

"Well, if it's not too late, I would like—"

"It's not too late," Brodie intercepted with boyish eagerness, unable to actually believe what his dad was saying.

Emmett smiled as much as Emmett ever smiled. "Good."

Brodie felt it like a punch of emotion in his gut. Had to brace himself with his old quarterback breathing. He knew football had to be good for something later in life.

"So, how is Zoey?" Emmett asked, maybe to give them both a breather from the previous subject.

"She's good, I think. I need to go see her. I have quite a lot still to learn about being a dad," Brodie admitted with a self-deprecating laugh.

"You can learn from my mistakes," Emmett said dryly.

"I think I've made enough of my own."

There was a pause while he felt his dad's eyes on him, then Emmett said, "You're doing well with her."

So surprised by the praise, Brodie wasn't sure what to say and found himself mumbling, "Thank you."

He watched Emmett's eyes crease fondly at the sides. Then he lay back, closed his eyes and said, "You better go see your daughter."

Brodie laughed. "Will do."

Chapter Forty-Eight

Brodie went straight to Maeve's house. He was unexpectedly nervous. He couldn't remember the last time he was nervous about seeing a woman, probably never.

He rang the bell. He'd brought a gift for Zoey but he should have brought flowers for Maeve. He would usually think to buy flowers. Before he could do anything about it, the screen door banged open and Zoey hurled herself into his arms. "You're back!" she cried.

He staggered, unprepared, but as quickly righted himself and wrapped his arms around her waist and gave her a big kiss on the cheek. "I *am* back. I'm sorry I had to go."

"It's okay, Mom said you'd be back."

Brodie frowned with surprise at the news. "She did?"

"Oh, yeah," Zoey said, nodding profusely, not taking her big eyes off him. "I was worried you'd left us again but she promised me right away that you hadn't and Mom doesn't make promises she can't keep."

Brodie couldn't quite process the news. It felt enormous, but there wasn't time to think it through properly because Zoey was saying, "Where did you go? You know I went to Bella and Logan's and I helped look after the sick horse? Logan thinks I'd be a real good vet. Mom had a milkshake. Your one—a Mudslide." She rattled off seemingly everything that had happened since he'd been gone.

Brodie nodded along, listening, but also thinking that Maeve had promised Zoey he'd be back. *I believe in you.*

Zoey slid out of his arms to the floor and, spotting the bag in his hand, said shyly, "Did you get me anything?"

"Did I get you anything?" Brodie pretended to think for a second. "Do you think there might be something in here?" He held up the bag. "But don't get your hopes up too much."

Zoey bit her lip in anticipation.

Brodie reached into the bag and pulled out a bright yellow sweatshirt with the words Jackson General Hospital written in a white arc on the front.

Zoey gasped. "My own one!"

Brodie tipped his head. "Your own one." Amazed how someone could be so thrilled with a hospital branded sweater, but pretty thrilled that only someone who knew her would know she'd love it—someone like her dad.

Zoey immediately pulled it on. It came down to her knees. "I love it. Thank you." She thew her arms around his waist, cheek pressed to his stomach. "I'm glad you're back," she said, looking up at him with her big brown eyes.

"Me, too." He bent down and wrapped his arms around her. "Me, too," he whispered again into her hair.

Chapter Forty-Nine

Maeve would have known Brodie was in her house even if she hadn't heard Zoey squeal from the back yard, even if she hadn't been able to smell his aftershave or hear his laugh. When Brodie was in the house, she just knew. She could feel him, his presence, his energy. Having him there was like turning the lights on, throwing open the doors in summer, or lighting the fire in winter. He gave the place life.

Still, it made her suck in a breath to see him down on one knee, hugging Zoey tight. His big arms wrapped around her tiny frame.

When he saw her, he let Zoey go and stood up. Before he could say anything, Zoey went, "Mom, look at my sweater!"

"That is a great sweater, Zo!"

"I know!" Zoey grinned then looked back at Brodie who was looking at Maeve, and narrowing her big eyes, said, "Are you okay, Brodie?"

He nodded quickly. "Yeah, fine."

Zoey led him into the living room to watch TV, then play *Uno*, then make bracelets, which they stopped pretty quickly because Brodie kept dropping his beads. When it was bedtime, he read Zoey her story, but Maeve heard Zoey say, "Brodie, I think you've missed a page."

"Oh, sorry, sorry!"

Maeve waited for him in the kitchen. When he came downstairs, she said, "It's a really nice evening, do you want to sit out the back?"

He nodded, uncharacteristically quiet, and followed her outside. The air was warm and the sweet scent of the orchard drifted in on the breeze.

Maeve grabbed a couple of sodas from the fridge and gestured for him to sit where she usually sat, on the wide back step. "I do have a table and chairs," she said as she sat down, "but they're in the shed and the best view is from this step." She pointed out to where the orchard trees stood in rows, like sentinels, and the mountains loomed, silhouettes carved from the blanket of navy sky.

Brodie said, "It's a great view."

She glanced at his profile, his jaw seemed tense, his forehead was sweating. "Are you sure you're okay?"

"Yeah, yeah," he said quickly.

Was he *nervous*?

"I meant to buy you flowers," he said, wiping his forehead with the back of his hand.

Maeve rolled her lips together to hold in a smile. It was funny to see him nervous when he was usually so confident. "I don't need flowers, Brodie." She gestured around her yard where all sorts bloomed, mostly of their own accord, occasionally kept in check when she had the time.

"Oh, right, yeah," he said, taking it in.

"Brodie, are you nervous?" she asked, voice laced with amusement.

"I think I am!" he agreed, pulling at the neck of his T-shirt. "I don't know why. I've *never* felt like this before."

Maeve bit her lip, she traced the silver rim of the soda can. "Felt like what?" she asked, her stomach starting to flutter.

He shook his head and looked at her suddenly serious. "Like I really don't wanna mess this up."

She swallowed. "Mess what up, Brodie?"

"This," he said, and taking her face in his hands, he leaned forward and kissed her. Gentle at first, almost wary, then as soon as their lips met all trace of hesitation went. He cupped the back of her head, drawing her closer, his touch gentle but the kiss urgent, like there was both all the time in the world and barely any left at all.

Maeve's heart thrummed with excitement, relief, exquisite happiness. She wound her arms around his neck, crushing herself to him like she'd been waiting years—forever—for this. She never wanted to let go, tangled her fingers in his hair, slipped her palm beneath the neck of his T-shirt. Brodie smelt like summer vacation and the outdoors and he tasted like he did eight years ago, with a kiss etched in her mind like no other. It was the same and it was better. Like she had finally come home. With his lips pressed hard against hers and his arms tightening around her waist it felt like she was where she belonged. Somewhere she would stay forever if she could.

When he finally released his hold, Maeve found herself bereft and breathless, her heart racing, she said, "You didn't mess it up."

She saw the smile start to spread on Brodie's face. "No."

She felt her own smile mirror his, bit down on the giddiness soaring through her. He reached and took her hand, pressed their palms together and let her fingers slot through his.

She bit her bottom lip, watching him, taking in his face, less tired than at the hospital, hair pushed to the side, T-shirt loose at the neck where he'd pulled it out of shape, golden-tanned skin. Eyes fixed on her. "So, you're back," she said.

He nodded. "Yes, ma'am."

She swallowed. "You staying?"

"I hope so."

She nodded, intoxicated by the familiar warm scent of him, the twinkle in his eye, the slow blink of his lashes. She leaned over and pressed her lips to his, soft, wanting. Felt a shiver of longing shoot down her spine. She let go of his hand and placed both of hers gently on his face, felt the sharp contours of his cheekbones, the softness of where his hair curled above the ear, the smooth skin of his temples beneath the pads of her fingers.

She breathed him in, the moment, the taste, the touch, the thrill as he threaded his fingers into her hair. And then as softly as she had kissed him, she pulled away, wrapping her arms around his neck and hugging him tight to her, pressed against the warm plains of his body, familiar like she'd always meant to be there, almost to tell herself he was real. And his arms went around her, palms flat on her waist, his head bent, his lips pressed against her neck. "I'm staying," he said.

She drew back, felt the smile in her eyes. This was *Brodie Carter*! "Yeah?"

"Yeah," he agreed, grinning now.

Bonus Chapter

He couldn't tell you how he got there. One minute he was standing outside the door of the military psychologist, next he was back in Autumn Falls. AWOL. His chest so tight he could barely draw breath.

He tilted his head up, found himself blinded by the glare of a street lamp. It was cold, he was shaking. No, it wasn't cold—it was summer, there were leaves on the trees. The night air clung to him, humid and close.

Breathe, Ethan.

He was immune to this, trained not to fall apart. He dragged a hand down his face, felt the rough scrape of days-old growth against his palm. Looked down at the cracks in the sidewalk, the curling bark on the trunk of a birch, the white picket fence that he'd vaulted more times than he could remember.

He frowned, head aching. So this was where he came when there was nowhere else he could be? He almost laughed. 11 Riverside Drive, Autumn Falls. Home of one Piper Adams.

The mind was a crazy thing. Took you to crazy places. And his head was a dark, dark place right then.

He looked around him at sights so familiar he saw them in his dreams. He could close his eyes and find his way to the ranch. But he couldn't go home.

He couldn't go back.

He thought about crossing the street. A few seconds' walk, yet a million miles away.

He wondered if Piper still lived there. Thought about her bedroom window, second floor. Whether she was sleeping.

Cross the street, Ethan, and find out...

But what would he do then?

His years of training were supposed to have taught him not to hesitate. Yet there he was, frozen in indecision.

Bang, you're dead.

The thought jolted him back to reality. Made him remember who he was, where he was. Made him look around and realize he had to get out of there.

There was nothing left for him now.

He stepped out of the light, started back the way he came. If he wasn't careful there'd be a warrant out for Ethan Carter's arrest before daybreak.

THANK YOU FOR READING
REDEMPTION RIVER

IT WOULD MEAN SO MUCH IF YOU COULD LEAVE A REVIEW ON ALL YOUR PREFERRED PLATFORMS AND SOCIAL MEDIA TO HELP SPREAD THE WORD!

YOU CAN ALSO FOLLOW ME ON INSTAGRAM @TAYLORGRAYAUTHOR FOR ALL THE UPDATES ON MY LATEST WORKS.

FALLEN IN LOVE WITH THE CARTER BROTHERS?
DON'T MISS OUT ON WHAT HAPPENS NEXT...

The Carter brothers were once inseparable – five boys, a band, and a bond that seemed unbreakable. But it's been ten years since the band broke up and even longer since they left the family ranch and the wide-open skies of Autumn Falls. Fame, secrets and time have left cracks that no one wants to face...

Acknowledgments

My thanks go, as always, to the amazing One More Chapter team, especially Charlotte, Sofia and Kara. Creative minds extraordinaire. And thanks to my agents for this book, Rebecca Ritchie and Euan Thorneycroft.

I also want to thank my great friends—Emily, for being such an enthusiastic Autumn Falls cheerleader, and Lucy, for letting me join her on her dog walks when I'm stuck on something and always having a brilliant idea about how to fix it.

A special mention goes to my son for taking the *Harry Potter* Sorting Experience test way more times than is strictly allowed and still never managing to be a Gryffindor.

Most of all, thanks to all the readers and reviewers for stepping into the world of Autumn Falls and taking the time to get to know these characters. I hope you love them as much as I do.

ONE MORE CHAPTER
YOUR NUMBER ONE STOP FOR PAGETURNING BOOKS

The author and One More Chapter would like to thank everyone who contributed to the publication of this story...

Analytics
Imogen Wolstencroft

Audio
Fionnuala Barrett
Ciara Briggs

Design
Lucy Bennett
Fiona Greenway
Liane Payne
Dean Russell

Digital Sales
Laura Daley
Lydia Grainge
Hannah Lismore

eCommerce
Laura Carpenter
Madeline ODonovan
Charlotte Stevens
Christina Storey
Rachel Ward

Editorial
Janet Marie Adkins
Rosie Best
Kara Daniel
Charlotte Ledger
Jennie Rothwell
Sofia Salazar Studer
Emily Thomas
Helen Williams

Harper360
Emily Gerbner
Ariana Juarez
Jean Marie Kelly
Kamrun Nesa
emma sullivan
Sophia Wilhelm

International Sales
Ruth Burrow
Bethan Moore
Colleen Simpson

Inventory
Sarah Callaghan
Kirsty Norman

Marketing & Publicity
Occy Carr
Chloe Cummings
Grace Edwards
Katie Sadler

Operations
Melissa Okusanya
Vanessa Coubrough

Production
Denis Manson
Simon Moore
Francesca Tuzzeo

Rights
Ashton Mucha
Alisah Saghir
Zoe Shine
Aisling Smyth

Trade Marketing
Ben Hurd
Eleanor Slater

The HarperCollins Contracts Team

The HarperCollins Distribution Team

The HarperCollins Finance & Royalties Team

The HarperCollins Legal Team

The HarperCollins Technology Team

UK Sales
Isabel Coburn
Jay Cochrane
Leah Woods

And every other essential link in the chain from delivery drivers to booksellers to librarians and beyond!

ONE MORE CHAPTER

One More Chapter is an award-winning global division of HarperCollins.

Subscribe to our newsletter to get our latest eBook deals and stay up to date with all our new releases!

signup.harpercollins.co.uk/join/signup-omc

Meet the team at
www.onemorechapter.com

Follow us!

@onemorechapterhc

Do you write unputdownable fiction?
We love to hear from new voices.
Find out how to submit your novel at
www.onemorechapter.com/submissions